DEAD SPACE™

CATALYST

DEAD SPACE™

CATALYST

B. K. EVENSON

TITAN BOOKS

Dead Space™: Catalyst
Print edition ISBN: 9780857681768
E-book edition ISBN: 9780857686572

Published by Titan Books
A division of Titan Publishing Group Ltd.
144 Southwark Street
London
SE1 0UP

First edition October 2012

10 9 8 7 6 5 4 3 2 1

This edition published by arrangement with Tor Books, an imprint of Tom Doherty
Associates, LLC.

This is a work of fiction. All of the characters, organizations, and events portrayed in
this novel are either products of the author's imagination or are used fictitiously.

Did you enjoy this book? We love to hear from our readers.
Please email us at readerfeedback@titanemail.com or write to us at
Reader Feedback at the above address.

To receive advance information, news, competitions, and exclusive offers
online, please sign up for the Titan newsletter on our website:
www.titanbooks.com

A CIP catalogue record for this title is available from the British Library.

Printed and bound in Great Britain by CPI Group UK Ltd.

PART ONE

1

When he was young, Jensi Sato had no idea that anything was wrong with his brother. Istvan had always been the way he was—always a little off, obsessed with patterns and numbers, entranced by shifts in light, prone to sudden fits of rage or mental absence. Or he had changed so gradually that Jensi, around him every day, hadn't noticed how different he had become.

As boys, they roamed the projects together, raising hell, heads always aching from breathing the thin, imperfect atmosphere of the dome they lived in on Vindauga. Really, it was Istvan raising hell and Jensi, younger, following along. But Jensi was glad to be included. And even if he didn't always quite understand why Istvan did what he did, he did want to get out of the house, did want to get away from their mother.

By the time he was in his teens, Jensi had begun to see how different Istvan was. His brother wasn't like other people. Most of the time, he didn't know how to talk to other people, and when he did the things he said didn't have the effect he thought they would. He saw how the other boys looked at Istvan strangely, how they drew away from him, then from both of them. Soon Jensi and Istvan were pretty much left to themselves.

It wasn't as easy as saying that Istvan wasn't normal, because in basic ways he was, more or less. He could get by if he had to, could usually make his way through brief and ordinary interactions without a tremor. But the more time you spent around him, the stranger he seemed. He lived in his own world, always getting caught up in the shapes and patterns he saw around him—patterns that Jensi often couldn't see. Istvan grew frustrated with other people quickly. He was less able to pay attention to others. It never occurred to him to care what other people thought of him, and he also wasn't afraid. Really, the only person he ever listened to was Jensi, and he only listened to him sometimes, only reluctantly letting himself be coaxed out of real trouble.

At age twelve, Jensi was out with Istvan, wandering through the compound where they lived, searching for something to do. The Mariner Valley compound was kept separate from the larger domes that comprised the rest of the town by a tube, and it was only later that Jensi realized this was because they lived in low-income housing into which all the undesirables on Vindauga were pushed.

That day, there had been a half dozen children a few years younger than them crouched near the outer wall of the dome, near a place where the inner wall had been cracked and rendered opaque. There was a slow leak there, quickly compensated for by the dome's oxygen protocol. The kids kept daring one another to get close to it. Holding their breath, one of them would run to the dome wall, touch the opaque section, and run back. The others would slap him on the back in congratulation and then would push at another boy until he did it, too.

"What kind of game is that?" asked Istvan, directing the question to none of them and all of them at once.

Most of the boys just ignored him, looking away as if they hadn't heard. One, the biggest, just shrugged. "Just something to do," he said.

"But it's not even dangerous," said Istvan. "How can it be fun pretending something's dangerous when it's not?"

Jensi put his hand on his shoulder. "Come on," he said. "Leave them alone. Let's go."

But Istvan shook the hand off. "Don't you want to play a real game?" he asked them.

Defensive, the leader of the boys said, "It *is* a real game."

"No," said Istvan. "It's not. You can't just run up close to it and run back. It's calling you to perfect it. That's the game it wants to play. Can't you see the shape is wrong?"

"It?" said one of the boys. "What do you mean?"

Isvtan gestured toward the damaged section of dome. The boys glanced that way and Jensi followed their gaze. What would make the shape of it right or wrong? he wondered. What was Istvan seeing?

"Do you want to see a real game?" asked Istvan.

The boys stayed huddled together, arms crossed, silent.

"Come on," said Jensi again to his brother. "Let's go."

"It doesn't matter if you want to see or not," said Istvan. "It wants to play." He leaned forward, locking his arms behind his back. He pawed the filthy ground with his feet and then, suddenly, screaming, he charged.

The group of kids scattered. But he wasn't aiming at them. He rushed past them without a glance and ran smack into the opaque portion of dome wall, his forehead striking it hard. Jensi felt his heart leap in his throat.

There was a hiss, and the cracks worsened, the shape of the opaque section expanding, but the plate, luckily, did not give. Istvan, though, did give, collapsing in a heap, his forehead smeared with blood. The scattered boys re-formed and stood huddled at a distance. Jensi ran quickly forward, knelt beside his brother.

"Istvan?" he said, shaking him. "Istvan? Why would you do that?"

Blood dripped slowly from his forehead. For a moment Istvan's eyes were glazed and loose in the sockets, and then they slowly focused on his brother. And then he smiled and let his gaze drift back to the opaque part of the wall. "There," he said. "Now the shape is right. Now we know what's really there."

Jensi had tried to ask him about it later, but Istvan had been unable to explain in a way that Jensi could follow. Istvan's brain was always hunting for patterns, always making connections that Jensi had a hard time seeing himself. Istvan had seen the crack in the dome and had known, he claimed, what he needed to do. The crack had called to him. He knew what it wanted him to do and what it would take to make it whole.

"What the hell's that supposed to mean? Make it whole?"

Istvan had tried to explain, but he just couldn't. His attempts at making sense of his thinking for Jensi just led him further and further into confusion until Jensi finally stopped him.

"Look," he finally said. "You sound crazy. You shouldn't tell anybody this."

And for once his brother listened, and stopped talking. Which made it so that any hope that Jensi had of figuring out what Istvan meant was drastically reduced.

When Jensi was fourteen, a group of girls chalked on the ground an old game one of them had read about in the vid library: a series of numbered squares, all connected, that you had to hop through, skipping squares according to a predetermined pattern. The girls were standing around the game, arguing about how you knew which squares you had to skip. Istvan, though, had been drawn by the numbers in the squares, his head rapidly swiveling from one to the next. He had simply walked through the group of girls, almost as if he didn't notice them. He knocked one of them down, scattering the handful of rocks they had gathered, crushing the chalk. The girls were yelling at him, the one on the ground crying and holding up her skinned elbow accusingly, but Istvan was now standing over the squares. Gingerly, he stepped into one, then leaped into another, then leaped back, following a complex pattern that only he could see until with a final leap he came to the top of the game and stepped carefully out again.

Once out, he stopped as if paralyzed. He stared at the uneven ground past the game. Jensi, not knowing what else to do, went to him.

"That was mean," he said.

But Istvan didn't answer. Instead he squatted and brushed his finger along the ground, tracing an irregular shape on it.

Angrily, Jensi batted his brother's shoulder. "Hey," he said. "Why did you have to be so mean to them?"

"Don't you see it?" said Istvan. "How they drew the right pattern and then it led me here?" He traced the shape again, his eyes gleaming. Jensi, squinting, could barely make out what Istvan was looking at, an unevenness in the ground, a tusk-shaped discoloration that made the ground just slightly different. "It's perfect," said Istvan, and reached down to stroke it again.

"Istvan," said Jensi. "What's wrong with you? It's just the ground."

"Huh?" said Istvan. "What?" It was like he was coming out of a trance. Quickly he stood up. Then he turned and looked back at the girls. They stood with their hands on their hips, still angry, though no longer yelling. "What's wrong with them?" he asked.

"You ruined their game."

"I did?" said Istvan. He seemed genuinely puzzled, as if he really didn't remember. He stayed staring at them a moment, then his features grew hard. "They didn't know what they were playing," he claimed. "I'm the only one who knows."

Jensi thought of the many times he had woken up in their bedroom late at night to hear his brother. Istvan would be mumbling, talking in his sleep, but the same pattern of words would be repeated over and over again, endlessly. Or he would be sitting on the edge of his bed, somewhere between sleep and wakefulness, rocking back and forth, rattling about a sequence of numbers, his voice almost worshipful. He was like that; he loved numbers and patterns, could get lost in them. They were almost like people to him, but people were less interesting. He also seemed to pick up things naturally about computers, had been hacking since he was nine, and had taught Jensi how to do the same. But here it was numbers, mumbled, repeated again and again.

"Istvan," Jensi would whisper. But Istvan wouldn't hear him.

Sometimes Jensi was lucky and his brother would simply stop on his own. Other times, though, he threatened to rock back and forth forever. Jensi would get up and shake him but sometimes even that wouldn't stop him. It was as if he were elsewhere, as if he had stepped outside of his body for a while. Sometimes it took a very long time for him to step back in.

I should have known, thought Jensi once he was grown. *I should have known how wrong things were for him. I should have known how damaged he was. I should have tried to get him help. I should have been able to save him.*

But how—another part of him wondered, a part he tried hard to suppress—how could he have known? He was the younger brother, after all. There was only so much he could do. And his mother, no, she didn't believe in doctors, thought that God would sort everything out on his own and that you shouldn't interfere. He had, actually, tried several times to tell her that something was wrong with Istvan. But each time she had looked up at him with bleary eyes.

"Wrong?" she said. "Of course there's something wrong with him. He's evil."

"No," he said. "Something's gone wrong inside of him. Something's wrong with his mind."

"Evil is in him," muttered his mother. "He needs to have it driven out." And then, with horror, he realized that he'd given his mother an excuse to hurt his brother.

But as Istvan grew older and bigger his mother started leaving him alone. She would curse him from the other side of the room, tell him that he was vile, but she no longer touched him. She was a little afraid of him. And that meant she no longer laid a finger on Jensi, either. She became more and more withdrawn. Or maybe she had always been that way and Jensi hadn't realized. Had Istvan gotten whatever was wrong with him from her? Was it something genetic, something inherited? And did that mean that Jensi might have it inside himself as well? No, he didn't want to be like his mother. He didn't want to be like his brother, either, but he loved his brother, felt responsible for him. Istvan had always looked out for him. Maybe now, now that his brother was becoming strange, it was Jensi's turn. It was time for him to look out for his brother.

Istvan was seventeen, Jensi fifteen, when things started to go seriously wrong. It started with their mother.

They had come back from another day of wandering through the Mariner Valley compound. When they arrived, their apartment door was ajar, their mother's passkey lying on the hall floor. They pushed open the door and saw a spill of dropped assistance packages, their mother lying in the middle of them, her body shivering.

Jensi crouched down beside her. He tried to turn her over to see her face, but it was hard. Her body was stiff, resistant.

"Help me, Istvan," he said to his brother.

But Istvan just stayed where he was. He was looking not at his mother, but at the packages. Jensi watched him mumble, gesture at them with his finger, tracing a figure through the air.

"Istvan," he said again. "Help!"

But Istvan was in a trance, mesmerized by the pattern made by the fallen packages. He was muttering under his breath, and then his eyes traced the pattern round again and then began to stare into empty air. Their mother, Jensi saw, was foaming at the mouth. The foam was red-flecked and he could see between her teeth and lips her tongue, partly bitten through.

"This is serious," he said. And when Istvan still didn't respond, he screamed his brother's name.

His brother flinched, then shook his head, then looked down. His expression was unfathomable.

"She might die," said Jensi.

"Yes," said Istvan, but he made no move to help. "Don't you see him?" he asked slowly.

"See what?" asked Jensi.

"The shadow man," said Istvan. "He's choking her."

The shadow man? "Istvan," said Jensi slowly. "Go to the vid and call emergency."

And slowly, almost like a sleepwalker, not taking his gaze away from the boxes, Istvan did.

Jensi held his mother, talked to her, and stroked her face until the emergency crew arrived. He massaged her jaw over and over until it relaxed enough to release her tongue and then he turned her head to the side so she wouldn't choke on the blood. Istvan, after making the call, simply stood on the opposite side of the room, watching. He refused to come close. *The shadow man?* wondered Jensi. *What did he mean by that? He was crazy.*

If I hadn't been here, thought Jensi later as they took his mother away, *Istvan would have let her die.*

Istvan had come through the door only to stop stock still, breathless. There it was, he could see it, the same pattern, just the same, glimmering. He had seen it so many times before, again and again, just waiting for someone to come along and see it and put it together—just waiting for *him* to come put it together, because the world called to him in a different way than to others. There was his mother, lying sprawled on the floor, but that wasn't important, she wasn't important. She wasn't part of the *arrangement*. She didn't tell him anything about what was real. She was just in the way.

No, what was important were the things she had been holding and the way they had fallen when she had dropped them, the way that each of them, tumbling out of her hands, had found its true and proper place. Things were like that. They told him something. They gave him a rough sketch of something else, something grander, something hidden. He could feel it, sense it, but it was far away, too deeply buried to make out completely. So he could only have this, this arrangement of packages that marked out something else, pointed to something else that he could almost see but couldn't quite.

Only maybe he could have more than that.

He held himself very still. He held his breath. He stared as hard as he could, letting his eyes follow the lines between things, connecting them, spinning from object to object. He could begin now to see the blaze of the lines of connections, was beginning to peel back the cover of the world and peer inside.

His brother was saying something, calling to him, but Istvan couldn't hear him, couldn't pay attention, because no, this was important, something was really happening.

For among the lines and between them he could see something beginning to emerge. A shape. A shadow that at first he mistook for his own shadow. But was it his own shadow? It didn't seem to belong to him exactly. It was attached to him, sure, but he didn't feel as though he were controlling it. It was its own creature. It was bound up in the objects around it and was, he realized, looming over his mother as well. It was a shadow but it was also a man, a man but also a shadow.

He moved his hands to try to touch it. When his hands moved, the shadow moved as well and placed its hands around his mother's neck. Then it turned its smoky mouth toward him and spoke.

Watch this, it said. *Here's how you do it. Here's how you'll kill her.*

He heard his brother scream his name.

He could not move his hands. The shadow man was choking his mother, smiling, but no longer speaking. Why had he stopped speaking? "She's going to die," he heard a distance voice say, a voice that was not the shadow man, a voice that he realized belonged to his brother. He made an effort of will and spoke.

"Yes," he said. "Don't you see him?"

But when he tried to explain to his brother what it was he saw, just as when he'd tried to explain so many times before, it came out in ways that he understood but his brother did not. Jensi did not think right about the world. Istvan was helpless to make it make sense for him. And so, slowly, he was snapped again out of this world of arrangements that he so loved and that so loved him, and brought once again to see not the pattern beneath things but the surface of them. And on that surface was his mother: dying. But, unfortunately, not already dead.

By the time the emergency team took her to the hospital, Istvan seemed normal again, or as normal as he ever was. She was there a day, then was transferred to a mental ward, straitjacketed, put away for what potentially could be for good. A social worker, a severe elderly woman, came out to the house and told the two brothers that they would be taken into governmental care.

"But I'm almost eighteen," claimed Istvan in a moment of lucidity. "I don't need a guardian."

"Almost doesn't count," she insisted. "You have to have one."

But the mistake the social worker made was leaving them alone for a few minutes instead of whisking them into care immediately. As soon as she was gone, Istvan began to make plans for leaving. He got an old, stained backpack out of the closet, stuffed it full of clothes, then dumped in a random assortment of things from the pantry, including things that he would never eat. Other things that were more edible he left where they were, adjusting their positions slightly. All part of making the pattern, Jensi couldn't help but think. Istvan was in his own world, unaware of anything but the task he was completing. Jensi just stood watching him, feeling a greater and greater sense of despair for his brother.

When he was finished, Istvan zipped the backpack closed and looked up.

"Why aren't you packed?" he asked Jensi.

"Where are you going?" Jensi responded.

"You heard that woman," said Istvan. "She wants to put us with someone. We'll have to learn how they think and they'll be like mother only they'll be worse because we're not related to them."

"Maybe they won't be worse," said Jensi. "Maybe they'll be better."

Istvan shook his head. "That's what they want you to think," he said. "That's how they get you every time."

That's how they get you every time, thought Jensi But it was not *they* that were getting Istvan, but Istvan who was making things hard for himself. The idea of Istvan being his own guardian—or being the guardian for both of them—that would never work. Istvan could hardly care for himself, let alone someone else.

"Come on," Istvan said. "No time to pack—they'll be back soon. You'll just have to go as you are. That's what the room is saying."

"The room?"

"Can't you see it?" said Istvan, gesturing around him. "Can't you feel it?"

Later, this would seem one of those decisive moments where his life could go either one direction or another, where Jensi could take a step toward his brother and whatever skewed version of the world existed inside of Istvan's mind or where he could step closer to the real world. The terrible thing was that even as young as he was he couldn't help but feel that either choice he made would be, in some way or another, not quite right. Either way he would lose something.

"Come on," said Istvan again, anxious.

"I . . ." said Jensi. "But I—"

"What's wrong with you?" said Istvan. "Can't you see what's happening here?"

But that was the problem: he *could* see. He could see that if he went with Istvan no good would come of it, even if Istvan could not.

"I can't go," he finally said, not looking his brother in the eye.

"Sure you can," said Istvan, his eyes darting all around the room. "It's the easiest thing in the world. All you have to do is walk out the door."

"No," said Jensi. "I'm sorry. I'm not going."

For a moment Istvan just stared at him, his face blank, and then Jensi watched something flit across his brother's expression as he took in what Jensi was saying. Then all at once his face was creased with genuine pain.

"You're abandoning me?" he asked in a voice that was almost a wail. It was nearly unbearable for Jensi to hear.

"No," Jensi tried to say. "Stay here. Stay with me. It'll be okay." But he knew that to Istvan that was as unimaginable as leaving was to him. For a moment Istvan looked stunned. And then, heaving the backpack onto his shoulder, Istvan went out and Jensi found himself alone.

2

Nothing was really wrong about the guardian the court appointed to Jensi, but nothing was all that right about her, either. She was what his mother might have called *the lukewarm*, neither one thing nor the other, but for Jensi that was all right. He could survive with someone like that. He could get by. For once in his life he didn't have to worry about where his meals were going to come from.

He threw himself into his schoolwork and was surprised to find that he enjoyed it, that he even excelled at it. The sort of kids who before had given him a wide berth now began to circle closer, sometimes even speaking to him.

One of them, a kid named Henry Wandrei, started hanging out around him, silently standing a few feet away from him during breaks between classes, sitting across from him at lunch but at first without speaking or meeting his eye. Sometimes he shadowed Jensi for a few blocks when he walked home. At first Jensi tolerated it, then he got used to it, then he started to like it. He started to notice when Henry wasn't there, like his shadow or ghost.

"What?" Jensi finally said one day at lunch.

"Nothing," said Henry. And then they sat silently for a while until Henry asked "What music do you like?"

Music? wondered Jensi. What did he know about music? Helplessly, he just shrugged. "What about you?"

Henry rattled off a few names of bands, then when Jensi didn't say anything in reply, began to try to explain what each one sounded like. He was, as it turned out, good at it, capable of talking in a lively and surprising way that didn't really describe the music so much as say something slantwise that still gave a sense of what it sounded like. Jensi was surprised to find he enjoyed listening to him talk. Henry, silent for so long, now seemed unable to be quiet. And later, when he gave Jensi the music to listen to, Jensi found that the descriptions felt right.

Henry was his first real friend, apart from his brother. But you couldn't really think of a brother as a friend, could you? How had he gotten to be fifteen before having a real friend? Thinking that made him resent Istvan, which made him feel guilty. Here he was, living an okay life, with a decent guardian and one real friend, while his brother was wandering alone somewhere out in the domes.

He had glimpsed his brother once or twice, usually from far away though once up close. That time, his brother had seemed not to know him. Istvan had not acknowledged him as he went past, and though Jensi wanted to reach out and speak to him, he hadn't been able to bring himself to do so. He couldn't, not if Istvan wasn't going to meet him halfway. But later he wondered if his brother hadn't simply been lost in his private world of patterns and numbers. Maybe his brother was so deep within his own head that he couldn't see Jensi.

His life was like that in those days. It was like he was on a teeter-totter, slipping from feeling all right to feeling guilty and then back again, but never stabilizing.

After a few months he trusted Henry enough to tell him about Istvan.

"That's your brother?" said Henry. He'd seen Istvan here and there, always from a distance, and didn't quite know what to think of him.

"I feel like I should help him," said Istvan.

Henry nodded. "Sure," he said, "he's you're brother. You have to feel that way." And then he shrugged. "But what can you do?" he asked.

For six months he did nothing, really, and then one day, walking home, he was talking with Henry about the apartment building he used to live in, trying to describe it as vividly as Henry had managed to describe not only music but other things since, and finding himself failing to make it come alive. Henry was watching him politely, eagerly even, but he kept tripping and stumbling over his words, unable to make them into images that Henry could understand. Slowly he ground to a stop.

Henry watched and waited for him to continue, and when he didn't simply said, "You could just show it to me."

Jensi thought *Why not?* So they trekked the mile or so over to the valve that led to the Mariner Valley compound.

The valve operator stationed there stared at them quizzically. "You sure you want to go in there? Two nice kids like you?" he asked from beneath a bristling mustache. "It's a little rough."

"I used to live there," said Jensi.

The operator wrinkled his nose. "If I'd lived there and gotten out, I don't know that I'd be eager to go back." But he let them through.

They watched the valve twist closed behind them, and then walked the thirty meters down the tube to the second valve. By the time they got there, Jensi was beginning to have his doubts. He had a new life now, he should be moving on. Why would he want to show any of this to Henry?

The valve twisted open and they stepped out. To Jensi the compound on the other side looked at once familiar, just as he remembered it, and different, too. Having changed himself, he could see it for what it was: a slum. The valves were a way of cutting off the Mariner Valley compound in case the people inside decided to revolt. The streets that had seemed normal to him as a child he could now compare to the streets where he currently lived. Everything was run-down, a little filthy, a little pathetic.

"You lived *here*?" asked Henry.

Jensi shrugged. For a moment he considered turning around, going back to the valve and leaving, but then Henry asked, "So, where's your building?"

He showed Henry the worn concrete steps, the cracked floor of the hallway leading down to their apartment, and then the door itself, discolored and scraped ragged along one side. They stared at it. Jensi didn't know what else to do, and Henry didn't seem ready to go back yet. The door was sealed where it met the frame with police tape. *Why?* wondered Jensi. He was surprised that someone new hadn't moved in by now.

But looking more closely, he realized the tape had been slit, very carefully, so that at first glance the door still looked like it was sealed. Henry must have realized that as well, for he reached out and placed his hand on the door's handle and pushed down.

The door was not locked. As both boys watched, it slid slowly open. Behind it was the largely empty living room, floor coated now with a thin layer of dust. There was the uneven couch, the small vid screen with its cracked corner, the makeshift coffee table made from a discarded and bent shipping container that they'd found and then beaten back flat. The wall was discolored, now beginning to go gray with mold in the corners, unless it was just dust gathering there.

"We probably shouldn't be here," said Jensi. The memories in the room were palpable to him, most of them bad.

"It's okay," said Henry, already poking around. "There's no one here. Even if someone comes, we can talk our way out of it." For Henry, Jensi realized, it was a game.

And then Jensi noticed the path that had been scuffed through the dust from the front door to the entrance to the back bedroom, the room he and Istvan had shared. He followed the path with his eyes. He could see a light coming from the crack under the bedroom door.

He reached out and grabbed Henry's arm.

"What?" asked Henry, starting to shake free.

"Quiet," whispered Jensi. "I think someone's here."

. . .

If he'd only turned and left, things might have been different. But he didn't. Why? Perhaps it was because Henry was there with him and that, for Henry, this was still an adventure. Knowing someone was there made it even more of an adventure for Henry. It was simply an escalation of the violation that had begun when they found the police tape slit over the door. They were sneaking in, and now they were risking something, but from Henry's perspective probably the worst that could happen was they might get scolded or warned off or kicked out. Or maybe, at very worse, turned in to the authorities for trespassing and then released with a reprimand.

But Jensi had grown up in this neighborhood. He knew it could be much worse, that if the wrong person was in the back room they might end up badly hurt or even dead.

And so when Henry started moving forward, deeper into the apartment, Jensi was not quick to follow. He watched his friend go, his feet tracking a new path through the dust until he stood beside the bedroom door. Maybe, thought Jensi, there would be nobody there. Maybe someone had come and gone but left the light on. But as Henry reached out and touched the door's handle, Jensi knew that he was fooling himself.

And indeed, before Henry could open it, the door opened of its own accord and a blotchy arm reached out and jerked him through.

Jensi started for the outer door, already beginning to run.

But there was nowhere to run, nobody to tell until he had gone through the valve and into the larger city. By then it would be too late. Henry would either be dead and lying broken on the floor when he got back, or he would have been carried away and would be gone.

And so, barely out the door, his feet slowed, he stopped, and he turned back. He was big enough, he told himself, and tough, too, and he had grown up here and knew how to fight. If he could just get a jump on whomever it was, there might be a chance for both him and Henry to get away.

He quietly approached the door to the bedroom and carefully pushed the handle down until the tongue slid out of the lock's groove. He could hear a voice inside, whispering, insistent. Taking a deep breath, he threw the door open and rushed in, fist already cocked and ready to strike.

On the floor, kneeling on top of Henry, holding him down, keeping him from struggling, hand clamped over his mouth, was a filthy man. His hair and skin were wretched and stinking. *Who sent you?* he heard him whispering loudly, without lifting his hand from Henry's mouth to let him answer. *What do they want from me? Why are they after me?* And then Jensi was on the man, clipping him in the ear and knocking him enough askew that he turned and shifted his balance and Henry began to wriggle free.

But at the same moment the man turned, and Jensi was surprised to find that his was a face he recognized.

It was Istvan.

But though he recognized Istvan, his brother didn't recognize him. His eyes were glazed, crazed even, and as he half fell, half clambered off Henry, it seemed almost like his brother wasn't there at all. It was like it was just his body but with someone else or even something else in charge.

Henry had managed to scramble to his feet. Isvtan, stumbling, gathered his balance against the wall and then bared his teeth.

"Istvan," said Jensi. "It's me."

Istvan made a noise that was a kind of snarl, his eyes darting everywhere, looking perhaps for some hidden pattern but as a result unable to see what was in front of him, and then he ducked his head and charged.

He struck Jensi hard, right in the center of the chest, knocking him off his feet, coming down hard on top of him. For a moment, Jensi had the awful feeling of suffocating, the room fading around him, and then he managed to suck in a deep, pain-racked breath. Istvan was on top of him, striking out, pummeling his shoulders and neck and face with his fists. Henry was behind him, trying and failing to tug him off.

Istvan, he tried to say again. *It's me, Jensi.* But nothing came out. He tried to grab Istvan's hands but failed. He tried to protect his face with his forearms, but Istvan kept punching him, the blows glancing off his arms but sometimes getting through, with Jensi catching here and there a glimpse of his slack, troubled face.

There was a moment when he thought he was about to fade from consciousness, and then it passed and his mind suddenly felt sharper but also more distanced, as if he were observing himself from the outside.

He suddenly realized that Istvan might very well kill him.

Istvan had been searching for something for a while, though he was never quite sure what. It was often like that, aimless, but he knew if he searched long enough it would eventually nudge its way out from the world it resided in, the world that was real, and come find him. Before, when his brother had been there, there had been things to pull him out, to interrupt his search, so that only rarely could he wait long enough for the surface of the world to peel back. But now he had all the time in the world.

The first thing was to limit the world itself, to get rid of all unnecessary distractions. Of anything and everything that did not encourage an arrangement that would crack the world open. Being out in the dome proved too much. There were signs and symbols there, patterns of all kinds, but they drew him in all directions at once. There were people there too who shook him and disturbed him and would not let him stay put.

A pattern, an arrangement, out in the dome had led him back to his mother's apartment again, just as a pattern, an arrangement, in the apartment had first coaxed him out into the dome. A voice had come to him and told him to slit back the tape sealing the door and told him too where his mother had hidden the key that would let him in. It was a voice that was not attached to a body, or if it was, he couldn't find the body. It was a voice that somehow was inside of him but separate from him too.

He had left the pantry as it was, the pattern was good there, it had been made whole when he had left, though it was not complete in and of itself. He had arranged the couch just right. The coffee table he had left as it was, but he had used his fist to dent it further until his fist was bloody, and then had stared at his distorted, gray reflection in its surface. *There*, he thought, *the shadow man*, and waited for him to come out.

Only he didn't come out. If it was the shadow man—he

could not be sure if it was or was not, not yet, not until he came out. Maybe he was too gray and was another man entirely. Or maybe it was nothing at all. And so, sitting on the couch, he had waited for hours, sometimes bringing his face down close to the metal surface but still unable to coax the shadow man forth.

But after a time he had felt the pattern pushing at him. The pattern was right, but he was the one who was out of place. No, he had to be elsewhere for the pattern to do its work.

So he had stood and stepped his way across the room and into the room that his brother and he had once occupied.

There, in the bare room, he waited. When it came, it would come now to find him. He stared at the door, patient, ready for whatever would come.

How long he waited, how many hours or days, he couldn't say. But in the end there came sounds outside and he knew the moment had arrived. He stood and pressed his ear to the door. And then when he heard footsteps approached, he yanked the door open and grabbed what was on the other side and pulled it in.

But no, it was not what he was hoping for, not what he expected. It was not something from the other world, but something from this world, an invader, an intruder, someone who had come to disrupt the pattern and to keep him from succeeding. Who had sent him? There were forces, he knew, out to disrupt him, forces that meant to keep him from finding what he was meant to find and fulfilling his purpose. They had been there at all moments, disturbing him. He shook this one, letting him know what he thought of him. To get him to tell him who was after him, who was trying to ruin him, he kept shaking, kept shaking. Yes, he told himself, he would get somewhere, he was getting somewhere.

And then something struck him hard on the head, dazing him. The invader beneath him wriggled out from under him and away and there were, he saw, at least two invaders now in the room. He scrambled up and away to face them, trying at the same time not to see them too closely, not to lose sight of the pattern, for if he lost sight of the pattern then they would win.

But there at last was the shadow man, curling there in the air, splaying from the feet of one of the intruders, the one who had struck him. The way to him was through the body of the intruder, he knew. He shook his head and then struck out and the intruder was beneath him and the shadow man was beneath both of them, being held by the intruder, but if he tried to dig his way through him then maybe he could get to him. The intruder was trying to speak, but no, he could hear a voice within his head telling him not to listen. And the other intruder was behind him now, striking him, but he was ready for that this time, he could keep his balance. It had happened, he had seen what he wanted, what he needed, and there would be no stopping him now.

3

There were nine of them gathered at the table. Some of them were clearly scientists, others military, others bureaucrats, still others it was hard to say exactly what they were. Most, but not all, of them were Unitologists, and here, among friends, they all wore their amulets exposed and hanging around their necks, publicly professing their creed.

"So we're in agreement," said one of them. He was a military man and seemingly the leader, of an impressive mien and bearing, named Blackwell. Of very high rank, his uniform studded with insignia and commendations.

"I still think it's too dangerous," said another, a wiry little man, a scientist named Kurzweil. "Despite all precautions, the Black Marker experiments went quickly out of control. We lost the majority of our team. We're very lucky that there wasn't an outbreak, that we were able to stop it within the walls of the compound." He gestured to the scientist next to him. "Hayes can attest to that."

"And yet, I'm for it," said Hayes. "As is everyone here but you, Kurzweil. In any experiment there is risk, and the potential gains that we have from unlocking the power of the Black

Marker far outweigh the risks. We are the vanguard meant to lead humanity to Convergence. Now that we've recovered the data, we should have the means to build a new Marker."

Some of the others nodded in agreement.

"Fine," said Blackwell. He turned to the first scientist. "You're outvoted, Kurzweil, as you knew already."

Kurzweil shrugged. "Can we at least agree not to build the new facility on Earth? We need to be somewhere where, if there is an outbreak, it'll do a minimal amount of damage."

"So where do we go now?" asked Blackwell.

"To the moon?" suggested one of the men.

Kurzweil shook his head. "Too close, not private enough."

"We need to go somewhere where we can allow things to develop and see how they go, get as much data as possible, and then nuke the planet if need be," said one of the men whose profession wasn't identifiable. His hair was cut short and he had cruel eyes. His skin had a dullness to it, was almost gray. "Somewhere off the beaten track."

Blackwell nodded. "I'll send a ship out," he said. "I know just the man for the job. We'll see what he can find."

They stood and prepared to go, but the two men without identifiable profession or affiliation beckoned to Blackwell to stay behind. He did, remaining silent with his arms folded, waiting until the three of them were alone in the room. But even once everyone else was gone, the men didn't say anything.

"That went quite well, I think," Blackwell finally said.

"Who do you have for the job?" asked the larger of the two, ignoring Blackwell's comment.

"Who? Commander Grottor. We've used him often in the

past. He has impeccable credentials and is very discreet, as is his crew."

The other man nodded. "We'll want to meet him," he said.

"You've never asked to meet them before," said Blackwell.

"This is much more important than anything we've done before."

"Don't you trust me?" asked Blackwell.

The two men just stared at him, as if he hadn't asked a question.

"We'll want to meet him," the man repeated.

Blackwell nodded. "Of course," he said.

4

Istvan seemed to be growing tired, the blows coming slower as he struggled not only to keep hitting Jensi but to keep pushing Henry away. Jensi waited, still trying to protect his face, and then, when Henry fell again on his brother's back, he lashed out, punched Istvan as hard as he could in the throat.

Istvan started to gasp but remained solidly straddling him. Henry kept trying to pull him off. Not knowing what else to do, Jensi sat up as far as he could and wrapped his arms around his brother, drew him as close as possible.

Up close, Istvan smelled of stale sweat and something else, something gone rotten. He began struggling the moment he felt Jensi's arms close around him, but Jensi locked his hands behind his back and held on. He pressed his face against Istvan's neck.

"Ssshhh," he said, as calmly as he could. "It's okay now, Istvan. It's okay. It's just me."

Istvan kept struggling. Behind him, Jensi caught a glimpse of Henry, looking puzzled now, arresting for a moment his attempts to tear Istvan off him.

"It's me," Jensi said, his voice a soothing whisper now. "It's me, Jensi. It's your brother. I'm here now, Istvan. I'm here for you."

He kept it up, holding on as Istvan continued to try to break free. Henry had taken a few steps back, confused. Half of him seemed to want to wait. The other half seemed poised to flee. Jensi kept whispering, trying to soothe his brother, until the latter started striking the side of his face with his forehead.

He held on as long as he could, his head aching, feeling like something inside his skull was in danger of giving way. Something was wet and at first he thought he was sweating, but when Istvan's head reared back, he saw that his brow was flecked with blood. *My blood*, thought Jensi. And then Istvan brought his head down again and Jensi's hands slipped free and he felt himself pass out.

Disconnected thoughts, a strange fleeting round of faces, as if all of his past has been condensed into a particular moment, a single space. They swayed all around him and began, slowly, to spin, flitting close and then fleeing away, more like grotesque swollen birds than human faces. And then they became birds, fluttering across the sky but strangely stretching too, as if they were leaving parts of themselves behind even as they progressed forward, so that they were more like snakes than birds, only not that either. And then, as suddenly as they had come, they had faded and were gone.

In their place came a strange repeated noise, a noise which it took him a long time to realize was the sound of a man sobbing. He felt something, too. Someone shaking him.

When he opened his eyes, it was to find his brother still on top of him, but something had changed. His eyes looked different, as if there was someone else inside of the body now: human, alive. Istvan. He had a hand on either side of Jensi's head and was caressing his face. His forehead was still smeared with blood. Henry was far behind him, huddled near the back wall, still tense, still ready to flee.

When he saw Jensi open his eyes, Istvan's tears changed suddenly to a weird, flat smile.

"You're alive," he said.

Jensi struggled to sit up, managed to lift himself to his elbows. "Of course I'm alive," he said. "Why wouldn't I be?"

"I thought I killed you," Istvan said.

"No such luck," said Jensi. He straightened further and winced.

"What?" asked Henry, incredulously from near the door. "You're friends now? Basically he just tried to kill you. We should get out of here."

"We're not friends," said Jensi. "Henry, this is my brother."

"I don't care who he is," said Henry. "He tried to kill you."

"I didn't mean to," said Istvan.

"He didn't mean to," said Jensi. "He just got confused."

"Who's to say he won't get confused again?" asked Henry. "Look at him. What's wrong with him?"

"I didn't mean to," Istvan claimed again. "You just got in the way."

"It doesn't matter if you meant to or not," said Henry. "Jensi, let's get out of here."

Jensi slowly shook his head. "I can't," he said. "He's my brother."

"He's dangerous," claimed Henry, but the steam seemed to be running out of him. He was no longer poised to run, seemed even to want to be convinced.

"He just needs to be cleaned up a little," said Jensi. "He's been on his own a while and he's gotten confused. He needs someone to take care of him."

"But why should that someone be you?" asked Henry.

"Who else is there for him?" asked Jensi. "There is only me. If I don't help him, nobody will."

Henry just shook his head. "It's not supposed to work that way," he said.

"No," said Jensi, "but that's the way it is."

Quickly, he found himself feeling even more responsible for Istvan than he had before. He got Istvan to take a bath, scrubbed him down, then left him shivering and naked while he went out and found him an old but clean pair of clothes from a local church basement. But it didn't stop there. Soon, he was scrounging up food for him, then finding scissors and trimming Istvan's hair and beard, then stealing an old blanket or two from his foster family so that Istvan would be able to stay warm. Not knowing what else to do with Istvan, he left him there in their old apartment, hoping that the complex was unappealing enough that the apartment would remain unoccupied until he could figure out what to do with his brother.

At first, Henry would have no part of it. He followed Jensi around, trying to talk him out of helping his brother, telling him that he had a good new life and it'd be a shame to ruin it.

Jensi stopped him. "I'm not going to ruin it," he said. "I'm not planning to leave my foster family. But that doesn't mean I can't help my real brother out a little."

When he started walking, Henry continued following. "But it's not as easy as that," he said. "It won't stop there."

At first it was easy. He stole a little food for his brother, not enough to be noticed, at least not at first. But then he saw that his foster mother was buying less, and keeping a closer eye on what was in the pantry, so he told Istvan he'd have to find his own food.

"But how do I do that?" asked Istvan.

"How were you doing it before?" asked Jensi, and Istvan pointed to the cabinets in the old apartment. Istvan had simply gone through them one after another, as it turned out, eating everything, including the sauces, before carefully returning each bottle to what he felt was its proper place.

So what could Jensi do but keep sneaking food out, even if now he did it less than before? After a while, though, his brother kept insisting he was hungry, still hungry, and so Jensi started saving half of his own food and hiding it, smuggling it out whenever he could. He was hungry all the time. But he was helping his brother.

Henry kept his distance for a while, then started hanging around him again. When he realized Jensi was eating less so as to smuggle food to his brother, he started passing food along himself. "Not for your brother," he said at first. "For you." But even when he must have realized Jensi was giving most of the food away, he still kept bringing it.

. . .

A few weeks later, Henry even started going along with Jensi to see Istvan. The first few times he was nervous, ready to bolt if Istvan did anything odd. But when the first incident wasn't repeated he started to calm down, began to get used to the idea of Istvan. He helped Jensi, became his collaborator in the support of his brother.

The three of them might have gone on together like that for a long time. True, it hurt Jensi's schoolwork to spend so much time looking after Istvan, but Henry was willing to help there, too, slipping him the answers during a quiz or writing all or most of his papers for him. No, they could have gone on like that forever if it hadn't been for Istvan. One day, sitting on the couch, staring in front of him, he said:

"I want to come live with you."

"You do?" asked Jensi.

Istvan nodded. "It's what I'm supposed to do." He traced a figure in the air. "See?" he said.

Suddenly he stood up and left the room.

Henry and Jensi exchanged glances. "What was that about?" asked Henry. "He can't come live with you."

"Maybe he should."

"Even if he wanted to, they would never allow it. They never put two siblings together in foster care. Particularly if one of them is troubled."

Jensi opened his mouth to retort and then realized that Henry was right. He closed his mouth again.

"You have to tell him no," said Henry.

Jensi shook his head. "He'll probably just forget about it.

He probably already has. He didn't even wait for a response—he just left."

But when he came back into the room, he had filled a small box with his few possessions. His blankets were over his shoulders, and he was wearing both pairs of his pants and all three shirts all at once, looking like a child that had tried, and failed, to dress himself.

"I'm ready," he said. "Let's go."

The two boys just stared. Henry looked at Jensi expectantly a moment and then, when Jensi had still said nothing, shook his head and left the apartment.

"What are we waiting for?" asked Istvan.

"Istvan . . ." said Jensi, and sighed. "You can't go."

"Why not?"

"They won't let you," said Jensi.

Istvan furrowed his brow. He traced another figure with his finger, stared at the empty air. "Then you come live here instead," he said, somewhat reluctantly.

Jensi shook his head. "I have another life now," he said. "I can't give it up."

He watched Istvan's face cloud. "Don't you love me? I'm your brother."

"You are my brother," said Jensi. "And I do love you. I'll help you in all the ways I can. But I have a life, too."

Istvan's mouth twisted in pain, as if he'd been struck. And then he turned around and went back into the bedroom, slammed the door.

Jensi tried the handle, found it locked. "Istvan," he said. "Don't be like this. Let me in."

He waited, but there was no response. He knocked again, still no response. Parts of his mind were imagining what might be going on behind the door, imagined Istvan huddled in a corner, crying or trying with a rusty nail to slit his throat or hanging himself. He shook his head to clear it, but the thoughts kept crowding in.

"Istvan," he said, louder this time. "Open up!"

But Istvan wouldn't open. Indeed, even after minutes of knocking, he remained resolutely silent. How long Jensi had been knocking exactly he wasn't sure. He only knew that suddenly Henry was there beside him, grabbing his arm and pulling him away from the door, trying to lead him away.

"But he might be hurt," said Jensi. "Or he might be planning to hurt himself."

"He's not hurt," said Henry. "He's sulking. Come on, Jensi. We should leave before he gets mad."

They made their way back through the streets, passing through the valves and into the neighborhood beyond, Jensi letting Henry lead him along. He couldn't stop thinking about his brother. He wondered if he should have handled the situation differently. But what could he have done with Istvan? It wasn't like he could take him home, like a pet or something. Wasn't he already doing all he could realistically do?

But for Istvan, whatever he did would never be enough. There would always be something more to do, something left to be done.

"What was that?" asked Henry beside him.

"What?" he asked listlessly, hardly bothering to look around.

"I thought I saw something," said Henry. "There, behind us." He shook his head. "Sorry," he said, "I'm jumpy."

They kept going, past the colony's headquarters, and down Luna Avenue toward their neighborhood. Jensi felt like his connection to his brother was a thread stretching all the way back to his old apartment, his old neighborhood, a thread growing thinner and thinner and now in danger of snapping. They passed at last into their neighborhood.

Before they knew it they were at Jensi's house. The two boys stopped on the porch and just stood looking at one another.

"Are you going to go back?" Henry finally asked.

"I don't know," said Jensi.

"You probably shouldn't," said Henry.

"I know," said Jensi. "But that doesn't mean I won't."

Henry nodded once and then raised his hand to say goodbye. He had just stepped off the porch when Istvan appeared.

"So this is our new home," said Istvan. He was panting, and out of breath.

"How did you find us?" asked Jensi.

"I have a right to be here," said Istvan. "It's my home, too." He gave a flat, dead smile. He slowly lumbered forward and onto the porch. He opened his arms and made a move as if to hug Jensi, but when his brother stayed where he was, he let his arms fall. "Aren't you happy to see me?" he asked.

"Istvan, go home," said Jensi.

"But this is home," said Istvan. "I'm hungry. What do we have to eat?" He reached out and opened the front door and pushed his way in.

. . .

Jensi's foster mother was standing near the stairway, a shocked look on her face. Istvan was in the kitchen. He sounded more like a bear than a human. He was rattling pots and dumping cans, slamming cupboards, searching for something.

"Jensi?" said his foster mother, her voice rising. "Who is this man and why is he wearing so many shirts? Can you tell me what's going on?"

Not knowing what to say, Jensi pushed past her, Henry following. Istvan had dropped most of the cans into a heap on the floor. Now his arms were full of food from the fridge, some of it dropping and falling. He carried it out into the hallway, past Jensi's foster mother, and into the living room, where he dumped it on the floor. He sat down cross-legged in front of it and began indiscriminately to eat, his eyes flitting from item to item, trying to construct a pattern.

"I'm calling the authorities," his mother said.

"No," said Jensi. "He's not a threat. I'll get him out."

"No," said Henry. "You should call them."

Jensi heard the sound of his foster mother's heels snapping against the floor as she made for the vid to place the call. He went to his brother, desperately dragged at his arm.

"Come on, Istvan," he hissed. "Stop it."

"I'm hungry," Istvan said. "A man's got to eat."

"She's calling the police," he said. "You've got to go."

"The police?" Istvan said, as if astonished. "But why would she call them? This is our home."

"It's not your home," said Jensi. "It's my home. Please, Istvan."

Istvan sighed and stood up and for a moment Jensi thought he had won the battle. But then his face went purple. Instead of heading for the door, he went deeper in the house. *This is my home!* he was yelling, *This is my home!* Jensi turned the corner and saw his foster mother crouched in the corner, arms flung up to protect her head, weeping. Istvan was over her, almost snarling, spittle flecked on his lips. He watched, horrified, as his brother struck her. When Jensi tried to pull him away, he shook him off.

Help is on the way, flashed the vid screen. *Help is on the way.*

"Istvan," said Jensi. "You have to leave. Now!"

"It's my home!" he said. "You go!"

"The police are coming," said Jensi, shaking him. "They're going to take you away."

Istvan suddenly stopped, his face growing weirdly slack. "The police," he said. "You called the police?"

"No, I didn't call the—"

"Why would you call them?" he asked, his voice filled with a certain confused wonder. He turned and looked at Jensi. Or didn't look at him exactly but rather seemed to look through him. The look reminded Jensi of that earlier time, when Istvan had tried to kill him.

"You're with them," said Istvan, his voice a hissing whisper. "You're one of them!"

"No," said Jensi. "What are you talking about?"

"Get away from me!" said Istvan, and, reaching out, pushed Jensi hard in the chest. Jensi stumbled back, crashed into the wall, then slid the rest of the way down. "You're one of them," Istvan said again. "You're just as bad as they are because you're one of them."

"No," he said weakly, not completely believing it, "I'm not one of them." But he didn't get up. He did nothing to stop Istvan when, hearing the sound of a siren coming closer, his brother stumbled past him and out into the hall, and from there into the kitchen and out the back door.

There were a few days when he couldn't do much. First there was his foster mother to comfort and help off the ground, then Henry to calm down and straighten out his story with, and then, shortly after, the police. They questioned him—more of an interrogation, really—about the man who had invaded the house and assaulted them. Who was he? He claimed not to know. How then, had he known what his name was?

"But I didn't know what name to call him. I didn't call him a name."

The officer shook his head. "You called him a name. Your mother told us," he said.

"She's not my mother," he said. "She's my foster mother."

The officer shrugged. "I don't care," he said. "That's not important. How did you know his name?"

Jensi kept talking, kept lying, feeding them little bits and pieces, half-truths, until they had poked enough holes in his story that he felt he had no choice but to fall silent, to not say anything at all. But he held out, he felt. He didn't reveal that the intruder had been his brother, didn't give the police a name. And that was, he felt, an act of loyalty on his part, and should be considered by Istvan a redeeming gesture. He hadn't exactly stood by his brother, but then again he hadn't betrayed him, either.

But four or five hours into the questioning, the officer had smiled and placed his hands flat on the table.

"Istvan the name was," he said.

Jensi felt his heart begin to beat harder. "Are you sure?" he said. "Maybe my foster mother heard it wrong."

"Oh, we didn't get it from her," said the officer. "We got it elsewhere. From your friend Henry. Maybe he's not as much of a friend to you as you want him to be. Istvan Sato," he said. He pretended to read from a piece of paper in front of him. "Hey," he said, "isn't Sato your last name, too?"

He kept his mouth closed.

"Not talking, eh?" said the officer. "Doesn't matter. We've already gotten everything we need to know to identify him from your friend. Shall I read off what I know?"

Jensi shook his head.

"I'll take that as a yes," said the officer. "But before I do, there's just one question I want to ask." He leaned forward. "How could you have ever hoped to hide from us the fact that the so-called home invader was your brother?"

He wanted to hate Henry for telling. At first he thought he did, but then gradually he began to take stock of all that Henry hadn't said as well. It became clear as the officer continued to talk that Henry hadn't told them where Istvan had been living or that they'd been seeing him regularly. Henry, as he discovered later, after the interrogation was over, had given very little away beyond the fact of Istvan being his brother. And Jensi had to admit they probably would have come across that fact on their own eventually.

Later, once the police were gone and Jensi was left to have to sort out things with his foster mother, Henry stood by him, told her that yes, Istvan had approached them, that they had met him, but that they had had no idea either how disturbed he was or that he had followed them. It was largely Henry and his arguments that calmed her, that kept her from sending him back to the agency to be placed in another family. He had Henry to thank for being able to continue on with his new life.

As for Istvan, it was as if he had disappeared. It would be a mistake, Henry convinced him, to try to make contact again. Istvan was unstable. If he came back, then that would be the end of Jensi's new life—he'd be sent to a new family, maybe even sent off planet where Henry would never see him again. Henry was right, but still Jensi felt guilty. He felt he was abandoning his brother, and who did his brother have but him? He couldn't stand the thought of his brother entirely and completely alone, living more in the warped world within his head than in the real world.

And so even though he knew it was the wrong thing, he found himself one day after parting from Henry after school, walking not toward his home but back toward the valve that led to the Mariner Valley compound.

The valve operator recognized him as the boy who had visited earlier, nodded once, and let him through without question. The compound looked the same as it had looked the last time he'd been there: same crumbling buildings, same dirty streets.

This time, the door was locked. The slit police tape was still there, but had been covered over with more police tape, this set intact.

He knocked and then waited, but heard nothing from inside. He knocked again and waited. Still nothing.

After a while he went out and walked around the building, trying to figure out which windows were the ones to his apartment. Once he thought he knew, he was disappointed: the windows seemed firmly closed and there was no sign of light or movement behind them.

What now? he wondered. For a while he just stayed staring at the building, waiting for something significant to happen. Nothing did. Down the street, he could see a group of four scruffy children playing, one of the same futile games he and Istvan had played as kids. Otherwise the street was empty.

Eventually, he went back inside. He stripped the police tape away. He wondered if he had the strength to break the door open. He hurled himself against it a few times until his shoulder began to hurt, without any apparent effect on the door. He stood staring at it. In the end, he went down to the super's apartment and rang the bell there.

The super seemed surprised to see him. "You're that kid," he said. "The one with the mother who went crazy."

"I used to live upstairs," Jensi said.

"Yeah, that's the one," said the super. "That's you. What do you want?"

"The key to the apartment," he said.

The super shook his head. "It's a crime scene," he said. "The police have taped it off."

"Not anymore," said Jensi. "They came and stripped the tape away."

"Yeah?" said the super suspiciously. "When did they do that?"

Jensi shrugged. "How should I know?" he asked. "It was already done when I got here." He held out his hand. "Give me the key."

"Why should I give you the key?" asked the super. "There's still back rent owed on the place. Who's going to cover that? Whoever covers that gets the key."

"My foster father's a lawyer," lied Jensi. "I am going to go up and take a look at the place, make sure the police didn't steal anything. If they did, we're going to sue their ass, and yours, too."

The super stared at him, a little stunned. And then he smiled and shook his head. "Naw," he said. "Can't be true."

Jensi crossed his arms and stood there, waiting.

After a while the super began to get nervous. He scratched the top of his head. He reached out and began to shut the door, but, when Jensi didn't react, stopped.

"A lawyer, you say," he said.

"A lawyer," said Jensi, holding his gaze steady and unblinking. "And very litigious."

The super sighed. "Five minutes," he said. "In and out." He went to fetch the key.

He opened the door not quite sure what to expect. Maybe his brother's body hanging from a rope, its tongue swollen and purple and pushing through the lips. Or on the floor with a bullet through his head, a spray of blood and brain on the wall behind him. Or simply dead from lack of food and water, a heap of skin and bones lying on the floor.

Or maybe he would still be alive but naked and shivering, crouched in the corner, and when Jensi took him by the shoulder and turned him to face back into the room, he would simply look through him without seeing him, without, indeed, seeing anything around him. Alive, but for all intents and purposes, not really there.

Or maybe he would be crouched behind the door with a knife and would immediately come at Jensi, slitting his throat before realizing who he was. Or even slitting his throat *because* he realized who it was.

But none of this happened. Instead, the door opened onto an empty room. Behind it, through the door to the bedroom, was another empty room. The bathroom and his mother's former room were empty as well. There was nobody there and no sign that anybody had been there in a long time.

5

Jensi grew. He was admitted to a university off world, back on Earth, but couldn't afford to go. Instead he studied at the technical college in the colony there on Vindauga. He studied computers, learning some solid programming skills and, on the side, improved on the hacking his brother had taught him. He might have gone into computers if he hadn't become interested in piloting. Henry, whose grades weren't quite as good but whose parents had more money, did go off world and Jensi figured that was the last of him, that he probably wouldn't hear from him again. But in a year Henry had flunked out and was back on Vindauga, at the technical college as well. "I'm the family failure," he claimed to Jensi. "They can hardly stand to look at me." Which made Jensi wonder if he was at fault for whatever had gone wrong with Henry. Perhaps he had ruined him by distracting him, giving him hints of a different, stranger life.

Jensi never went back to the house, but he still walked sometimes through the Mariner Valley compound, hoping to catch a glimpse of his brother, gaining some reassurance from the familiar griminess of the streets. Then one day that was gone, too, carried away in a public works effort to clean up the compound. For a few days the streets stayed clean, the smell of disinfectant replacing the stench of trash, but quickly they began to revert to what they were before.

Several times, while walking through one part of the city or another, Jensi thought he caught a glimpse of his brother—hair crazed and overgrown, shambling—but he rarely managed to catch up with these apparitions, and the few times he did, they turned out not to be his brother after all.

And so, three or four years went by with Jensi moving forward with his life. At first he thought often of Istvan, but as time went on he thought of him less and less. He could go for days without thinking of him at all. He managed to finish his associate's degree in flight and cargo manipulation, and would have gone on to complete his bachelor's if the planetary government hadn't cut school funding. When that happened, he moved out of his foster family's home, took a small apartment near Vindauga's space hub, and began to work.

He was a picker, working every time a ship bearing supplies came in. His job was to help crew a surface-to-atmosphere ship that would meet the huge cargo ships that came into orbit, transferring a fraction of the load from one ship to the other over and over again until the cargo was on the surface. It was a simple job, but he didn't mind it. They were busy building an orbital docking station and he wondered if this wouldn't eventually make his job obsolete. For a while Henry did the job as well, but the moments of near-weightlessness proved too much for him. He went back into training on his family's money, preparing for first one surface-based job and then another.

Picking either was very busy or very slack, never simply steady. He was either working sixteen-hour shifts or lying idle in his apartment, scrolling through something on the vid screen. Was it the life he had dreamed of? No, but it was better than any life he probably would have had if he'd ended up staying in the Mariner Valley compound.

He met a woman, a little shorter than him and slightly plump, and somewhat neurotic. He saw her for a while and then broke it off. Then he met another, long-legged and a little taller than him, generous and kind, whom he liked much better. But he managed to sabotage the relationship despite that. He was leery of getting involved, leery of establishing new ties, remembering the hell that had been his family growing up. He wondered if he should see someone, a psychiatrist, a specialist, maybe they could help him, but he didn't know who to see or where to start looking.

It could have gone on a long time, maybe even for a whole life, but it didn't, for one simple reason. The reason was Istvan.

Nearly four years after his brother had suddenly disappeared, Jensi was on a long pick, thirty-six hours solid clearing out a freighter on overtime. He would catch a little sleep here and there on the trip up and down, but not enough not to be exhausted by the time the pick was finally over.

When he went home, he found his apartment unlocked. *Weird*, he thought, but shook it off, figured he'd been called away on the pick on short enough notice that he'd simply made a mistake and forgotten to lock the door. Inside, nothing seemed to be out of place or missing, either in the living room or the bedroom. But when he went into the bathroom, turned on the light, shucked off his clothes, and pulled back the shower curtain to climb in, there was Istvan.

"Hello, brother," Istvan said, and offered his flat, dead smile.

At first Jensi thought he was much more tired than he'd realized, that he was hallucinating. But no, after screaming and stumbling back into the wall he found Istvan reaching out and steadying him, stepping out of the tub, undeniably real.

"What are you doing here?" Jensi asked, heart still thudding.

"I came to see you," claimed Istvan.

He had cut his hair short, in a crew cut, and was clean-shaven. His right cheek was marred by an angry red scar, puffy and relatively fresh. Jensi could feel something strange about one of the hands steadying him, but it was only when Istvan let go that he realized it was missing two fingers.

"How did you find me?" asked Jensi.

"I always knew where you were," said Istvan. "I've been watching over you."

Watching over me, Jensi thought, and shivered. He pushed Istvan gently away and slipped back into his clothes.

"Why were you hiding in the bathroom?" he asked once they were in the living room.

"How did I know it was you?" Istvan asked. "It could have been someone else. It could have been *them*."

Jensi nodded. He wasn't sure what to say or what to do. Did he really want to see his brother at all? But already the weird mixture of guilt and affection that he thought he'd managed to eradicate years ago was beginning to well up within him. The unhealthy bond with his brother was already starting to form again.

"You can't stay here," he managed to say.

"I don't want to stay here," Istvan said. "I have a purpose now."

"What do you mean, a purpose?"

Istvan smiled and shook his head. "It's my purpose, not yours," he said. "It's for me to know."

Jensi ran his fingers through his hair. "Why are you here?" he asked.

"I wanted to see you again," said Istvan. "One more time before fulfilling my purpose."

"What's that supposed to mean, 'fulfilling my purpose'? What are you on about?"

But Istvan just smiled flatly again.

"You look well," said Jensi.

"You look tired," claimed Istvan.

"I am tired," said Jensi. "I'm exhausted." He tried again. "What do you mean by your purpose?"

"They told me not to tell."

"Who told you?"

"They."

"Who's they?"

Suddenly Istvan giggled. He pressed his hand over his mouth to stop himself, but couldn't help giggling through it.

"What's wrong, Istvan?" Jensi asked, trying to keep his voice as calm as he possibly could.

Istvan giggled again, then closed his eyes. He sat there on the couch, trying to breathe slowly until finally the giggles stopped entirely. Then he slowly moved his hand away and opened his eyes.

"There," he said. "See? Everything is all right. There is nothing wrong with me."

"I don't know what you're planning," said Jensi, "but whatever it is, don't do it."

"There is nothing wrong with me," said Istvan again, but this time it sounded more like a question.

"Istvan . . ." Jensi said.

But Istvan was already standing. "I have to go," he said. "I just wanted to see you first."

"Before your purpose," said Jensi.

"Before my purpose," he said, and smiled. He walked almost drunkenly to the door, turning around just as he got there. "I'll be on the vids tomorrow," he said. "All the vids. Watch for me. I'll be famous." And then he was gone.

He's crazy, thought Jensi. *Certifiable. Just like mother.* His brother had been going on about some imagined encounter he had, some delusion of glory and fame that he'd invented for himself, which would amount to nothing. His brother had reentered his life for a brief, somewhat painful moment, and now he was gone again, maybe for good this time. *I should be thankful he's gone*, Jensi told himself. *He's nothing but trouble.*

But he wasn't thankful, couldn't feel thankful. Instead, despite being exhausted, he found himself having difficulty sleeping. What had his brother been talking about? His *purpose*? What if it did mean something?

He turned over and tried to ignore the thoughts. He closed

his eyes and lay there watching little bursts of imagined light flicker over his eyelids. He tried all the tricks he could think of to coax himself to sleep: counting sheep (even though he had never seen an actual sheep), thinking through a math problem mentally, repeating to himself the same rhythmic phrase over and over again, trying to imagine the weight of his body growing heavier and heavier and falling asleep limb by limb. But nothing worked. There, beneath the exhaustion he was feeling, like an inhuman, baleful eye, was his worry about his brother, staring at him, staring into him, keeping him from sleeping.

He kept trying to fall asleep, until finally he felt like he was going mad. Then he got up, vidded Henry.

"Do you know what time it is?" Henry asked, his face and hair scruffy through the vid.

"All too well," said Jensi. "I couldn't sleep."

"So you thought you'd wake me up and make it so neither of us could sleep." He yawned.

"Istvan was here."

"What?" said Henry. "Really. You mean you dreamt about him?"

Jensi shook his head. "He was really here. In the flesh."

"I thought by this time he was probably dead," said Henry. "What did he want?"

"He wanted to see me one last time."

"One last time before what?"

Jensi explained the little he knew. "He's crazy, right?" he asked once he was finished.

"Maybe," said Henry slowly. "I don't know. Maybe he's planning to do something."

"What?"

Henry shrugged. "I don't know," he said. "Something drastic maybe."

"Like what?"

"What's he capable of?" asked Henry. "I know you love him and that he's your brother, but you remember how he was when we first found him? He might have killed us. If he's in the right mood—or the wrong one, I guess—I think he's capable of anything. A bomb, maybe?"

"A bomb?" said Jensi. "You've got to be kidding. It could break one of the domes, put everyone at risk."

"Doesn't have to be a bomb," said Henry. "Anything happening tomorrow?"

"Like what?"

"A speech, a rally, some sort of protest march, a meeting of two officials. Something along those lines?"

"I don't know," said Jensi. "I've been picking. I haven't been following the vids. Have you noticed anything?"

Henry shook his head. "I don't think so. If there is, maybe he's planning to disrupt it. He claimed he was going to be on the vids?"

"That's what he said."

Henry shrugged. "Look through the vid notices, see what's happening tomorrow. We can try to figure it out, stake a place out if it sounds right. Otherwise, we just wait, watch the vids for something that seems likely and then, if we find it, try to make it there before he does."

Jensi cut the link and tried to sleep, again without success. He lay there staring up into the dark until, slowly, the room began to brighten. Then he got up and began scrolling through vid notices. A school was being opened, someone from the colonial authority coming to cut the ribbon. There was a press conference on the steps of the municipal hall, run by a politician named Tim Fischer, about a methane leak in one of the outlier domes and to what degree if any, the government was responsible. A political rally for the opposition candidate, David Vernaglia, held not far from the municipal hall. An ambassador from EarthGov named Jedrow Berry landing at the spaceport. There were other things mentioned but they seemed less likely: the revamping of a new low-income housing project, the demolition of a now-deserted microdome, etc. If it was anything, it was probably one of those four events.

But which one? Henry would help him, but that still meant they could only cover two. School-ribbon cutting, press conference, political rally, ambassador . . . Any of them might be what he was looking for: a place for Istvan to be visible, to be seen on vid while he did whatever it was he planned to do. Was he likely to be violent? Crazy? Yes, Jensi had to admit, either of those things were possible, even likely. Would he try to hurt someone? Kill someone? Would he try to kill himself? All possible. But it was equally possible that his *purpose*, whatever he meant by that, might be something else entirely, something relatively benign. Maybe he would throw a pie at the ambassador. Or maybe he would take his pants down at the press conference and moon the crowd. He tried to tell himself that Istvan was doubtless capable of those sorts of things, too.

Though Jensi knew he was fooling himself, that violence was most likely.

And what, suddenly worried Jensi, still exhausted, his eyes throbbing in his sockets, a migraine just beginning to create an aura in front of one eye that he knew would travel across his vision until it filled both eyes and then dissolved into pain, *what if Istvan, in saying he was on the vids, was not referring to some event or occurrence that he was going to hijack, but to the fact that whatever he did, wherever he did it, it would be featured on the news after the fact, that he would be made famous by having fulfilled his 'purpose'?* What if it wasn't that he was going to borrow the celebrity of an event, but that he was going to make his own fame, by doing something rash?

If that was his plan, he could do that anywhere.

If that was the case, there was no way to find him until it was done, until it was too late.

The next six hours were the worst Jensi had ever lived, the most anxious, the most exhausting. Until close to the time of the events themselves, there was nothing he could do. He just had to wait, all the while trying to guess which might be the most likely place to find his brother, trying to ignore the fact that his brother might not be at any of the events he'd keyed on. He kept imagining Istvan strapping himself into a jacket with sticks of explosives sewn on the inside of it. Or his brother suddenly appearing out of the crowd, running toward the steps or the platform or the security guards, brandishing a knife. He was worried both that his brother would kill someone and that, trying to do something foolhardy, his brother would be killed. He didn't know for certain which was more likely.

In the middle of the morning Henry showed up and together they talked things through.

"Does he care about politics?" asked Henry.

"He didn't use to," said Jensi. "Now, who can say? I haven't seen him in years."

"His 'purpose,' he said? Was there a way he said it? A particular way he phrased it? Did it sound political to you? Religious?"

Jensi shook his head. "It didn't sound like anything. It just confused me."

"Let's try to think," said Henry. "There are only two of us. We can only cover two things. We have to narrow it down."

Jensi nodded.

"Or we could call the police," said Henry. "Tell them there's been a threat on the two that we can't cover."

"That might make things worse."

"For who? For Istvan? Certainly it won't make things worse for whoever he might hurt."

Jensi shook his head. "No," he said. "He'd see it as a betrayal. I can't do it."

"You may have to do it," said Henry. "You don't want anybody's death on your conscience."

"It could lead to his death. To Istvan's. I don't want his death on my conscience, either. I don't want to do it."

Henry just looked at him with a steady eye.

"Only as a last result," Jensi finally said.

"All right," said Henry, and sighed. "Only as a last result."

"Political rally seems likely," said Henry. "How about that?"

"I don't know," said Jensi. "I'd think so, but since it's for the opposition candidate, I'm not so sure. He always supported the underdog. But maybe he's changed."

"So, possible, but maybe not likely. What about the school ceremony? Does he have anything against education?"

"He didn't want me to join my foster family," said Jensi. "School might be tied into that for him, something that he feels separated us."

"But it's a new school opening," said Henry. "Not a school that you went to. I know his mind is broken, but as a symbolic gesture it doesn't amount to much."

His mind is broken? thought Jensi. And then thought, *Yes, Henry's right*.

"Someone on the colonial authority is cutting the ribbon," continued Henry. "Is it anybody he knows?"

"Who is it?"

They looked at the vid notice. "It doesn't say," said Jensi. "No way to tell without going."

"Even then, we probably won't know," said Henry. "Who knows what he's been up to or who he's met over the last several years. Still, not likely. What about the ambassador from EarthGov? What's his name?" He scrolled through the vid until he found it. "Jedrow Berry. Name ring a bell?"

Jensi shook his head.

"All right," said Henry. "That's okay. Doesn't mean anything. He's a representative of EarthGov authority. That might be enough." He sighed. "Basically nobody seems all that likely. Nobody is jumping to the top."

They sat across from one another in silence until, finally, Jensi said "So what do we do?"

"Do? We draw straws."

Jensi felt like he was going mad, his mind straining to see a connection that either wasn't visible or simply wasn't there. He felt like Istvan, always searching for a pattern, trying to see something that nobody else could see.

How would Istvan think? he wondered, his head throbbing. He tried to put himself in the place of his brother, tried to re-member the erratic way he had responded to those situations that had seemed clear and straightforward to Jensi, but they were all moments from childhood, and even thinking back on them he could neither understand them nor extrapolate them into something relevant to the present situation. He had long understood that something was seriously wrong with the way Istvan viewed the world, as if he were seeing everything through a different lens than everyone else, a dark and smoky lens that distorted everything and made it false. But how could Jensi, more or less normal, simulate that way of seeing the world?

Solemnly, Henry took four scraps of paper and wrote a word on each one: rally, press, school, port. Then he folded each into a smaller square and jumbled them in one hand.

"Do you want to choose first, or shall I?" he asked.

Jensi reached out, took a piece of paper from Henry's hand.

"Open it," Henry said.

"You go first," said Jensi.

Henry closed his eyes, felt around among the pieces of paper, chose one. Together they opened them. *School*, said Henry's. *Port*, said Jensi's. Henry reached out, placed his hand on Jensi's shoulder. "Good luck," he said, and they both left.

Commander Grottor stood at the helm, hands clasped behind his broad back. There was nothing about his stance to suggest that he was anything but relaxed, but within his head the thoughts spun back and forth. He knew altogether too little about the project to be comfortable. He was not sure exactly what he was getting into.

He turned and looked behind him. There on the bridge to one side was a technician named Jane Haley. She was young, fairly fresh out of the academy, but smart and ambitious. He had seen her scores—off the charts—and read the reports on her and chosen her. Indeed, the whole crew was handpicked by Grottor, excellent crew, notable as well for being willing to follow commands to the letter and for their unquestioning loyalty. Though he had chosen Ensign Haley precisely because she was not like that, because she might stand up to him when the others would not.

On the other side of Grottor was Ensign Erik Orthor, a thin and tubercular man who was the only person that Grottor hadn't chosen as part of his crew. Blackwell had insisted on him, which made Grottor wonder if Blackwell trusted him.

He'd done what Blackwell and the two somewhat odd men he'd introduced him to had asked of him, but perhaps Blackwell still had his doubts as to his loyalty. Grottor was a good commander, inflexible in his own way, but smart enough to get out of scrapes when he needed to. And working for Blackwell, he often needed to.

Orthor too was a Unitologist. That was fine—Grottor technically was, too, but in name only. It had been one way up the promotion ladder and he had joined because it was expedient at the time. He didn't believe in it exactly, but he'd seen enough of the footage and records from Michael Altman's time to know that there had been power to the Marker. Blackwell, too, he imagined, wasn't much of a believer, maybe wasn't even a Unitologist at all, but he saw the potential for power as well. And those others, the ones who went unnamed but seemed really to be the ones in charge—he'd met them only once, but once had been enough.

Yes, he knew too much about the project to be comfortable. He was to locate a planet for a secret facility that would allow for the continuation of the Marker project. What all the specifics of that continuation would be, he didn't know, but the fact that they wanted to make sure the planet was uncharted, away from the usual trade routes, and far from civilization, told him it wasn't good. With Blackwell he had chosen several likely planets, but had rejected them one after another. The last on the list they were approaching now. It was one Blackwell had hesitated over for some reason, but had finally said yes, go ahead.

It was listed as uninhabited. No breathable atmosphere, but Earthlike gravity. They had approached it and circled around it, and had been surprised to find signs of life, a small colony of some sort, completely enclosed. It was small enough that he'd almost missed it, but Haley, with her sharp eyes, had caught it. Except for that the planet was perfect. He double-checked— it wasn't in any records; they were illegals.

"Do we recommend it, sir?" asked Haley.

"No," said Grottor. A colony, even an illegal colony, wasn't possible. Who knew what connection they might have to other people in other places, and when someone might come looking for relatives they had down there. No, it wasn't secure.

"So what do we do, then?" asked Haley.

Grottor shrugged. "We keep looking," he said.

When the vid sounded, it was one of the two men Blackwell had introduced him to, the one with cruel eyes and grayish skin. He cut right to the point. "I hear you've rejected Aspera," he said. "Care to explain?"

"There's an uncharted colony there," said Grottor. "It won't do."

The man shook his head. "It's not a colony," he said.

"No," said Grottor. "Then what is it?"

"A containment facility. We have a share in it. Apart from that, Commander, is everything else about the planet up to specification?"

He referred to Haley's notes, gave a rundown to the man. Yes, everything did seem to be right, everything else was fine.

"Then we'll move forward," said the man. "You're to contact Tim Fischer on Vindauga. He's one of us, and very discreet. He supervises the shipping for the containment facility. He'll arrange to have building supplies shipped out, ostensibly for the containment facility, but in actuality for you." He looked more closely at Grottor. His eyes narrowed.

"What's wrong?" he asked.

"Nothing's wrong," Grottor said.

"You can speak freely," claimed the man.

"It seems like a risk factor," Grottor said. "Word of the project could get out through them or the guards in the facility. In addition, there's the risk of what might happen if the project goes awry and there's an outbreak."

"They're prisoners and they're in a secret containment facility," said the man.

"Yes?"

"That means they're expendable," the man simply said.

Grottor nodded curtly.

"Besides," said the man, "we might need human subjects."

For a moment Grottor was silent. Then "Yes, sir," he finally replied.

7

No, thought Jensi on the way over. *The rally's more likely. I should go there.* But it was only more likely, he realized, if it were he rather than Istvan doing the thinking. *Stick with the plan,* he told himself.

But when he reached the port, he found that the EarthGov ambassador's arrival was delayed, there having been a problem with the surface skimmer that had met his ship. There was hardly a crowd, only a dozen people, most of them there in an official capacity. He scanned over them quickly looking for Istvan's face, but wasn't surprised not to find it.

There was still time, if he hurried, to go to one of the other sites. *Rally or press conference?* he asked himself. *Which one?* Both were roughly in the same direction. He started to run.

He went down the wrong alley and got turned around, routed back in the other direction, but he realized his mistake quickly and worked his way back out. He was running faster by now, but still unsure where he was going. One or the other. Which was closest? The rally, but not by much. He could already hear the sound of it, the echo of the loudspeaker, the words so distorted that he couldn't begin to make them out.

He cut through a back alley and came out on the main avenue, and suddenly there he was, on the fringes of a crowd.

On a platform down near the end of the street, David Vernaglia had just begun to speak, his voice booming from speakers all around the crowd. Jensi pushed his way forward, looking for his brother.

"Now, I wouldn't say that the current administration is doing a terrible job," said Vernaglia. "But then again, I don't have to say it, because you already know it. You wouldn't be here if you didn't."

The crowd erupted into applause and shouts. Jensi pushed further in, the people he pushed shoving back, giving him dirty looks. As he got closer, the crowd got tighter. He stood on his tiptoes and tried to peer around, looking for his brother in the sea of faces. It was hopeless—too many people.

Now what? he wondered. *Did I make the wrong choice?*

Vernaglia was still talking, really getting the crowd going now. Vernaglia was, at least, still alive, and the rally hadn't been interrupted by anyone, which probably meant that this was the wrong place to be. Was there still time to make it over to the press conference?

He pushed his way sideways through the crowd, ignoring the complaints of the people around him. If he could get to the edge, he could go back down the alley he'd come out of and take back streets to the press conference. It was worth a try.

And then he noticed a man in a black suit pushing through the crowd at a little distance behind him, speaking into a headset. Someone official, part of the candidate's security force probably. Another was there to his left, deeper in the crowd, but wading his way as well. *Maybe my brother's here after all,* he thought, and glanced around a moment for him before suddenly realizing that, no, it wasn't Istvan they were moving toward, but him.

Suddenly he realized how he must have looked, pushing his way into the crowd, causing ripples, forcing his way toward the front, then swerving away, going sideways again.

Oh my God, he thought. *They think I'm a threat.*

The man behind was slowly gaining on him. The one to the side was in a thicker part of the crowd, and was having a little more difficulty. If he started pushing and running, Jensi knew, they'd be on him all the more quickly, and people in the crowd would probably start trying to catch hold of him as well. As long as he didn't panic, didn't give the game away, he hoped the two security guards would stay at the same pace, trying to slowly gain on him, but not wanting to panic the crowd.

He kept moving roughly sideways, doing his best to follow the quickest, most open path.

And then, suddenly, he saw his chance: a path opening up in two directions and a large, tall man there in front of him. He ducked and scooted around him, striking the man's left leg as he did so, following the tightest of the path but moving as quickly as he could and as far as he could while still trying not to jar or knock the people in front of them and give his location away. He risked a glance backward and saw that the man he had struck in the knee on the way past had turned and bent to feel his leg, and in so doing effectively blocked the path.

He could only go maybe three meters before the crowd thickened up again, but he hoped that would be enough.

He stayed crouched and hunched over and out of sight for a

moment, and then carefully raised his head, peering over the shoulder of the man behind him. He could only see one security guard, but the one he could see was stationary, staring all around him, trying and failing to catch sight of him. Jensi moved just a little and caught sight of the other one. The man had crossed over Jensi's path without seeing it, was pushing toward the back of the crowd, scanning the people around him carefully but never looking back over his shoulder.

Keeping his head down, Jensi began pushing forward again, more gently this time, trying not to attract the attention of the two security guards. In a few moments he was in a less populated section of the crowd. A few minutes more and he had darted down an alley and was away.

The press conference was only three or four minutes away—the rally must have been set up where it was partly to disrupt it and negate the colonial government's attempts to smooth things over—but that was enough time for Jensi to realize that there was something he had overlooked, that maybe there had been a reason to favor the press conference over the other options after all. He remembered the strange moment when his brother and he had come across the children playing near the crack in the dome, daring one another to get close, remembered, too, Istvan's obsession with the crack and when Istvan had rushed at the crack and struck the dome hard enough with his forehead to bloody it. The press conference was about a crack in a dome. That wasn't much of a connection, but it was the only connection he'd been able to come up with so far.

His heart was beating fast by this time, and he was short of
breath. He ran along the street until he figured he'd passed
the last of the rally, then cut back toward Luna Avenue.

There, just a few hundred feet away, was the municipal hall.
It was a much smaller crowd than the rally, the merest fraction
of the number of people. Still, the steps were crowded, perhaps
close to a hundred people, though as many people seemed to be
looking back toward the rally as toward the man fielding questions up on the steps.

Not wanting to be conspicuous, he slowed his run to a
quick walk, then slowed further still. He drifted into the edge
of the crowd and stopped, waited.

"No," said Councilman Tim Fischer, frowning. He stood
flanked by two security guards, their faces expressionless. "The
government can hardly have teams of wandering assessors
moving from dome to dome, reporting on the integrity of each
structure. We simply can't afford it."

Jensi looked around. A first sweep didn't reveal his brother.

"But," said a reporter, perhaps the same one who had asked
whatever the initial question was, "how can you afford not to?"

Fischer remained unruffled. "We can afford to do a little of
it," he said, apparently thoughtfully. "But we do not have endless resources and so we have to focus them. As most of you
know, we do have a team for the dome we are in today. We felt
that this dome, as the largest dome, should be a priority."

Jensi kept scanning the crowd, more slowly this time, moving from face to face.

"It is also the richest dome per capita," stated another reporter.
"That's beside the point."

"But the poorer domes are not a priority," said the second reporter. "That's exactly the point."

"It is a sad thing," said Councilman Fischer, "but we do have to make choices. We depend on citizens to let us know when they see signs of stress or potential indications of failure. Whenever they let us know, we do our best to correct the problem as quickly as possible. In this case, it's not a governmental failure that's the problem. It's a failure on behalf of the citizenry. *They* should have been on this sooner."

A dull, dissatisfied rumble moved through the crowd, people turning to one another and whispering, and in that moment Jensi caught sight of Istvan. He was mostly hidden behind a large middle-aged woman, on the other side of the crowd, near the top of the steps, close to the councilman. He was standing motionless, his head down, and he remained that way even when the people around him were turning to one another to discuss something the councilman had said. But Jensi could tell by the tension of his neck and shoulders that he was as tautly wound as a spring.

Istvan was waiting for a sign, something that would tell him when to go, what to do next. He already knew what he would do, they had taught him, they had given him his purpose and explained to him what would happen when he did it, how funny it would be, but the question now was *when*. And they were not the ones that could tell him that. The world around him had to be the one to tell him that, a voice had to come, to signal to him, to show him its pattern and shape and draw him forward.

They had suggested to him that there was no reason to hesitate. He had a *purpose* and so as soon as he saw his opportunity he should spring forward. But no, he was almost seeing a pattern but it wasn't quite there yet. Something was missing. Someone had not felt it yet and was standing wrong, the lines could not be traced, the shadow man remained hidden, unspeaking. Or something else was just slightly out of place and needed to be adjusted. And yet it was not his task to adjust the pattern. No, his task was only to see it, and once he saw it, to let it call him forward to his purpose.

He would wait. Would wait as long as he had to.

Patience, he told himself. Patience.

The man in front of him spoke on, answering questions but in ways that made no sense to Istvan. He pretended to be listening but he was not listening. He was watching and waiting. In his head he was saying the numbers, calling the pattern forward, reminding himself, and his voice, he realized now, was mumbling too, not too loud, not loud enough to be heard. But if the pattern did not come soon, he would, he knew, get louder and louder still.

And then he caught out of the corner of his eye a flicker of motion and the pattern slipped into place and he saw the life beneath things rear its head just a little, a voice forming inside him, calling him forward to fulfill his purpose.

Jensi passed back out of the crowd and circled around to the other side, began cautiously working his way up the steps, trying not to cause a disturbance. He kept his eyes open for other security in the crowd. There was nobody obvious: either there was nobody or somebody was undercover. There was Istvan's head and shoulders just a few steps above him.

All I have to do is get to him, thought Jensi. *If I can get to him and touch him, I'll be able to coax him out of doing whatever he's thinking of doing.*

But even as he thought this, Istvan lifted his head and began to move.

"Don't you think—" a new reporter began to say, and then stopped when she saw Istvan suddenly dash toward the podium. The security man nearest to him had been caught napping, too, and by the time he'd uncrossed his arms and begun to react, Istvan had kicked him hard in the knee. Even from where he was, pushing desperately forward through the crowd to try to get to his brother, Jensi heard the snap of the bone.

The man went down in a heap, with an unearthly cry. The other guard turned and rushed forward. He was now grappling with Istvan, trying to pull something out of his hand. Someone in the crowd started screaming and suddenly everyone was fleeing down the stairs and away, the flood of moving bodies carrying Jensi along with it. He tried to resist the current, then turned and fell. Someone stepped on his hand, hard, and somebody else stumbled over him and careened farther down the steps, and then he had scrambled to his feet again and was rushing forward. He saw Istvan head-butt the guard he was struggling with. The man let go, stumbling back a little bit before falling down. Fischer now was crouched behind the podium, cowering, protecting his head with his hands. Istvan spun and pointed what was in his hand at the man, and Jensi realized it was a gun.

"Istvan, no!" he shouted.

But Istvan didn't seem to hear him. He had a strange grin on his face—strange because it did not seem malevolent or malicious, but only like the grin of someone who was playing a joke.

And then he pulled the trigger and there was a roar and Councilman Fischer's head broke apart to spatter the podium. For a moment the body swayed there and then all the joints went loose and it collapsed. Istvan's face had changed: he was no longer grinning. Instead he seemed genuinely shocked. He turned the gun around and brought it close to his face and stared into its barrel, as if it could tell him something. Then he lifted his head and suddenly met his brother's gaze and this time seemed to see him. Shaking his head, he said, "This is not my purpose."

"Put the gun down," said Jensi. "Please."

But Istvan kept holding it. "Brother," he pleaded, "help me."

Jensi took a step forward, but it was already too late. The second security guard had regained his feet and plowed into Istvan, knocking him down, the gun clattering away. Istvan didn't resist. He allowed the man to force his head against the concrete and hold it there while he zip-tied first his arms and then his legs. And Jensi, watching all of this, remembered above all else the way that Istvan's expression remained puzzled, confused.

"Who are you?" shouted out one of the reporters who had remained behind. But Istvan didn't answer.

Jensi tried to get close but the security guard waved him

back and, when he kept on coming, pulled out a pistol, threatened him. "If I need to, I'll have you taken away along with him," he said. The other security guard was still lying on the ground, groaning, holding his leg.

"Why did you do it?" asked one of the few people who had stayed, apparently a reporter.

"No vids!" said the security guard brandishing the gun, but more than a few people were already taking them with their mobiles.

This time Istvan did speak. He licked his lips and said, softly enough that Jensi himself could barely hear. "My purpose. But no, it wasn't . . . it was wrong."

"What was that?" asked the reporter. "Speak up."

"Shut up," said the guard, and kicked Istvan in the ribs.

"Who gave you your purpose?" asked Jensi.

"They did," said Istvan.

"I told you to shut up," said the guard.

"What is it you want to tell the world?" asked the reporter. "All eyes are on you now. What do you want the world to know?"

"Who's they? Who gave you your purpose?" said Jensi again.

"*They* did," said Istvan, and grimaced.

A moment later the steps were flooded by SCAC officers in riot gear, and Jensi wondered fleetingly if they were the "they" that Istvan had been talking about. One of them was in front of Jensi now, pushing him back and down the steps, the others moving rapidly to establish a perimeter. Jensi tried to resist and found himself pushed over and clattering down the steps.

Through the gap between the officer's legs he caught a brief glimpse of his brother's face, still as confused as ever, and then they had forced a bag over Istvan's head and were hustling him away.

The news was in people's minds for a day or two, the subject of discussion on the vids, and then it disappeared almost as suddenly as it had first begun. Jensi had a hard time not thinking it had been deliberately quelled. For a week or two you could find the vid if you looked hard enough, hiding in some of the backwaters of the system. It showed nothing of the assassination itself, since the killshot had been hidden by the podium. No, you had to be to one side, as Jensi had been, to see Fischer's head burst and scatter blood and brain. But what you did see was the look of confusion on Istvan's face directly after the shot, a confusion and puzzlement that continued well after he'd been knocked down and tied up.

Jensi kept whirling the footage back, looking at it, trying to understand exactly what had happened. Was it simply an indication that Istvan had come out of his fantasy world, was now realizing that the blood and brains were real? Had he convinced himself that the gun, when fired, would do something else? Or had he, in fact, been *told* that the gun would do something else: fire blanks, fire a flag, not fire at all? Was it a question of Istvan's madness, or had he been set up?

And, more importantly, was there any way in watching the vid to know for certain? After a few dozen viewings, Jensi guessed not. He might, he realized, never have a clear handle on what had happened to his brother. Yet he could not stop himself from continuing to watch the vid, continuing to hope that this time, by slowing the footage down to a crawl, he'd see something that he had missed before.

Henry had shown up shortly after they'd carted Istvan away, when Jensi was still standing there at the scene, trying to take in what had happened. "I came as fast as I could," he claimed. "As soon as I saw it on the vids. I'm so sorry." Without Henry, Jensi did not know how long he might have gone on standing there, shocked. But he let Henry gather him around the shoulders and lead him away.

Back in his apartment, he slept the sleep of the dead, not waking up for almost twenty hours. When he did, he found Henry still there, asleep on the couch. Once Henry realized he was awake, he roused himself and made Jensi something to eat.

"I've been asking about him," said Henry. "Trying to find out what they're going to do with him."

Jensi nodded listlessly. "They arrested him," he said. "I was there. I saw it. He shot the man. What other choice did they have?"

Henry shook his head. "They took him away, but they didn't arrest him."

"What?"

"No. He's not at the police station or in any holding facility

I could locate. Or if he is, they won't tell me. Since you're a relative, you might have better luck."

But when he began contacting people, he had the same results, or lack thereof, as Henry. Nobody in the police station admitted any knowledge of Istvan. None of the facilities in the incarceration dome had received him, either.

"But he has to be somewhere," said Jensi to a prison representative on the other end of the line.

"No doubt he is somewhere," she said acidly. "But he isn't here." And then she broke the connection.

They tried again. Henry called his father and got him to talk to an acquaintance on the police force. He reported to Jensi that yes, there had been a man brought in with a bag over his head, surrounded by SCAC forces, but almost as soon as he had arrived he had been taken away again. He didn't know where or why—this wasn't, he made clear to Henry's dad, standard procedure. The man promised to ask around if he could do so without raising too many hackles, see what he could find out.

After that, they didn't know what else to do. They sat silent for a while, trying to come up with other ideas of how to locate Istvan.

"Maybe they killed him," Jensi finally said, breaking the silence. And then, when Henry didn't contradict him, said, "Say something. Did they?"

Slowly Henry shook his head. "I don't think so," he said. "It doesn't seem like a smart move on their part, particularly with the vids still available."

"But they seem to be getting rid of the vids."

"They can't get rid of all of them. They don't know who has

them on private systems—it could come back to haunt them. It's not in their best interest to kill him unless they're sure he won't be needed later. I don't think they could possibly know that yet."

"But you think it's possible they killed him?" asked Jensi.

Henry nodded. "It's possible," he admitted.

He took sick leave. He watched the vids over and over, still looking, still searching for something that would mean anything. If only he'd tried to keep Istvan from leaving. Maybe if he hadn't been as tired as he was, he'd have managed to do that. But then again, maybe not. Or if he'd asked Istvan more questions, tried to coax what he meant out of him. Then, even if he hadn't managed to get him to stay, Jensi would have more of a sense of what he meant by his purpose and of who "they" were.

Or maybe, he couldn't help but think, even though he didn't want to, *I couldn't have done anything to make any difference at all.*

When Henry's father showed up at Jensi's door, it was only to tell him that his contact hadn't been able to find anything out. Nobody seemed to know anything at all, though it was clear that a higher authority was at work, maybe even that Istvan was no longer on the planet.

"No longer on the planet?" asked Jensi. "But how can he stand trial if he's not here?"

Henry's father fell silent. "He can't," he finally said. "And he probably won't."

"What do you mean, won't?"

"He's a political prisoner. An enemy of the state," said Henry's father. "The rules don't apply to him in the same way."

"The law applies to everybody the same," said Jensi.

Henry's father reached out and squeezed his shoulder. "Surely you've been around long enough that you can't actually believe that," he said. "Your brother has been taken away, somewhere secret, somewhere where the laws don't apply. There, they'll torture him until he tells them whatever they want to know about why he did what he did. After that, they'll imprison him in an undisclosed location." He gave Jensi a look of pity. "In all likelihood, you'll never see your brother again."

But still, even having been told that, he couldn't help but try. He went to the police station, inquired after his brother, and when they turned him away and told him Istvan wasn't there he simply returned again the next day. He kept coming, they kept turning him away, until finally they told him that he couldn't come anymore. He insisted on seeing the chief of police, who also claimed to have no idea what had happened with his brother, claimed that the police had had nothing to do with it, but did actually listen to him. When he had finished and the police chief was still shaking his head, Jensi asked, "Who do I have to talk to next?"

The police chief was happy to send him up to the superintendent, just to get rid of him. From there he got shuffled between politicians and the military, one sending him to the other and vice versa for a while, like a ricocheting bullet, until finally a councilman named Richard Savage was staring across a table at him and asking him to repeat the story one more time, and once he had he took pity on him.

"Do you have a lawyer?" Savage asked him. Jensi shook his head. "If you had one," said Savage, "he might be able to cut through some of this red tape."

He didn't have enough money for a lawyer, but he got one anyway, a young, independent fellow named Lee Tomkins who was more interested in the politics of the case than in any money he might earn. Even with the lawyer it took a while, more shunting and shuttling, but finally he and Tomkins were in an office with a military official by the name of Granon.

"What brings you here?" asked Granon. He had clear, pale eyes and a steady gaze, and a stony face that gave very little away.

"You know why we're here," said Tomkins, and began to unload signed and stamped forms from his bag. He placed them on the desk, but Granon ignored them. "We've followed protocol," said Tomkins. "We've done everything that the law requires of us. Now you are required to tell us where this man's brother is."

"That information is classified," said Granon.

"We have all the approvals," said Tomkins steadily. "You can't stonewall us."

"I'm not stonewalling," said Granon. "I'm just not in a position to answer your question." He leaned back in his chair, tented his fingers. "I can admit we have his brother. But he is a political prisoner."

"My brother doesn't have a political bone in his body," said Jensi.

Granon shrugged. "He killed a politician at a public ceremony," he said. "He's political."

"It's all a misunderstanding," said Jensi. "There's something not right about him; he didn't know what he was doing. He shouldn't be in jail. He should be in a facility, somewhere where he can get help."

"He isn't in jail," said Granon. "He's in a containment center."

"Where?"

"I can't say where. That's classified information."

"How can you take someone off without even a trial and hide them in a containment center where nobody knows where they are?"

Granon didn't answer.

"Is it off world?"

"I can't answer that," said Granon.

"What can you answer?"

"I can tell you that we have your brother. I can tell you that he is still alive. I can tell you as well that he will not be released anytime soon, perhaps ever."

Jensi shook his head. "Who else can I talk to?" he asked.

"Nobody else," said Granon. "I'm the end of the line. I'm sorry, but this is as much as you're ever going to know."

Jensi turned to Tomkins. The lawyer nodded. "I'm afraid he's right. Next step is the courts. We can file a suit, but it'll take years for it even to get heard. For all intents and purposes, we've run out of possibilities."

Jensi kept trying, even after Tomkins drifted away and on to other cases, but he realized more with each passing day how hopeless it was. Eventually, it became almost a hobby, a way of stirring things up a little even though he knew there was no hope.

He returned to picking, slowly started thinking of his brother less and less, though when he did think of him it was with a twinge of guilt and pain.

But he had his own life to live. He had to keep on.

Henry just squeaked by in school, then left to work off world for a while, the plan being to get a job that would let him build up some quick capital and then return and invest in real estate. Jensi was sorry to see him go. After that, it was just him, and picking, and lying around his apartment. Occasionally an evening out with an acquaintance or a friend. Or wandering the streets, late at night, alone, stumbling through endless self-accusations, making vows to himself about what he would do to get his brother back. But part of him wondered if he would ever see his brother again, and deep inside he knew the chances weren't good. He would have to learn to live with that fact. He would have to learn to move forward alone.

PART TWO

When he pulled the trigger the gun did not do what he had been told it would, did not make a funny joke. Instead, it killed the man Fischer. Who had told him? He couldn't remember now, not for certain, not after all he'd been through. And he wasn't entirely sure that it had been someone outside of him. There were voices inside of him as well, and these were the voices that, at times, he could not help but listen to. But no, this had been, he was sure, an outside voice. Or not *sure* exactly, but almost sure, nearly sure. Jensi was an outside voice, so was his mother, but his mother, now that she was gone, had become an inside voice, too. And Jensi, when he was away from him, could become an inside voice as well. How was he to keep it all straight?

But still, Istvan was pretty sure that the voice that had given him the gun had been an outside voice, not an inside one. He had been more than pretty sure until the gun had gone off and instead of spraying red dye like it was supposed to, had blown apart the man Fischer's head. Who was the man Fischer? He didn't even really know. Just a man that someone inside of him or outside of him wanted sprayed with red dye to humiliate him. A kind of joke, the voice had explained to him.

No, it must have been an outside voice: he remembered seeing a body along with it. There had been a man with a pale face, missing most of his hair. He had spoken with him for a while, and Istvan had been fed by him, and it had gone on for days perhaps or longer than that, the voice attached to the man asking questions, little needles sticking into his skin, and then the man nodding when Istvan answered them in a way he liked and gently or roughly teaching him other answers when Istvan answered in a way that he did not like. And it had been through that, through their conversation, that his *purpose* had developed. It wasn't like the voice was exactly telling him what his purpose was, more like he was coming to it on his own, but he had to admit, now, now that he had time to think, that the voice had been like a funnel, directing him, guiding him in, slowly narrowing out all other possibilities. Like those chutes in the vids you drive cattle down just before you shoot them in the head with a bolt gun. Or pigs.

Was the voice outside or inside? That was the question now. If it was inside, it would come back and he would talk to it, try to understand what had gone wrong, what he had done wrong, why he had managed to kill the man Fischer instead of fulfilling his purpose. If the voice was outside, then it was a trickier question. It might come back or it might not, there was no way of saying. And voices outside, he knew from long experience, were not always direct, not always honest. They would say things they didn't mean. Voices inside weren't like that. Not usually, anyway.

. . .

Where was he now? For a while he had been in a sack. Or his head had been in a sack anyway. His arms and legs had been tied and were slowly going numb and then a bunch of men wearing uniforms had appeared and put his head in a sack. It reminded him of what they used to do with horses, he had read about it, as a way to calm them when they had to go past something difficult or impossible, like a fire. They put their heads in bags and then they couldn't see enough to get frightened. Did they think he was frightened? Of what? Horses also would eat food out of a bag hanging from their faces, but that wasn't exactly the same thing since the whole head wasn't in a sack. *I'm like a horse,* he had thought, though it was hard to think that with his arms and legs tied behind his back. You couldn't do that with a horse, he thought, unless you broke their limbs and folded them back the wrong way. That would kill the horse, probably. At very least cripple it. And that made him feel like maybe they had done that to him, had broken his legs and limbs, and so he began to struggle. The inside of the bag smelled like sweat. And then suddenly there were hands on him, hands all over him, and they were lifting him up and carrying him away.

He was in a vehicle. He could tell by the way the floor he was lying on was rumbling, and by the hum of the electric motor. Then someone sat him up and leaned him back against something and cut the straps holding his wrists together and he began to chafe his hands to bring the feeling back. Someone, too, maybe the same someone, cut the straps on his legs and feeling also began to come back there. He started to reach up to remove the sack that was over his head, but someone grabbed his hands and pushed them down. *No,* a voice said, *don't touch it. Leave it on.* He was pretty sure it was an outside voice, but since all he could see was the inside of the sack, how could he be absolutely sure? He decided in any case to listen to it, to do what it said.

They were in the vehicle for what felt like a long time. *Maybe not all that long,* a voice inside his head suggested, but no, he had to disagree, it *was* a long time. Then the vehicle stopped. For a while he just sat there, listening to muttering voices around him and inside of him. And then there was the sound of metal scraping and rough hands had grabbed him and were helping him to his feet and then pushing him out. He almost fell while leaving the vehicle but they were there to catch him. For a moment he could hear the sounds of the dome, and he could see the light, a hint of it, through the weave of his sack, but quickly they were in another space where it was quieter, enclosed.

"Where are we?" he asked. But maybe his voice was muffled by the sack because they didn't answer, nobody answered him. Though whoever was holding his right arm did, at least, tighten their grip. A clattering sound as he was propelled forward—his shoes now on a different sort of flooring, something slick and hard—and then was abruptly jerked to the right. He knocked against something that must have been the side of a doorway and then hands were pushing on the tops of his shoulders and it took him a moment to realize that they were trying to get him to sit. *Why don't they just say sit?* he wondered. *Like they would to a dog? Why aren't they talking?* Slowly he lowered himself down until he found something solid beneath him and then relaxed into it.

For a few minutes, there was the noise of bodies moving, a tramping back and forth in the space around him, the sound of breathing, the scrape and scuff of boots against floors, all of it slightly dampened by the fabric surrounding his head. Then, slowly it faded, all of it moving away and retiring to a safe distance. A door slowly closed, and noise became silence, apart from the sound of his breathing within the sack.

He sat there, waiting. Was he alone? He didn't know, but suspected so. For a moment he held his breath and listened, but still heard nothing. What, he wondered, should he do?

Carefully he lifted one hand to the sack, felt his face through it, waiting for a hand to come and push his hand down and away. When it did not, he slowly pulled the sack off his head.

He was facing into a corner, not more than a foot or so away from each wall, like a schoolboy being punished. *First horse, then dog, then schoolboy*, he thought. *I'm evolving.* He rubbed his face, then slowly turned.

Behind him was a stretch of open floor. Then a large table, on the other side of which sat a small gray man. The man was motionless, just watching him. When he saw that Istvan had noticed him, he smiled.

"Come pull your chair closer," he said, and patted the table.

"Why should I?" asked Istvan.

"Why shouldn't you?" the man responded, and Istvan,

having no ready response to this, considered for a moment and then pulled his chair to the table.

"Do you know what you've done?" asked the small gray man.

"Why are you gray?" asked Istvan.

"Excuse me?"

"Why are you gray? That's not a normal color. Are you real? Are you the shadow man?"

"Do I look gray to you?"

Istvan nodded.

"Interesting," said the man. "I don't know if it's a normal color or not. I don't know how you typically see things. I've always thought of myself as having a normal color. And yes, I am real."

Istvan nodded again, then stared at the table.

"What about you?" asked the gray man. "Do you think of yourself as real?"

"Me?" said Istvan, surprised. "Of course I'm real. Why wouldn't I be?"

"That's good," said the man, and smiled. "Then, both of us being real, we can speak seriously."

"About what?"

"About what you did."

Istvan folded his arms. "I don't think it went right," he said. "It wasn't supposed to happen that way."

"No? How was it supposed to happen?"

"He wasn't supposed to get hurt."

"Are you sure?"

No, Istvan realized. He wasn't sure. That was what was troubling him. Maybe the man Fischer *was* supposed to get hurt.

Maybe he had been tricked. Or maybe he had simply misunderstood. Not knowing what to answer, he simply didn't answer. He looked up and the gray man was still there, across the table, watching him with unblinking eyes.

"You'll be with us for a long time," said the gray man.

"Why?" asked Istvan.

"Because of what you did," said the gray man. "You killed someone. Not only that, you ended up killing someone political. You assassinated him. He was only a councilman, but he was important in other ways, important to us. That means you belong to us now. To me."

Istvan felt anger rising in him. "I don't belong to anybody," he said.

"It's just a figure of speech," said the gray man affably. "What I mean is that you are now an enemy of the state. We have to understand what you did and who convinced you to do it. We know you didn't plan this yourself. We're eager enough to understand that we'll use any means necessary to have our answers."

"I won't tell you anything," said Istvan. "Why should I?"

The gray man smiled. "We're patient," he said. "We don't need the answers right away. But eventually you will tell us everything we want to know."

Istvan shook his head and waited for the gray man to disappear. But he didn't disappear.

"You're not real," Istvan claimed.

"We already agreed I was real," said the man.

"Did we?" asked Istvan. "Or was that someone else?"

The gray man smiled. "I like you, Istvan," he said. And then a moment later, everything around Istvan started to go strange, the light changing, going bloody. The gray man started to fold himself up. First he folded one arm up and then the other arm, and then he bent in the middle of the back and folded backward. When he was done, he was nothing but a strange gray square lying flat in the chair. Istvan reached across the table and picked it up.

Open it, open it, a voice inside him was saying.

And so he did, slowly unfolding it until it had become a man again. He set it up in the chair and then took a step back to look at it. When he did, the light went back to normal. It was a man all right. Only it wasn't the gray man. It was a man in a uniform and with a red face, and from the face was coming a voice that was yelling.

When it stopped for a moment so that the man could draw his breath, Istvan stuck his hand out. "I'm Istvan," he said. "Put it there." He closed his hand around the man's hand and shook it, only it wasn't a hand at all, but a neck. As it turned out, the man's neck. Abruptly he was lying on the ground with other people's hands on him, holding him down. *What have I done?* he wondered. *What's wrong with me?*

He was like that for a while and then they hauled him up and set him in the chair again. This time they tied his hands to the arms of the chair. There were more men in the room, one to either side of him in fact. The red-faced man was still there, sitting on the other side of the table now and rubbing his neck, looking a little frightened.

"What about you?" asked Istvan. "Are you real?"

"What's wrong with you?" the red-faced man said, which was enough to make Istvan think that yes, this man was real, since he had heard that very question posed to him so many times before by people who actually were real.

He and the red-faced man talked for a long time. The red-faced man had a lot of interest in the politician and what had happened to him, in why Istvan had shot him. He seemed to want to ask the same questions again and again in slightly different ways. Each time a question was asked, Istvan did his best to answer, but the man never seemed satisfied. "Who told you to do what you did?" the red-faced man might ask. And Istvan would answer, "They did." "Who are they?" the man would riposte. "The ones who told me," Istvan answered, quite truthfully. It went on and on like that, sometimes very much like a merry-go-round, sometimes like other rides at the carnival, rides Istvan had never ridden but which he had seen vids of. He wished he could ride them. They might be fun. As long as he could think about carnival rides it did not bother Istvan to have this conversation, but it seemed to bother the red-faced man, and he would get very angry and lean over the table and sometimes shout into Istvan's face. This shouting, too, he could think of as a carnival ride in a way, as long as he thought hard enough.

After a while, the red-faced man got so irritated with him that he threw up his hands and left. Istvan was on his own, sitting in the chair, waiting. He did not mind being on his own, even preferred it in a way. So he just sat there. There was, somewhere deep in his head, a slow staticky sound that he could listen to, and so he listened to it, wondering if he would begin to hear the inside voices hiding in the static. That sometimes happened to him. But no, he did not hear voices, just the static. It was soothing, relaxing, and for a while he forgot where he was.

When he remembered where he was again, the red-faced man was back, shaking him this time, yelling again. Then he picked Istvan up by his shirt and lifted him off the chair and let him go so that he fell sprawling on the ground. Istvan lay there, confused, looking up at him, wondering why the man had done that to him when all he had been doing was just sitting minding his own business.

"Get up," the man said.

Why? wondered Istvan. *I'm fine where I am.*

He lay there a while longer, just staring at the man.

"Get up," the man repeated, and gave him a kick in the ribs.

This man is not your friend, a voice told him. It was an inside voice, he knew, because he could tell that the red-faced man did not hear it, too. It was a voice just for him. Voices like that, voices just for him, made him feel special.

Not your friend, the voice repeated.

"He's not?" he said.

The man standing above him creased his brow in confusion.

No, he's not. In fact, he's your enemy. You need to get rid of him.

"Rid of him how?"

The red-face man had taken a step back. "Who are you talking to?"

Start by getting up. Sit back in the chair. I'll tell you what to do.

It was good to have a voice with him. It was good especially when the world around him was confusing and he didn't know what to do. The voices seemed to know more about the world than he did, even if sometimes they told him to do things that later he wasn't certain he should have done. But yes, he would listen to it. Slowly he pulled himself around and stood up, then went to the chair.

"There, that's better," said the red-faced man.

No, said the voice, *it isn't. But we will make it better.*

"Yes," said Istvan. He was talking to the voice, but the red-faced man thought he was talking to him and so he nodded.

"Good," the man said. "Now are you ready to tell me what happened?"

Tell him 'yes,' said the voice. And now the voice was no longer feeling like it was inside him exactly, it was more than that somehow. He was beginning to see now a shadowy shape forming there right next to the red-faced man. Not a body exactly, it would never be a body. But, he knew from past experience, eventually it would be *like* a body. It was like his vision was slowly adjusting so that it could begin to see what was really there. He smiled.

"Yes," he said.

"Good," said the red-faced man. "Let's start at the beginning. Who were you working for?"

The shadowy shape was now more or less human, though still a little blurred around the edges. He watched as the shadow man put its hands around the red-faced man's throat and pretend to choke him. The red-faced man didn't seem to notice. Then the shape turned to Istvan and nodded encouragingly.

Now you, it said.

In an instant he had sprung out of his chair and thrown

himself across the table, knocking both the red-faced man and his chair backward. The man gave a startled cry and then his head struck the cement floor and his body was suddenly loose. Istvan clamped his fingers around the man's throat and squeezed.

Yes, said the shadow man, now kneeling beside him, an awful smile on its blurry lips. *Do it. Harder!*

And then the door burst open and other hands were on him tearing him off, dragging him away.

10

They bound his hands again. After a while, they brought him back into the interrogation room, unless it was a different room. Curious, he tried to look to see if there was blood on the floor that had leaked out of the man's head but either this was a different room or they had cleaned the blood up. Then more questions, from several people this time, back and forth, none of them giving him a chance to do much. Where was the voice? Now that it had a shadow body, had it simply walked off? In any case, he couldn't hear it. He kept listening for it but couldn't hear it, but it was so hard sometimes to hear the inside voices when there were so many outside voices talking.

Whatever he was saying to answer the questions didn't seem to be satisfying them; they kept on asking him the same questions again and again as if he had another answer to give to them. So, he stopped answering. This didn't seem to help any, though: they still kept on asking, and now they started acting like his body might have the answers as well. They kept yanking on his hair or pushing his head down or pushing his head up or edging him out of the chair. When he hit the ground he lay there, wondering if the inside voice would come back. But nothing happened. They were right there, all around them, but it felt to him like they were moving farther and farther away, like he was burrowing deeper and deeper into his own body where they couldn't get at him.

After a while, they took him away, down a hall and to a cell, and locked him in. Once he was alone, he felt himself slowly beginning to fill up his body again, until the things around him felt like they were real and there again. His body, he realized, hurt a lot, ached all over. There were bruises on his arms and legs where they had hit him, and probably bruises on his face, too, though there was no mirror or anything reflective he could use to examine it. There was the taste of blood in his mouth and he seemed to be missing a tooth.

He groaned a little, pulled himself onto the narrow cot and lay there. How had this happened to him? Why were things always happening to him in ways that he had a hard time understanding? Was it the same thing for everybody or just for him? He thought back to Jensi—Jensi always seemed to understand the world around him more clearly. Why would that be the case? *What's wrong with me?* wondered Istvan again.

After a while he fell asleep.

He awoke to the sound of someone groaning. It took him a while to realize that it was him. His body hurt all over, and was stiff now. He sat up slowly holding his head. When he looked up, it was to see the gray man.

"You," said Istvan.

"Me," said the gray man.

"Are you real?" asked Istvan.

A flicker of amusement passed over the man's face. "We decided earlier I was," he said. "Don't you remember?"

Istvan thought for a moment, then nodded. "But maybe I was wrong," he said.

"Does it really matter if you were right or wrong?" asked the man. "Who else is there to talk to?"

"What do you want to talk about?" asked Istvan.

"You know what I want to talk about," said the gray man. "Who told you to do what you did?"

Istvan just stared at him, then shook his head. "I've tried to explain it," he said. "I can't."

"You won't, you mean," said the man.

"No," said Istvan. "Can't. I don't know why."

The man stared at him thoughtfully. "You really believe that, don't you?" he said. Once Istvan nodded, he continued: "I'm afraid it doesn't matter what you believe," he said patiently. "The information is there. We're going to get to it. Even if we have to break your skull open and filter it out bit by bit. And in the process, we'll make sure that you never are able to do anything like what you did again." He smiled. "We have a reputation for being very thorough. It is not an undeserved reputation."

Istvan had an impulse to stand up and fall on the gray man, but he suppressed it. He was afraid that the same thing would happen that happened before, that the gray man would fold up again, into a gray box, and then unfold into someone or something else. He did not want to see that happen again. So he stayed there, waiting, part of him hoping the gray man would go away, part of him hoping he would say something else that would help him to understand better the situation he was in.

But when the gray man did not speak, Istvan finally cleared his throat. "What will happen to me next?" he asked.

"Normally you would go back into an interrogation room a few more times," said the gray man. "Maybe a dozen times, maybe two. But what you did to my colleague has sped the process up a bit."

"Your colleague?"

"The man you strangled," he said. "Or rather, started to strangle and then cracked his skull." He shook his finger at Istvan. "That wasn't very nice of you."

"But he told me to do it," said Istvan, and then noticed the gray man was staring at him with delicately poised attention.

"*Who* told you?" he asked.

Istvan raised a hand and let it fall helplessly. Who had told him? At the time it seemed so clear, but now it seemed so confused. A man that was not a man, a figure made of smoke, a voice that perhaps was there, perhaps not. How was he to explain that? Particularly to a man whose skin looked wrong?

"I didn't mean to," he finally said.

"You didn't answer my question," said the gray man.

"I didn't?"

The gray man smiled, shook his head. "No," he said. "You didn't." He sighed and rose from his chair, pushing up with his hands on his knees. "No matter," he said. "We'll have you for a long time. I don't need the answer today."

The gray man started to move toward the door, then turned back. "You asked what would happen to you," he said. "Next step, since you sped things up by murdering a man who was just trying to do his job, is for you to be taken off planet to a secure location, a place not subject to the laws in place here.

That'll make it easier to work on you." He smiled. "*Work on you* is obviously a euphemism," he said. "By the time we're done with you, I don't know how much of your mind will be left."

He struck the door twice with the flat of his hand. "Then again," he said, "it's an open question how much of your mind is there now." The door groaned and slid open. "Be seeing you," the gray man said, and slipped out.

11

But it was months, or what felt like months anyway, before he saw the gray man again. First they left him alone in his cell for a while without food or water, and then, once he was very weak, finally gave him water. Then they beat the bottoms of his feet with a steel rod until he couldn't walk or even stand. They they put a bag over his head and poured water over it, so that it felt like he was drowning. They stripped him and left him shivering in a cold bare room and then yelled at him and insisted that he talk until he felt he had no choice but to retreat deeper and deeper into his body and watch it all from a distance.

Most of it he watched with horror, but their growing frustration at being unable to crack him he watched with a certain delight. How many days that went on, he couldn't say for certain. But then abruptly it came to an end: they again put a sack over his head and bound his hands and hustled him careening down a corridor, laughing at him when he fell before yanking him back to his feet. *Is it the same sack?* he couldn't help wondering. They put him in a vehicle again, but he didn't think it was the same vehicle they had put him in before—it felt different somehow. The tone of the space, even through the sack, was different. There was someone next to him holding him firmly by one arm and someone on the other side of him holding him firmly by the other arm. They drove somewhere for a long time—*maybe not all that long,* suggested a voice somewhere inside of him and when he heard it he grunted with satisfaction into the hood. *Welcome, voice,* he thought. He felt one of the hands tighten on one of his arms. However long it was, eventually the vehicle stopped and he was rushed out of it and brought quickly into another place. At first he thought he was going into a building, but when they finally had him inside and seated and had removed the sack from around his head, he saw that he wasn't in a building at all, but in some kind of aircraft. He was alone except for two guards.

"Where are we going?" he asked.

But the guards with him would not answer the question. They would not even look at him. There was a grating sound above them and he saw light begin to flood in and realized they were in the spaceport, and then the ship's engines began to rise and they were lifting straight up and into the air. That, of everything he had experienced so far, turned out to be the thing most akin to a carnival ride. He could feel his stomach pushing down, threatening to leave his body, and his whole body felt heavy and he had a hard time breathing, and the voices in him drifted tingling down from his head before getting tangled within his legs. And then they were through the upper lock of the dome and the pressure began to diminish, to become less and less until it was almost nonexistent. Soon they were circling a space station, synchronizing speed with it and slowly coming closer until with a gentle *thunk* they had docked.

"Is this where we're going?" he asked. But neither of the guards answered. It felt strange to be weightless, to feel like you hardly even had a body. It was like how sometimes the inside voices didn't have a body, he thought, and then thought, *Maybe I am becoming an inside voice.* Or maybe the inside voices weren't inside at all, he told himself, but in space, where they could exist without a body. He was webbed into his chair, but floating now, jostling gently back and forth against the webbing. But the two guards seemed to be sticking to the floor, something about their boots holding them in place. He didn't have boots. Why not?

They unwebbed him and, grabbing him by his elbows, propelled him gently through the air, but as they got closer to the hatch, he started to feel his body come back to him and by the time they had gone through and into the station, he weighed nearly as much as he always had. Having a body again was something of a disappointment.

They dragged him down around the wheel of the space station and to a bigger bay where a larger ship was waiting, not a planet hopper but an interstellar vessel. Near it was the gray man, holding a rubberized sack.

"Ah, Istvan," he said. "I've been waiting for you."

"Why?" asked Istvan, astonished.

"Now that these fine gentlemen have tried their best," he said, gesturing to the two guards, "it's my turn." He gestured to the guards. "Take him in."

The guards dragged him up the ramp and into the ship. They passed a series of crew members, many of whom regarded him nervously.

"No need to be alarmed," said the gray man to one of them. "You never saw this."

The gray man directed them down a flight of stairs and through a thick metal door marked RESTRICTED AREA on the outside. Inside was a chamber lined with metal cabinets, a grate cut into the floor. The room was freshly washed, water still puddled on the floor, but there was nevertheless an odd smell to it, something that Istvan couldn't quite place. In the room's center were three reclining rubber and metal chairs, all of them bolted securely to the floor, each equipped with a series of restraints.

"Strap him in, boys," said the gray man.

Eventually they did. First, though, they removed his restraints, and then removed his clothing, making a neat pile of it to one side. For a moment Istvan thought of trying to break free but he was too weak to do much of anything. They led him to the chair and strapped down his arms and his legs, and then affixed a head strap as well, something to keep him from turning either left or right. Then they saluted the small gray man and left the room.

"They can see you. You're real," said Istvan.

"I thought we'd already agreed that I was real," said the gray man. "Can't you accept anything as meaning something once and for all?"

No, thought Istvan. *No, I can't.* He had been hurt too many times, burnt too often by a world that seemed to be constantly changing, constantly shifting out of his grasp.

The small gray man came forward and stroked Istvan's hair. "Now we're alone," he said, and then he reached into his sack and took out a razor and began to shave the hair roughly away, sometimes nicking and gouging Istvan's scalp.

"We have lots of things to play with," said the man, gesturing to the cabinets. "We've got a lot of time before we arrive where we're going and where the fun will really start." He reached into the rubberized sack, bringing out a hypodermic and a needle in a plastic casing. He affixed the second to the first and broke the casing away. "No reason we should wait until we arrive to get things started," he said, and smiled.

He primed the needle, and then brought it slowly down until it was no longer within Istvan's field of vision. Istvan felt a sharp prick in his arm, followed by a burning sensation, and he winced. The burning pushed its way down toward his fingertips and began to climb up his arm.

"How does that feel?" asked the small gray man, almost in a whisper. He was holding the hypodermic up again and Istvan could see that it was empty, the needle slick with blood.

Istvan felt the burning push its way past his shoulder and then insinuate itself into his chest and neck, and then suddenly it felt like the top of his skull had been torn off and the skull filled with liquid fire. He gasped, could see in his wavering vision the smiling face of the gray man.

And the worst part was that—even as he struggled to catch his breath, even as he tried and failed to stay focused and keep a grip on his mind, even as pain rapidly transformed into the worst thing he had ever felt—he experienced a brief moment of lucidity, and couldn't help but realize that this was only the beginning, and that before it was over it was sure to get much, much worse.

PART THREE

12

In a dream Jensi found himself in an unfamiliar room, strapped into something that resembled a dentist's chair but wasn't quite that exactly. Besides, why would a dentist have to strap someone down? Still, it moved like a dentist's chair, rising slowly up and falling slowly down according to how a technician next to him applied pressure with his foot to the controls. The technician was wearing a white coat, like a dentist's coat, but he wasn't a dentist: Jensi could tell because of his teeth. Some were crooked and thrust every which way and others were simply missing and all of them were stained a yellowish-brown. His breath was bad, too, almost unbearable. And his coat was spattered with what looked like old blood.

"What am I doing here?" asked Jensi in the dream.

The technician laughed. "What are you doing here?" he asked. He lifted both hands and Jensi caught a flash of metal in one. "You've always been here," the technician said.

There was, hanging from the ceiling, a strange rubbery contraption, like an inverted dentist's chair, and once the technician had lifted and lowered Jensi's chair to his satisfaction he reached up and pulled it down. It was some sort of pliable plasticene substance and it closed around Jensi, molding itself firmly against his body. Mostly it was soft, but here and there it pushed at him, hard little points touching his arms, his legs, in a way that made it difficult to move. What was hidden within it? And then he felt a little pricking as one of the hard points pushed its way farther into him, a needle of some sort, then another, then another, until it was hard for him to breathe since it made the needles, if they were needles, sink in even deeper. The technician slid his hand underneath the plasticene covering and when he slid it back out again it was slick with blood. It was hard for Jensi not to feel alarm, but the harder he breathed the more his chest hurt, the needles jabbing deeper and making him burn, so he tried to breathe in short, sharp breaths and raise his chest not at all. But he was, he suddenly realized, beginning to hyperventilate, his head getting exceptionally dizzy and black spots beginning to appear before his vision—unless the needles were injecting something into him and it was the drug he was feeling.

"I'm going to ask you a few questions," said the technician, his voice extremely flat.

"No," said Jensi, and felt a stab of pain.

The technician ignored him. "Let's start with an easy one," he said. "What is your name?"

Jensi shook his head.

"Wrong answer," said the technician. "I'll ask again. What is your name?"

"I—" said Jensi. "Please—"

"These answers are also incorrect," said the technician. "Please try again." He leaned forward, and for a moment his voice wasn't flat but friendly. "I'm surprised at you!" he said.

"This is the easiest question. If you struggle to answer this one, how are you possibly going to manage the rest?"

Before Jensi could respond, the technician leaned back, his face becoming neutral again. "I will repeat the question. What is your name?"

The black spots had nearly overwhelmed his vision. He could barely see the technician now, and what he could see of him was covered in overlapping circles of darkness, as if the man was either just coming into or just fading out of existence. "I—" he tried again, and then screamed as the needles jabbed, and then managed in a half-strangled voice, "Jensi."

"Closer," said the technician. "But still wrong. Would you care to try again?"

But no, thought Jensi, trying to plead to the technician with his eyes, *that's my name, that's really it. I've answered correctly, let me go.*

The technician waited there patiently, his face expressionless, while Jensi kept taking quick, shallow breaths. Finally he said, "Would you like me to give you a hint?"

Very slowly and deliberately the technician raised his hand, and Jensi saw that the flash he had seen before was not metal after all, but a mirror. For a moment the technician misdirected it and Jensi only saw in it bits and pieces of the walls, and then it caught the light and flashed hard at him, momentarily blinding him.

And then he caught a wavering glimpse of his reflection, and realized that the face he was seeing was not his own, but that of his brother Istvan.

His body was tingling when he woke up. He rubbed his arms, almost expecting to see marks from the needles, but there was nothing there. He had to get up and go look at his face in the mirror, just to make sure that it was really him and not Istvan. For once, he was reassured to see his own haggard face and red-rimmed eyes, the proof of another night of uneasy dreams and little sleep.

After that, he had trouble falling back to sleep, was worried about having the same dream over again. He made the bed and then lay on top of it, thinking.

I did everything I could for Istvan, he told himself. *When we were together, I tried to help him and keep him out of harm's way. Later, I tried to stop him from doing something rash. Later still, I spent months and then years looking for him. I did everything I could.*

Still, despite saying it, he did not quite believe it. He had not found his brother. How could he say he had done everything he could when his brother was still missing?

It was a hard day. He was, for one thing, exhausted, even more so than usual. For another, he found his thoughts returning throughout the day to his brother, wondering where he was now. Enough had started to come out now about the methods used by the SCAC against political prisoners and terrorists that he couldn't help but think that Istvan had likely been through a lot. Maybe they had driven him mad, made him even madder than he already was. Or maybe they had crippled or maimed him. Even killed him.

Did he really want to know what had happened to his

brother? Would Istvan even be the same person if he were to get him back?

I'll think about him for a few days and then slowly forget about him again, he told himself. *Life will continue on as normal. Even if I didn't find him, I can hardly be blamed.* But a few days came and went and he was still thinking about his brother, unable to help himself. And so he did what he usually did when this happened: he filed another request with the military to be allowed to have contact with his brother, knowing that it, just like all the petitions he had filed before it, would simply vanish. It would not even be acknowledged. But at least his conscious mind could now tell his unconscious that it had tried to do something.

He was still working the same picking job as he had been four years earlier, back when his brother had disappeared. He piloted a small cargo ship designed to shift freight from local orbital spacecraft to the larger shockpoint ships in orbit and vice versa. He showed up in the morning, was given a series of deliveries and pickups, and worked with a small crew until they were done. If everything went right, he could do the job in eight hours or so. If anything went wrong, though, he'd have to stay until things were taken care of, and even if he went over his eight-hour shift he never got overtime. But it was a job and the economy was bad—he was lucky to have anything at all. The piloting was far from intense—nothing beyond what he might be trained for in the first few weeks of military flight school except for the docking procedures—but it was something anyway. He wasn't making much money, wasn't saving any, but he was getting by.

And then, a few weeks later, he came home to find a vid message waiting for him. It was from his mother. It was surprising: he hadn't heard from her since her confinement in the asylum where, he could tell from the background the vid showed, she still was. She looked relatively okay, though: her hair combed, her eyes drifting a little but not darting about like they used to do. Plus, she was able to form coherent, unslurred sentences, even if she only said a few words.

"Jensi," she said. "I need to see you. Come see me."

It didn't make sense. Why would his mother call? She'd always blamed him for Istvan's disappearance, and the few times, early on, that he'd tried to see her, she'd turned his requests to visit down. Even then he hadn't particularly wanted to see her, but he'd felt obligated. He didn't want to see her now, but at the moment, still worrying in the back of his mind he'd failed Istvan, still feeling guilty about his brother, he couldn't stop himself from trying to contact her. But by vid rather than in person. No, in person would be too much.

It took a while for the hospital staff to acknowledge that he had a right to communicate with her, and then even longer for them to track her down and bring her to a vid. She didn't look as good as she had in the first vid. Her hair was sticking out in all directions now, and her face had a slackness to it as well, as if she had perhaps just been medicated. Seeing her like that, he couldn't help but say:

"You haven't called me for years. Why are you calling me now?"

He had to repeat it twice before she understood what he was saying. For a moment she stumbled over her words, babbled almost, and then managed to say, "But I've finally forgiven you."

"Forgiven me?" said Jensi. "For what?"

"For what you did to your brother," she said. "I forgive you."

Jensi felt himself beginning to fill with rage. "But I didn't do anything to Istvan!" he said. "Whatever happened to him is not my fault. Whatever happened to him, he brought upon himself."

"I need you to come," she said, her voice strange now—high pitched and screeching.

"Why should I come? What did you ever do for me?"

"Come and receive my forgiveness," she said. "Come and be saved."

He cut the feed, angry as hell, feeling it had been a mistake to humor her and talk to her at all.

A few hours later, he had a brief prerecorded message from Henry, who was now working off world, doing security for a special facility. "Very hush-hush," he said, and winked. "Can't tell you much about it. Very lucrative as well. It'll give me the step up I need, the capital to start something decent back on Vindauga. I hope you'll be part of it." When he tried to examine the location marker of the message, Jensi found it had been stripped. Not only did it not indicate a particular location, it didn't even pinpoint a specific planet or even solar system. What could Henry be up to?

. . .

His dreams had faded and he had almost forgotten about Istvan again, when he had another live vid feed from the hospital. Thinking it must be his mother, he rejected it, but the call came back immediately, this time with an emergency designation. Curious despite himself, he accepted it.

It was the director of the asylum. "There's no easy way to put what I have to say," he said.

"Then just say it," said Jensi. His mind was racing out in front of him, imagining his mother going berserk and attacking another patient or a doctor or a visitor. Or imagining the director saying that the public assistance funds had reached their end and that they could no longer take care of her. Because of that, paradoxically, it was almost a relief when he learned that his mother was dead.

"She had a cerebral hemorrhage," the director informed him.

"A cerebral hemorrhage?"

"She'd had a brain scan not long before and nothing was there to make us worry. But things can change quickly. There was probably nothing that could have been done."

Jensi thanked the man and hung up the telephone. He sat down and tried to feel something, but wasn't sure what to feel. He felt some anger, some loss, some grief, but it was nothing compared to what he felt over the disappearance of his brother. And his mother was gone, was dead. His brother might still be alive.

I need to find him, he thought. *I haven't done enough.*

But he was helpless to know where to start.

13

Grottor sat up on the bed and ruffled his hair, then leaned over and answered the vid. On the screen was one of the men who Blackwell had introduced him to.

"Ah, it's you," Grottor said.

"Expecting someone else?" said the man.

Grottor shrugged. "Do you know what time it is here?" he asked.

"Last I checked, you were on a ship rather than a planet," said the man. "Which means time doesn't really apply."

Grottor grunted. "What am I even supposed to call you?" he asked. "What's your name?"

The man gave a strange smirk. "You can refer to me as the gray man," he claimed.

"The gray man?"

"It's a name that someone gave me," said the man. Yes, Grottor realized, his face did look somewhat gray. "It'll serve as well as any other."

"What do you want?" he asked. "Where's Blackwell?"

"Now we get down to it," said the man. He smiled. "We figured it was time to cut out the middleman. Saves time and saves confusion. It's simpler." And then he added, without transition, "Fischer's been killed."

"Killed?" said Grottor, surprised. "What happened?"

"Shot," said the man. "Head blown off. We've interrogated the man responsible, one Istvan Sato. He doesn't seem to know anything. Strangely enough, it seems actually to be a coincidence, which means the project should be able to go forward without impediment. He's a man with severe mental problems. There's something about him, though, that intrigues me."

Grottor nodded. "Why are you telling me this?" he asked.

"Because he'll be arriving at the prison camp on Aspera," he said. "We don't expect anything to happen to suggest we were wrong about it being a coincidence, but we wanted someone there to be aware of him, just in case anything came up. That's why we contacted you. Blackwell didn't need to know."

"I appreciate the faith you put in me," he said.

"It's not a question of putting faith in you," said the man. "It's a question of us losing faith in Blackwell. His motives are . . . shall we say, impure?"

Grottor remained impassive.

"You'll notice we haven't contacted Orthor," said the man. "He's Blackwell's pawn, not ours. As for you . . . We've always preferred a knight to a pawn."

"I don't know whether to feel insulted," said Grottor.

"Of course you don't," said the man. "Now turn off the vid and go back to sleep and try to pretend this was all a bad dream."

14

In a fit of desperation, he considered joining the Colonial Marines. If he did that, maybe after years of hard work and faithful service he'd be in a position where he'd be given sufficient security clearance to be able to gain access to information about his brother. But then again maybe not. Still, what else could he do? Maybe develop his computer skills further and hack his way into the system? He'd never been terrible with computers, but he was hardly an expert, either, and how would he know where to start?

He was considering these and other schemes when a live feed changed everything. He was lucky to catch it—normally he would have been at work during that time, but he'd traded shifts with someone who had a funeral to attend. Even so, he was lucky to see it: the vid request came in without a name or a location marker and so at first he figured it was just an ad, something new put together by a vidimarketer.

But there flashed into his mind the recorded vid from Henry. That, too, had had no location marker. And so he connected.

It was Henry this time, too. He was hunched toward the vid screen, difficult to see. He was whispering. He looked nervous and cagey, and kept glancing back over his shoulder. It took him a moment to realize the connection had been made.

"Henry," said Jensi. "What a great surprise."

"Shhh," said Henry. "Not so loud. I shouldn't be calling out at all, let alone using this channel. If they find out I did, at the very least it'll cost me my job."

"What's wrong, Henry?"

Henry shook his head. "I'm calling you just so you'll stop worrying about your brother. He's here. He's alive, he's okay, you don't need to worry about him anymore. That's all I can tell you."

Jensi felt his heart leap. "Where's here, Henry? I have to know."

"I can't tell you," said Henry. "It doesn't matter. What matters is he's okay."

"Is he a prisoner? What's happened to him?"

"It's a penal colony," said Henry. "That's where I work. Yes, he's a prisoner. I saw him for the first time yesterday. Not in person, on vid. I almost didn't recognize him."

"What was wrong with him that you almost didn't recognize him?" asked Jensi, his voice rising.

Henry pressed his finger to his lips. "You don't know what I'm risking telling you this."

"It's not enough," said Jensi. "I need more. I need to know where you are."

"Classified," said Henry, reaching now for the off switch. "I wish I could, but—"

"Henry, think of everything we did together," said Jensi hurriedly. "You've already told me enough to get you in trouble. Now give me the rest."

Through the screen, he saw Henry hesitating, his hand still hovering near the cutoff.

"Please, Henry," he said. "I'm your best friend."

And for a moment Henry's nervousness stilled. He nodded almost imperceptibly, and said one word: "Aspera."

And then the screen went dead.

15

Aspera. At first he thought it was the name of the facility, of a penal colony on some backwater world, but a quick search turned up nothing of the kind. The only Asperas he could come up with were a school back on Earth, now defunct, and an uninhabited and uninhabitable planet, an uncolonized world far to the edge of the galaxy and away from normal trade paths. He found a satellite image of the school and saw it was collapsing. Definitely nobody there. No images seemed to exist of the planet. It had few valuable resources, and had been classified off limits to industrial concerns and other interested parties.

It was just one word, very little to go on, plus what Henry had said to back it up and the little he could infer. Maybe his brother was there somewhere on the planet.

Or maybe Aspera referred to something else, some off-the-vid corporation or lesser-known location on another planet. Or maybe he'd misunderstood what Henry had said—it could have been "Asberra" or "Hasparrow." Those were possibilities, too, he supposed, but exploring those names didn't turn up anything substantial either.

It was the first time in years he'd had any clear indication that Istvan was still alive. He had to ask himself: *Do I really want to go after my brother?* If he was in a penal colony, what could he do for him? Shouldn't he leave him where he was? But despite himself, like a bad reflex, he found the same protectiveness for his older brother kicking in. Now that he suspected he knew where Istvan was, how could he stop himself from going after him? Even if he wasn't there, even if he didn't manage to see him, at least he had to try.

16

There were many days in which Istvan did not say a word; days, too, when he had no real sense of who or even what he was. Very quickly, as the small gray man began to manipulate his body, drawing tool after tool out of the cabinets around him, Istvan found himself withdrawing deep inside, trying to reach a place where he would be safe, where he could watch what was happening to him but not feel it. Each time a technique would fail to get results, the small gray man would change the drugs or bring out a larger tool and he would begin to feel it again. He would burrow deeper, and deeper, until at last he had nowhere else to go. His body was awash with pain and suffering; he crouched there within it, on a tiny speck that was not free of pain exactly but better than everything around it. What his mouth was saying, what his body was saying, he had no idea. It was as if it was operating without him.

And each time he thought he couldn't stand it any longer, each time he felt like he might lose himself for good, the pain abated just a little. The small gray man would stand back and wipe the sweat off his brow, his lab coat now spattered with blood, and give him a moment to breathe. And then Istvan would feel himself stepping tentatively from where he was crouched inside, slowly starting to occupy his body again. But this was a trick, for soon enough it would start all over again and he would be forced deep into his corner again.

And then one day—how many days into the flight Istvan had no way of knowing—something happened. A twinge of frustration passed ever so briefly over the gray man's gray face and Istvan was not hidden deep enough within his body to keep his own face from smiling. The man's face darkened and he started in on Istvan again, harder this time that he had before. Either the drugs or the instruments that the gray man was sticking into him made him feel like his body was covered with ants, then like his body was not a body at all but just a swarm of ants. He retreated from the pain, going back to where he'd been securing himself, where he'd been hiding, and then felt the pain follow him, coming closer and then touching him lightly. This time, though, instead of receding just on the verge of becoming unbearable, it kept coming. He felt his footing eroding away, slowly crumbling around him, and suddenly he was thrust fully against his own skin, exposed all at once to all the pain his body was feeling. He screamed, and struggled, and heard the gray man laugh, but then the pain was too much for him and everything went dark.

For a long time, he simply wasn't there. When he did start to come back, it was at first as a mess of sensations with nothing to filter or connect them. Then slowly he began to feel like he had a vague shape and form, but that that form was on fire. He tried to move but found he couldn't. Then the fire faded to a low dull ache and he imagined it as a form of ash. He was, he momentarily thought, now a shadow man, but then his shape and form became sharper, clearer, and he could feel he was human. He could feel, too, that he was lying down on his side, one side of him pressed against something cold, flat and hard. He tried to open his eyelids and succeeded in getting them to flutter, light strobing vaguely into his brain.

He rested a little and then tried again. This time his eyes came open and stayed open.

He was in a small room, a cell of some kind, lying on a concrete floor. The walls behind him and to either side were concrete; the wall in front of him was made of iron bars, the metal door standing ajar. Next to his face was the dented metal underside of a toilet, and, a little farther away, a cheap cot. For a moment he thought he was back in the cell he had been in before, just after he had shot the politician. But no, he remembered, that cell had had a metal door, not bars. This was new.

It took him a while to pull himself up to his feet. He was weak, his muscles not at all like he remembered them, atrophied perhaps. It took some getting used to. Maybe they had changed his body, made him an inside voice and taken his body away and then given him a new one. How long had he been like this? Months? Days, maybe? He had blacked out before, it used to happen to him all the time when he was younger, but he had always woken up feeling pretty much like he had felt to begin with. This was new. This was different.

He stood there swaying, staring at the open cell door, and then went through it and out. It led into a slightly curving hall, lined on one side with cells, the other side a smooth metal wall broken at one point by a steel security door. If he followed the curve around, he suspected it would go on forever. All of the cells had their doors open. Most of them were empty, but in one a heavily tattooed man sat on the bed, legs crossed at the ankles, reading. In another a few cells down, a rail-thin man was doing push-ups. They were both dressed the same, pants and simple shirts with a number stamped on the sleeve and a name over the pocket, and he realized he was dressed the same way. Both of them looked up as he shuffled past, curious for just an instant before their eyes returned to what they were doing.

He was muttering he realized, and giving little strangled cries. He made a conscious effort to try to stop, and did for a moment, but before he knew it he had started up again.

He followed the hall around until there was a break in the cells, and an opening. Tentatively he went through it, found it gave onto a large open space surmounted by a dome. It was perhaps forty meters in diameter. Tables with built-in benches were scattered here and there, as well as a few vid screens. At the tables were seated several dozen men, all of them eating. He stood there watching, still mumbling, until one of them noticed him, a thick-lipped man with a scraggly beard.

"Madman's awake," the man said, shaking the shoulder of the man next to him. "Won't have to be force-fed today." He leaned to look at a man farther down the table. "That means you're out of a job, Bill."

Ambler, William it read over his pocket. He grunted. "Fine by me," he said.

"Where am I?" Istvan said.

"Where are you?" said the first man. "You're in hell, friend. Welcome."

"Hell?"

"Last stop for all political prisoners," he said. He stood up, came over to Istvan. "Only way to get out of here is to die. What's your name?"

"Istvan Sato."

"James Waldron," said the man, holding out his hand. Istvan stared at it, waiting to see what it would do. It took him a moment to realize that Waldron intended for him to shake it. "Hungry?" Waldron asked once he did. When Istvan nodded, he led him over to a console set in the floor in the middle of the tables and showed him how to automatically dispense a meal. Once he had his food, he held Istvan's arm and directed him back to the table, the other men scooting down to make room for him.

Istvan at first ate with vigor. "Don't overdo it," said Waldron. "That's your first solid meal in days." Istvan nodded, slowed down. A moment later he was glad he had: the little he had eaten weighed heavily in his stomach. He pushed the tray back a little. Waldron and the others were watching him.

"Where am I?" he asked again. "What am I doing here?"

"I already told you, it's hell," said Waldron.

"It's a penal colony," spoke up Bill, from the other end of the table.

"A penal colony?"

"For political prisoners," said Bill. "People that will never get out of the system and that they're not prepared to have killed. At least not yet. James is right: this is the end of the line. You'll be here until you die."

Istvan tried to take it in. Was all this real? What had happened between the gray man torturing him and this moment?

His body had been present but somehow he himself had not. Where, then, had he been?

"So, what did you do?" asked another man, clean-shaven and with a haircut.

"Do?" asked Istvan.

"To get here," said the man. "You must have done something."

"Oh," said Istvan. "Yes. Shot someone. A politician giving a speech."

"That's a hell of a way to express your disagreement with someone's political views," said Bill.

"I don't know what his political views were," said Istvan. "I'm not quite sure why I shot him."

The others stared at him for a moment. "But you're a political prisoner," said one of them. "Don't you have a cause?"

"I don't know," said Istvan.

"What do you mean you don't know?"

"I think there might have been some kind of mistake. It was supposed to be a funny joke. . . ."

"What's funny about it?" asked Bill.

Istvan stared at him, didn't seem to know how to respond. "It sounds like you were a patsy," said Waldron. "A pawn. A fall guy. Somebody wanted the man dead and figured they'd trick you into doing it."

Istvan hesitated, then shrugged.

"But now you're here," said Waldron.

"Too late for explanations," said Bill.

"What?"

"Bill's right," said the man who had originally asked him

what he'd done. He held out his hand. Again, it took Istvan a moment to realize that he was expected to shake it. "Michael Stewart," he said. "Once you're here, there's no talking your way out of it. Whether it's a mistake or not, this is where you'll die."

"Where's here?" asked Istvan again.

"We don't know," said Michael. "Somewhere off the beaten track. Some desolate planet out in the middle of nowhere that nobody is likely to accidentally stumble onto."

"The guards and technicians probably know," claimed Bill, "but maybe they don't, either. We hardly see them anyway."

Istvan looked around for the guards and technicians. He didn't see any, unless they were disguised. He looked suspiciously at the men around him. Were they guards? Were they technicians?

"You know where the cells are?" asked Waldron. Istvan hesitated, nodded. Waldron dipped his spoon in the gravy left on his plate, used it to trace a circle in the plate's center.

"Here's where we are," he said. "Right now. This is where we eat, we can walk or talk or play cards here most of the day." He drew a circle around the circle. "This is the corridor for the cells. That's where we go at night." He dipped the spoon again, drew a further circle around this. "The guards and technicians and anybody not a prisoner is out here. It may not look exactly like that—hard to say. They watch us through cameras hidden in the cells and on the struts of the dome. None of us really knows how many guards and technicians there are. Maybe just a few, maybe a lot. We hardly ever see them. When we do, they're in riot gear and we can't see their faces. If it's really as isolated a location as Michael thinks, they're almost as much prisoners as we are." He licked the spoon clean, smiled. "That's all we know."

Istvan waited for him to go on. When he didn't, he asked, "What is the spoon?"

"The spoon?" said Waldron, surprised. He stared at it. "The spoon's nothing. What's wrong with you?"

Istvan nodded. *Yes, now he understood, the spoon was nothing.* "How do we get out?" he asked.

Waldron's smile faded. "We don't get out," he said. "Haven't you been listening?"

"There must be a way out."

"Only dead."

"We could use the spoon to overpower the guards, take over."

"Forget the spoon. Haven't you been listening?" said Michael. "The guards are probably nearly as much prisoners as we are."

Bill nodded vigorously. "So we take over the outer ring, assuming that's what it is. Then what? Where do we go from there?"

"Out," said Istvan. His head was beginning to throb.

"There is no out," said Bill. "We're on a planet without a breathable atmosphere. Outside of the rings of the colony is death."

"We don't know that for certain," said Waldron.

"No, we don't," said Bill. "But we're certain enough. Why would there be a dome otherwise?"

"Maybe the dome's a trick," said Waldron, "to make us think we're on a planet with nonbreathable air." But the way he said it made it clear that it wasn't something he really believed.

There was, Istvan noticed staring down at his feet, something near the base of the table leg. A little something that looked plantlike at first, but strangely tentacular as well, a kind of weird mold or something. He prodded it with his boot. For a moment he thought he was imagining it, seeing something that nobody else could see, but then realized Bill was watching him.

"Don't worry about that," Bill said. "It's everywhere. It doesn't seem to be harmful, but when we try cleaning it up, it just keeps coming back."

Everywhere, he thought, everywhere. He looked around, and yes, there it was a little bit here, a little bit there.

Suddenly Istvan clutched his head. There was something wrong with it, like a tone or sound going off somewhere within it, but in a way that flattened everything. Next to him Waldron was saying something, but he couldn't hear it, could only see his lips move, no sound coming out. And then he was lying flat on his back on the floor, staring up at the dome. Something was strange within his vision, shadows darting back and forth before his eyes where no shadows should be. A roaring in his ears, inarticulate but yet somehow still human, still sentient. And then, suddenly, nothing.

17

On the ship above the planet, hovering several miles above the research facility, Jane Haley, technician first class, pressed her palms against her temples. There was something wrong with her head. It had come suddenly, a numbing wave of pain that had swept over her and made her almost fall out of her chair. And then, almost as suddenly as it had come, it was gone.

When she opened her eyes, Ensign Erik Orthor was staring at her, too attentive. "Anything wrong?" he asked.

She shook her head. "Bad headache," she said.

"Get those a lot?" asked Orthor, as if hoping to start a conversation.

She ignored him. She looked around and saw that some of the others on the bridge looked dazed as well, though nobody as much as she. Maybe it wasn't just a headache, but something else. But what? Orthor, though, seemed unaffected, as did Commander Grottor. The latter was staring at her, a look of deep curiosity in his eyes.

"Have you felt that before?" he asked.

"Headaches?" she said. "Sure. Hasn't everybody?"

He looked at her a moment more, then nodded, the curiosity fading. "Take a few minutes away from the bridge. Gather yourself," he said.

"But I'm fine, sir," she said.

"That's an order," he said.

She nodded and stood, left the bridge. *An order,* she thought. *Since when did you have to leave the bridge if you had a headache?*

But it was good to get away for a moment, catch her breath, gather herself. Ensign Orthor made her nervous. He was nice, or tried to be, but there was something strange about him, and he was always preaching Unitology. He seemed just one step away from either asking her out on a date or inviting her along to a religious revival, maybe both. And Grottor, she had noticed, treated her a little differently than some of the others. Not enough to notice unless you paid close attention. It was hard to pin her finger on what it was exactly, but she was sure he did it. But she had no idea why.

She made her way to her quarters, lying down on the bed for a while. The headache, if that was what it had been, was now completely gone. Strange, that. But it hadn't been a headache, exactly, or not the headaches like she usually knew them. There had been little flashes of something, images jagging like lightning into her head, but broken and incomplete, impossible for her to make into coherent shapes. It had been like watching a broken vid screen, one in the process of fuzzing out. She felt that there was something there to be seen, but she just couldn't see it.

She lay on the bed, staring up at the ceiling. It was no secret to her that there were tensions between the commander and

Ensign Orthor, and though Grottor did little to give himself away, she'd noticed that there were things that he'd say around her that he wouldn't say around Orthor. It was, she supposed, a mark of privilege that he'd say them to her. She tried to take it that way. But she also had to admit that when she'd signed up for the academy, she hadn't imagined it would be like this. She didn't know what was going on down on the planet proper exactly, but she knew enough to know that she wouldn't approve if she knew more. Which made her wonder why Grottor had chosen her as part of his crew. What did he expect from her? she wondered for the fiftieth time. Why was she here?

After she deemed sufficient time had elapsed, she washed her face and made her way back to the bridge. Orthor was still there, and he immediately tried to engage her. She mumbled an apology and slipped back into her work at her console.

But the work itself wasn't holding her attention. There was little to do; they were hovering above Aspera, not orbiting the planet exactly but doing a strange loop that unnecessarily expended fuel, it seemed to her, and which kept them in proximity to the structure below that she'd been the first to identify. Why they were doing it, she couldn't say. Grottor had hinted about what was taking place on the planet, and she'd seen the supply ships come and pass through, seen as well another structure being built below over the course of a number of months. It was a research facility of some kind, but of what and for what exactly, she couldn't say.

Someone had stopped to hover behind her. For a moment she thought it was Orthor. She prepared herself to become irritated, snap something at him that might drive him back.

But Orthor, she saw out of the corner of her eye, was still at his station. When she craned her neck, she saw it was Commander Grottor.

"Do you mind explaining where that came from?" he asked.

"What?" she asked, and then he flicked his finger at her vid pad.

With her stylus, she saw, she'd been tracing something. It looked like a pair of tusks of some kind, but instead of curving they twisted around one another. *Funny,* she thought, *it looks like the Unitology symbol.* All of Orthor's talk about Unitology must have sunk deeper into her skin than she realized.

But it was different from the Unitology symbol, too, or at least more articulated. It was covered with dozens of small squiggles, distinct but bizarre symbols

"I don't know," she said.

"What have you seen?" he asked. "What have you been up to?"

"I haven't seen anything," she claimed.

"This doesn't mean anything to you?" he asked. "Then why did you draw it?"

She shook her head. "Nothing, sir," she said. "I swear. I was just doodling."

"And what are these numbers?" he asked gesturing to the right edge of the pad. "These equations?"

Were they equations? Well, yes, they looked like them.

"Probably just the remnant of some old navigation computations," she suggested.

"No," he said. "They're not."

"No?"

"Who have you shown this to?" he asked.

"Shown?" she said, confused. "I . . . it was just a doodle, I haven't shown it to anybody. Why would I?"

"Not Orthor?" he asked.

"Of course not," she said.

He stared at her for a long moment, as if assessing her, and then nodded. "Forward it to me and then erase it," he said. "And then we need to have a serious talk."

18

Doctor Enoch Briden was already drifting off to sleep when he felt it: the pulse had gone off again. He could feel it tugging at his mind, just for a moment, as if trying to unknot something, and then came a brief, sharp pain that put him wide awake. *Interesting,* he thought. The pain at the end, that was new, different from the last time. Something was changing, developing.

He got out of bed and checked the time: three days since the last pulse, minus an hour or so. That made the fifth time. He pulled up the log and saw as he suspected, no regular pattern, no sense that they were coming in a particular order. Though they were, he noticed, coming closer together now, as if the object that was emitting them was, so to speak, feeling its way around. Looking for something.

The technician on duty still hadn't called. Briden knew not everybody was as sensitive to the pulse as he was—it was fortuitous that he was heading up the project—and even those who were sensitive to it didn't respond always in the same way. Some became nauseous or bled at the nose, some became agitated and violent. A few, a very few, didn't seem to notice it at all, and perhaps the current technician on duty was one of those. If he didn't call within the next sixty seconds, Briden would make a note of his name and have him reassigned to a job more appropriate to his level of awareness. Janitorial duties, for instance. No, there was no room for error: the project was crucial. It might, in fact, change the course of humanity. There was no room for mistakes.

Forty seconds. The technician still hadn't called and so Briden turned on his vid and called him. It took the man eight tones to answer, and when he did his eyes were red rimmed and his hair was ruffled, as if he had been asleep.

"Anything to report?" asked Briden.

"No, sir," the technician said, his eyes drifting to one side to look at his stats panel. "Yes, sir, I mean," he said. "A pulse just came in."

"Sleeping on the job?" asked Briden.

"No, sir," said the technician, without batting an eye. *Incompetent and a liar, too,* thought Briden.

"Give me your name," said Briden, and when the technician gave it he wrote it down. "When does your next shift end?" he asked.

"In about an hour," said the technician.

"Return to your quarters," said Briden. "You've done enough damage for one night."

The technician looked confused for a moment and then nodded, switched the vid off.

Do I have to do everything? wondered Briden as he got dressed. *Am I the only one who understands how important this is?*

He left his quarters and made his way down the hall, deeper into the heart of the complex. He had been there since the beginning, ever since they'd first started constructing the Red Marker. At first, they'd been told that it was a two-year tour, but then they'd been informed that the project was important enough that they'd have to remain on it, out of contact with the outside world, until further notice. One of the others, a man with a family named Pete, had complained about that, and then had kept complaining, and then, when that didn't work had started to try to sabotage the project. Result: he had been accused of treason, quickly tried, and then exiled from the research facility and remanded to the penal colony a few miles distant. Even then, Pete hadn't understood, had continued to complain and beg to be released, had begun, too, to reveal to the other prisoners the secrets of the research facility. So they had held another court, secret this time, and a few hours later Pete was found dead on his cot. Briden didn't particularly relish what had happened to the man, but then again he didn't object to it, either. He should, at very least have known better.

Besides, this was a sacred calling. Any scientist worth their salt would kill to have the chance that they had here.

It still made his skin tingle to see it. Each time it was just as amazing as the first time.

He reached the first set of doors, slid his card through, and entered the code. The door slid back. The technician, he was pleased to see, was gone, though he had left a mess at the console—wadded up food wrappers, a single glove, a crumpled manifest. He swept it all into the incinerator chute without a second glance, then went to the glass window.

There it was, just on the other side. Clear proof that humans were not alone, that humans were not the only form of intelligent life that had existed in the universe. Clear proof that Unitology was the only true religion, and that Michael Altman had been a true prophet.

It was perhaps twenty meters tall. It was a blackish red, cut in variegated stripes, and gave off at times an unearthly glow, the indecipherable symbols on its body burning with a curious light. Two slanting columns joined at the base then twisted upward, around one another. He and his team had constructed the Marker using the Black Marker research from Earth. It was more "grown" than constructed, really, as a fractal heuristic crystal lattice. It was almost like a brain. On activating it, they could hardly keep up with cataloguing the unexpected properties it exhibited, not limited to just these sudden pulses. It seemed to him to possess some intelligence, seemed to be trying to communicate with them. With *him*: Briden. The others sometimes scoffed at him when he suggested this, but somehow he was sure of it: he could feel its pulse prodding at his mind, trying to find something that would respond to it. What was it looking for within him? How could he help it to find it?

He opened the second set of doors and entered the chamber. Slowly, he moved toward the Marker, taking a moment first to take it all in. The floor of the chamber was bare exposed rock, rapidly cut so that they could begin. The prison colony site had been chosen because the military had realized that the life-sentence prisoners might prove perfect experimental fodder for the Marker experiments to come. They had started, though, by using some of them to build up the scientific compound where the Red Marker would be constructed.

Of course, those prisoners had had to be killed to preserve the secret, but they were doomed anyway, it didn't matter much. And with the way things were in the galaxy, there would always be new political prisoners to fill the colony and to be used if and when they were needed.

Near the Marker and a little farther out, near the walls, were little patches of what looked like fungus or rot, sloping tendrils. They were bigger than he remembered them being, and there were more of them. He'd begun to notice them in the halls as well, spreading somehow. He'd have to set the clean-up crew onto them.

He reached out and placed his hand against the stone, but felt nothing unusual. It was, he knew, still sending a signal, just not in a way that his body or mind could perceive. The computers, though, were picking it up, recording it, trying to decipher it. He tried to keep his thoughts free and his mind open, listening inside his head for whatever the Marker was trying to say to him, willing it to talk to him. *I'm ready*, he told it mentally. *Take me*.

How long he waited like that, he didn't know. When nothing happened, he sighed and went back through the doors and into the control room, and began to sort through the latest data.

It took only a few moments for him to realize that the new data was inconsistent with the earlier data. It seemed that the pulse itself had begun to change—not only during the moment of pain he had felt in the end, but earlier as well. And now that the pulse had subsided, the Marker was broadcasting on slightly different frequencies, something it had never done before. Apparently, the constructed Marker had started to reorganize itself, continuing to grow and develop even after they'd finished the process. It wasn't something he'd expected. *What did it mean?*

He was poring over the data, trying to assemble things into a coherent structure, when other members of the team began to arrive. Callie Dexter was the first. She was second in command, but Briden felt she did not have proper respect for what they were doing. She was a good scientist, but for her the Marker project didn't go beyond science. She didn't have the proper level of either faith or awe, and thus could not be counted on.

"Here already? What's on the docket for today?" she asked when she came in and settled in at her console, right next to him. Briden just grunted. "Anything new?" she asked.

"Lots," said Briden. "Major pulse last night."

A few minutes later Anna Tilton came in. She had dark brown hair, cut short so that it clung close to her face. Briden liked her better: she understood things properly. Like him, she was a Unitologist, and like him she had understood that the Black Marker had been a gift, a glorious proof of the truth of their religion, and their work here to reconstruct it was a holy cause. They were trying to decipher the mind of God. She nodded at him as she came in, settled right in.

A few moments later the room was full, a dozen or so scientists and technicians, all of them going over the data and thinking about it according to their own specialties. They exchanged a few comments here and there, asked one another for clarifications, and prepared for the day's tests and experiments.

Callie leaned over to Briden. "It's changing. What do you make of it?" she asked.

"I don't know," said Briden. "I think it's trying to speak with us however it can, and, since we didn't seem to be listening to how it spoke before, it's trying out new voices."

"You make it sound like it's alive," said Callie.

Briden shrugged. "It almost acts like it sometimes," he said.

"Careful, doctor," cautioned Callie. "Don't lose your objectivity."

It made him angry. *Doctor Dexter can't see what's right in front of her own eyes,* he thought. It was a mistake to have anyone on the team who wasn't a Unitologist, but when he'd suggested to the authorities having her removed, they'd denied his request. She was a good scientist, he had to admit that, but this wasn't just science. This was something bigger, something grander.

She was staring at him, he realized, her gaze hard. "Are you all right?" she asked.

"Of course I'm all right," he said, and gave her a cold smile. He had to tolerate her for now. But maybe a time would come when he wouldn't have to.

They worked in silence a while until Callie said, "Hmmm."

He ignored her, kept sending his own data through the modeling system. Then she cleared her throat and said "Strange."

"What's strange?" he asked.

"The vector," she said.

"Of course there's a vector," he said. "There's always been a vector, several in fact. Ours broadcasts out into space."

Dr. Dexter shook her head. "That's just it," she said. She scooted her chair closer to him, turning the screen so she could show him. "See here?" she said. "There's the unidentified signal we caught the other day."

"Keep your voice down," said Briden in a low voice. "Not everybody in this room has our security clearance."

Dr. Dexter smiled. "It hardly matters, Briden. With what we already know, we're all already a huge security risk." She reached up and traced her finger along the screen. "Now, something else is coming from here, a few dozen systems away. Looks like it could be on Kreemar, or that the signal cuts through it anyway. And here's us." She shadowed the other vectors, making them nearly invisible, and brightened this one. Then she scrolled it backward in time. "Watch this," she said. "Here we are, broadcasting indiscriminately, with an occasional pulse. But the pulses are wide. And then this morning, boom. Sharper focus."

"It's just a different frequency," said Briden.

"Okay," she said. "Could be. But the other pulses were all directed up into space, off planet. This one is angled differently. Half of it is simply bouncing off the ground. The rest of it travels the planet's surface pretty closely. It's never done that before."

Maybe that explained the pain at the end, thought Briden. *Maybe that was what made it different.* To Dr. Dexter, he said, "Why would it do that?"

She gave him a look. "You think it's alive," she said. "You tell me." When he didn't, she said, "Maybe it found what it wanted."

Briden nodded. "And what would that be?"

Dr. Dexter shrugged. "I don't know," she said. "Give me more data and maybe we'll find out."

19

A strange veil of light seemed to hang before Istvan's eyes, tattered and inconsistent, like a curtain made from bits and scraps of rag. In it he could see figures moving, swaying back and forth, hiding and coming forth. They were there and not there at the same time. *I'm dreaming,* he thought.

But no, he wasn't dreaming, his eyes were wide open. Through the veil of light, just on the other side of it, he could see the cell around him, and he could feel that he was lying on his cot. Someone was crouching over him, but the light was such it was impossible to see the man's face. For a moment he thought it was the small gray man, but then the curtain swayed and he saw enough to know it wasn't him. The man's head was too large, but still spun over with light, its features difficult to make out. He tried to move his lips to talk but found his teeth clenched tightly shut, his breath hissing angrily through them.

"Just relax," said the man obscured by light. "It's all right. Calm down."

He tried to calm down, but he couldn't. He could feel the man shaking his shoulder, and then that slowly passed and was gone, as if he no longer had a body anymore. A roaring filled his ears and the veil of light grew brighter and brighter until he could see nothing behind it and there was a buzzing pain where his head used to be. All he could see was the light, featureless and bare, and stretching on forever.

And then, slowly, he began to make out a flexing and falling of different shapes, like water boiling, but still all the same light, barely distinguishable. At first the forms seemed to make no sense, seemed merely random patterns, but then they began to adapt, to adjust. He could feel his mind working with them, making them something different, something he could understand. How did his mind know how to do such a thing? Was this like the voices? But there were no voices, only shapes. It was the opposite of voices, but his mind could make something of it somehow, and he was helpless to do anything but watch.

At first the shapes were geometrical, simple straight lines and then simple forms, slowly becoming more and more complex, dissolving into one another phantasmagorically. But then they began to warp and bend, becoming a collapse of form and then slowly taking on the shapes of faces. They were simple at first, cartoonish and immobile, but gradually they became more and more articulated, more and more human. They were still obscured, nearly lost in the light that created them, but they were more and more convincing. Here a head shot forth, even whiter light pouring out of its eyes, and burst. Another white shape arose and turned toward him and seemed to notice him. It was just a head, without body, but able somehow to move nonetheless, its neck pulsing it forward. It came toward him, its eyes curious, growing larger as it came until it seemed to fill nearly all his vision, as if it were just inches from his own head. It was hard not to imagine that he could feel its breath against his face.

And then it smiled, its mouth opening up jaggedly and too far as if its cheeks had been shut and its jaw dislocated.

He screamed.

The white face screamed back, mimicking his scream exactly, though loudly, too loudly, and then capsized in on itself, dissolving back into the light. He tried to slow his breathing, tried to bring his body back, but it wouldn't come, he couldn't find his body nestled anywhere under the light. And then he realized that something was forming again, a head coming up again, the same head as before, but a little more distinct this time, the light shot through with strands that were less illuminated as the muscles and sinews and tendons began to form into a slablike and brutal face, which it took him some time to recognize as his own.

It was a shock to see himself like that, embodied in light. He felt his mind push out against it and the face suddenly began to reform, becoming not his face but that of his brother. No, that was too painful in a different way, and he felt his mind push again until there she was: his mother.

He hated her, but here he didn't hate her exactly. No, here it was more like he was afraid of her. Seeing her like that, formed all out of light, was terrifying.

"What are you doing here?" he asked, and far away, down wherever his body currently resided, he felt someone squeeze his hand.

"Whatareyoudoinghere," the mother face repeated, its mouth moving awkwardly, wrongly. It seemed unable to make sense of the gaps between words, just ran everything together and then waited, staring expectantly at him. Which was, he realized, how he must be staring at it.

When he said nothing, the face let out a stream of raw sound, ululations and yelps, clamors and groans, a strange unearthly combination of sounds that left him feeling raw and damaged. And then it stopped, waited.

"What do you want?" he asked, as much to keep the face from sounding off as anything else.

"Whatdoyouwant?" the mother voice responded.

"You first," he said.

"Youfirst."

And then, as suddenly as it had gone, the light began to fade again, becoming first that tattered veil that half obscured things and then going away altogether and he was thrown panting, teeth aching, back into the world.

Waldron was there beside him, gripping his hand. "That's right," he was saying. "Just relax. It'll be okay." Several of the other prisoners were there, too, gathered around him.

Slowly he disentangled his hand, pushed them away enough to sit up and hold his head in his hands. He closed his eyes and when he opened them again the first thing he saw, in the corner of his cell, was a creeping tendril. Some of that moss or corruption. It hadn't been there before. But suddenly it was there. Was it real? Would the others see it, too?

"What happened?" asked Waldron.

He just shook his head helplessly, started at the tendril.

"Do you have fits like that a lot? You were shaking so hard it was all we could do to get you into the bed."

He lifted his head. "It saw me," he said.

"What?" said one of the other men. "What do you mean?"

"It was staring right at me," he said. "And then it spoke. But it was saying the things I was saying, only wrong. And then it spoke in a way that I couldn't understand."

"Istvan," said Waldron, shaking his head, "none of us know what you're talking about."

"It's out there, you just can't always see it."

"You're crazy," said Bill.

"We already knew he was crazy," said Michael.

"But this is a new type of crazy," said Bill. "It's worth noting."

"What is it exactly?" asked Waldron, his eyes narrowing.

"White, all white," said Istvan. "No, made of light. But maybe that's not really it, but just what I could see. Changing faces. Hard to remember it wasn't the person it looked like. For a while, it was me."

"You're babbling," said one of the others.

"For a while, it was me," said Istvan again.

Waldron patted him on the shoulder. "Well, if it comes back, ask it if it can help us get out of here," he said. He turned to leave the cell, shooing the others in front of him out. "Come on, boys. Show's over."

20

Every indication Jensi had was that Aspera was an unoccupied, uncolonized planet. It was off the beaten track, not even rich in resources, hardly worth a second glance. Which perhaps made it the perfect place for a secret political prison.

But since it was uncolonized and off the beaten track, the question Jensi kept asking himself was how was he to get there. He didn't have money to pay for passage on a ship, even if there had been a ship going there, let alone enough to charter his own vessel. Any attempt to enter the sector was likely to set off alarm bells—surely it was carefully patrolled and anyone coming close would be turned back.

He spent a few days thinking about what to do. He dug up what information he could, but there was almost nothing to indicate that Aspera was anything but an uncolonized, inhospitable world. Through a stolen pass, an unlocked terminal behind closed doors in the port, and a little of his brother's creative hacking, he managed to spend a few minutes with closed military records before being locked out, enough to come away with the impression that there was something happening on the planet after all, though what exactly it was remained vague.

Some indication that, yes, there was a political prison there, but perhaps more than that: another project was hinted at, but remained very top secret. It was only referred to as Operation Aspera. At first he thought that must be the name for the prison. But no, the prison was called, simply and relatively un-imaginatively, Hell. Operation Aspera was something else. But figuring this out brought him no closer to figuring out how to get to the planet.

It took a few days for it to hit him: if the planet was inhos-pitable then nothing could grow there. Unless they had a hy-droponic facility. . . . But even so, they'd need other supplies, so there must be someone bringing supplies in every few months or so, maybe more often, maybe less. That had to be his way in.

It was, in any case, the only possible way in he could think of.

It would take another trip to the spaceport, a balaclava, and the appropriation of a little more security clearance. He waited until the day shift was ending and then followed the security manager out of his office and forced him from behind into a supply closet, where he gagged and bound him. He took the man's key cards, used them to get back into his office, and onto a terminal. He had to go back and threaten the manager and his family to get the right passcodes, but in the end he was into the system. From there, it took a while but following what his brother had taught him, he cracked his way from there to the military side.

He was there for just a moment before the system shut him out, but saw enough to find mention of the name of a freighter with security clearance for the sector where Aspera was to be found: the *Eibon*. From there it was back to port records. He scanned through bills of lading for the *Eibon*, found it making a trip to a classified location every three months or so, the last one a little over two and a half months previous. That didn't give him much time. The cargo was as to be expected for a prison camp: food and medical supplies, vast quantities of water as well. But there was other cargo as well—specialized scientific equipment, computer ware, surgical supplies.

It was easy to locate the freighter. It was in a military berth, though, and well-protected. He scanned the vid listings to see if they were looking for crew; they weren't. From a terminal at his picker job, he could access past manifests for the *Eibon*, including names and pictures of the crew. There were two freight specialists, basically glorified pickers, one of them a large Swede named Swanson, the other a smaller man named Talbot.

Both were listed in the public directory. Swanson had a small apartment fairly near the spaceport, just a few blocks away from Jensi's own place. Talbot lived on the far side of the dome. For a few days Jensi followed Talbot home from work, then hung around his place afterward to see where he went. He never seemed to go anywhere; from the street Jensi could see the blue light of the vid flickering on the walls around him. The man hardly seemed to have any sort of life.

So he switched to Swanson, who went directly from the spaceport to a bar called the Martyr almost every night. He would always take the same place at one end of the bar, easing his large body carefully down onto the narrow stool. He was apparently enough of a regular that the stool was always empty when he arrived.

The first night Jensi took a stool around the corner of the bar, a few stools between him and Swanson. He waited until Swanson had ordered his beer and then nodded. The man crinkled his eyes at him in confusion and then nodded back. He watched Swanson order half a dozen beers, one about every ten minutes or so, and then, promptly at the end of an hour, leave. Getting up, he waggled his way off the chair, a slightly waviness to his stride, but basically okay. Jensi considered following him home, but instead stayed where he was.

The next time, Jensi was already seated when Swanson arrived. He nodded once to the man, who nodded back and sat down. Jensi waited until Swanson was nearly done with his third beer and then got himself another beer, ordering a round for Swanson as well. The Swede nodded his thanks and quickly drained the glass, but, taciturn, said nothing to Jensi, made no attempts to start a conversation. And, just as before, after an hour had passed he promptly stood and left, moving awkwardly and ponderously out the door.

Later that evening Jensi began to think, *What if this doesn't work? What sort of backup plan should I have?* But he could think of no plan. If he wanted to get on board the *Eibon*, this had to work.

The third night, when Swanson came into the bar, Jensi had already taken the stool beside his own. Swanson grunted once to him, nodded slightly, and then squeezed his way onto the stool. Jensi ordered himself a beer and turned to Swanson. "Want one, too?" he asked.

"You're paying?" asked Swanson.

"Sure," said Jensi. "Why not?"

Swanson nodded.

The bartender brought them their beers and they drank for a while in silence. Finally Jensi said, "You're at the port."

Swanson nodded. "You, too," he said.

Jensi nodded back. "I'm a picker," he said.

The big Swede cracked a smile. "A picker," he said. "That's no kind of life."

"No? What do you do?"

"Freight, too," said the Swede. "Not that much different than a picker, but the pay's a lot better."

He took a big sip of his drink and for a moment Jensi thought that was all he was going to say. He was afraid to push it. He didn't want to seem too eager. Indeed, it was all he did say for a while, through the end of his first beer and all the way through his second, until somewhere well into the middle of his third.

"You have to get on a ship going off planet," Swanson finally said, his speech slightly slurred now. "Somewhere that wants you to load up and travel with the goods and then unload, too. That's where the money is."

"Sounds good," said Jensi. "How do I go about it?"

Swanson shook his head. "Have to just ask around," he said. "Place I'm at is full."

"And where's that?"

"The *Eibon*," said Swanson. "Nice ship. New. Specialized."

"When do you ship out next?" Jensi asked.

Swanson frowned. "Week and a half," he said. "More or less."

That was as far as it went that night. The next night, though, Jensi was back, again buying the beer, and Swanson spoke a little more. "Best pay comes with cargo that you don't know much about," he said, and winked. "At least that's what it seems like on the *Eibon*."

"What do you mean you don't know much about it? Someone's got to know."

Swanson waved one meaty hand. "Oh, the captain, he probably knows something," he said. "But us, all we know are the basic categories listed on the bill of lading."

"That's all we usually know," said Jensi.

"Yes, but you're a picker," said Swanson, becoming more loquacious. "You just pick up the job at the beginning or the end. All you have to know is how fragile it is or isn't. We have to load the cargo and ride with it the whole way and unload it. Usual jobs, they give us pretty specific content listings so that we'll know what to do if something goes wrong." He swiveled on his barstool until he was looking directly at Jensi. His eyes, Jensi saw, were slightly glazed. "Something spills, say. Something goes wrong, it's good to know what you're carrying and whether it might blow up or explode or burn through the deck. But some of these jobs"—he said, and took a drink—"no, take that back, one job that we keep doing, they'll put a label on a box that says medical supplies but when it accidentally gets knocked open it isn't medical supplies at all but sealed vats of some sort of acid. I ask you, how can that be a medical supply?"

"So they're smugglers," said Jensi.

Swanson prodded Jensi's chest with his forefinger. "I didn't say that," he said. "These are government men. They just don't want people to know where they're going and what they're prepared to do once they get there."

"But you've figured it out," said Jensi.

Swanson shook his head. "No reason to figure it out," he said. "Better just to go along with it and get paid. People who start trying to figure stuff like that out always end up in trouble."

Which is probably exactly where I'm headed, thought Jensi.

. . .

By the end of the week, they were more or less friends, with Swanson talking almost as much as an ordinary human though prone to odd fits of silence as well. Several times Swanson slapped him on the back, said he was going to miss him once he shipped out.

"Maybe a spot will open up," said Jensi.

Swanson shook his head. "It won't," he said. "But if it does, I'll put in a good word for you. You're a picker, but I bet you could do it."

Two choices, thought Jensi as he waited in the bar the next day for Swanson to come in, just three days before Swanson shipped out. He could do as his original plan had suggested and simply drug Swanson, make him incapable of showing up for work. He had a twist of ground-up sleeping pills in his pocket that he could pour into the man's beer. It'd be enough to knock the Swede out, maybe would make him sleep for a few days. And then when he didn't show up for work, Jensi could be there, asking around for work, just happening to have a specialization in cargo.

But he liked Swanson, that was the problem. Talbot on the other hand he hardly knew. And Swanson was likely to think to call on him if Talbot didn't show up for work. The odds were better. But the question was how to bring it smoothly about.

And as ideas flitted back and forth within his head, he began to ask himself: *How far am I willing to go for my brother? I'll break the law for him, I'll force someone out of their job just to have a chance to see him, what else will I do? Would I kill someone for him?*

He shook his head. No, he had to be careful. He couldn't let this quest for his brother—a quest for a brother who might now be damaged enough to not even recognize him if he were to find him—make him into a different person than he was. He couldn't let go of himself just to find his brother.

That afternoon, he quit his job. His boss was a little surprised and started to protest that he needed some notice, but in the end he sighed, counted out Jensi's back pay, and shook his hand good-bye.

Jensi went out and bought a roll of duct tape, then went to the apartment building where Talbot lived. He rang several bells until someone buzzed him in. The apartment was on the third floor, the door a cheap affair, and by leaning into the door and jiggling the knob while forcing a card in, he managed to pop the lock out of its groove and go in.

Inside, the apartment was immaculate, nothing out of place. Two clean plates sat side by side on the counter with a knife and fork crossed over each in an X, with two glasses arranged in perfect symmetry above them. The cabinets were mostly empty, though one was full of identical cans of food. The bed was made, the bathroom exceptionally clean. In a way, it was hard to believe anybody lived there at all.

He wandered around the apartment for a while, thinking. In the office he found a pen and a piece of paper and wrote: "Your next job?" followed by the picking company's vid contact. Was that giving too much away, putting too much at risk? Maybe, but he'd had a hard enough life himself that he couldn't see himself taking away a man's livelihood, even a man as strange and repressed as Talbot. He left it on the kitchen table, where it lay awkwardly, the only object in the apartment to seem out of place.

By the time Talbot had come home from work and had opened the door, Jensi had his balaclava on and was hiding behind it. The small man came through and Jensi hit him hard twice in the temple, quick jabbing blows. Talbot gave a strange breathless cry and fell in a heap. Jensi dragged him over to a chair and taped his arms and legs to it.

When Talbot was secure, Jensi poured a glass of water and sprinkled the twist of crushed sleeping tablets into it. He waited for the man to come around. But nothing seemed to be happening.

He waited some more, then pulled a chair closer to him and placed his finger against his neck. No pulse.

It seemed absurd, an accident of fate. He stripped off his balaclava and quickly unbound Talbot and laid him flat, tried to give him artificial respiration, pumped his chest, but it had been too long. The blood was already seeping lower in the body and pooling, leaving the face pale and waxen.

He left the body and slumped into the couch, holding his head with his hands. It was his fault: he had hit the man too hard. Or maybe just bad luck: maybe Talbot had some sort of condition that he should have known about, a heart problem, say. In any case, the first thing he should have done when the man went down was check his pulse and made sure he was still breathing.

Now he had traded the chance of seeing his brother for another man's life. How many other lives would fall forfeit along the way?

After a while, he got up and removed the remaining duct tape from Talbot's arms and legs and from the chair. He dragged the man into the other room and positioned him in an armchair in front of his vid, then turned it on to one of the broadcasts. The body was already a little stiff, but it bent for him with a little pressure and settled into the chair. Maybe it would look like he died there.

He carefully positioned the kitchen chair back where it had been at the table, then washed out the glass containing the water and crushed sleeping pills, arranging it back where it had been before. The note he tore into fourths and slipped into his pocket, along with the twist of paper.

He took one last look over the apartment and then, thinking there was nothing else he could do, left.

The next morning he was down at the port early, ostensibly to see Swanson off. The big man, upon seeing him, came over and swatted his shoulder with his big hand.

"No more drinking together, eh?" he said, his eyes twinkling. "Now you'll have to drink alone."

He introduced Jensi to Captain Martin, who shook his hand. "My friend Jensi," Swanson said. "One of the best pickers there is, but ready to move on to more serious freight. Keep him in mind if you ever have an open position."

Captain Martin just nodded, made small talk for a moment, and then went back to making preparations and overseeing the loading of the shuttles that would take them up to the *Eibon*, currently in orbit. Swanson shook his hand again and then left.

Jensi hung around a little bit more and then, not wanting to seem too needy or conspicuous, went home.

The next few hours were hard ones, as he waited by the vid for them to contact him. What if they didn't? What if they had someone else in mind or simply decided that they could manage without an additional person to take Talbot's place? Then Talbot would have died for no reason, and he, Jensi, would have gotten no further toward figuring out how to see his brother.

He imagined the captain or perhaps Swanson or perhaps someone else realizing that Talbot wasn't there, then trying to call him by vid, then sending someone running toward his place to check on him and finding the dead body. Would it seem that he had died of natural causes? Would there be a suspicious bruise on his temple where Jensi had struck him?

An hour went by, then two, without word. He was close to giving up and abandoning it altogether when the vid flicked on and he saw the captain's face. He accepted the connection.

"Mr. Jensi Sato?" the captain said.

"Yes?" said Jensi.

"Didn't know that I'd find you at home," he said. "But here you are."

"Swing shift today," Jensi lied, hoping they hadn't managed to track down which picker he worked for and discovered that he had quit. "I go in in a few minutes."

"Maybe not," said the captain. "How'd you like to come work for me?"

"Work for you?" he said. "Sure." And then felt he had to backtrack and ask, "What's the pay?"

The captain gave him a figure that was nearly double his picking job. "You come highly recommended by Swanson," he said. "I trust his judgment. Only catch is that you'd have to start today."

Jensi pretended to think about it, then nodded. "What time do you want me?" he asked.

"Immediately. We're already in orbit and waiting for you. There's a shuttle waiting in the port. Pack your things and catch it right way. No delaying now: we'll leave as soon as you get up here."

He nodded and cut the vid. He took a deep breath. He was one step closer to seeing his brother.

21

Istvan could never tell when the world was going to change for him. Most of the time that other world was there but deep in the background, a dull whispery rumbling like a voice talking to him from very, very far away. But then, unexpectedly, pain would bloom in his head and the veil would descend again and then it was the world of the penal colony that was almost lost in the background and the whirr and rush of this other place that took over. Which was the real world? Or were they both real? Or neither? Each time that inversion took place, when things reverted to normal, that other world was just slightly less in the background, just slightly louder, just slightly more noisy.

He could tell that the other prisoners were beginning to feel it, too, though they didn't know that they felt it. Whatever was making the pain in his head and throwing up or tearing down the veil was simply tickling their hindbrain a little or scratching it enough to slowly rub it raw. They felt it, but didn't always know they were feeling it. They were more jumpy than they had been, and some of them seemed at times to have difficulty with their heads. They became angry, said things they not only didn't mean but didn't understand. For once, Istvan felt like he wasn't the one who was behind; he could see things that the others couldn't, and he could see its effect on them, even if they couldn't.

He tried to remain calm. He slept in his cell at night. When the alarm went off and the door automatically slid open, he went out with the rest of them, did his best to talk and converse and pretend like he was a person just like the rest of them. But he had never been very good at that, and soon he'd lose the thread. He knew he was different. The three who he'd first sat by at the table—Bill, Michael, and Waldron—seemed to tolerate him best and he found himself drawn to them as well, maybe because of that, or maybe just because he had sat by them first. He could see it affecting them as well, whatever it was, but differently. When the world began to recede for Istvan, it made Michael simply withdraw into himself. Waldron became manic, overexcited. Bill began to mumble to himself, his face slowly taking on a smile, until the world came back and they all became more or less like they'd been before. Though not quite. Each time, they had a little farther to come back, and each time they stopped a hair or two shorter.

Maybe it was partly the penal colony itself that made it worse. There they were, free in a manner of speaking, but with their world limited to a circle with another circle around it, knowing that there was a third circle that they could not enter and that from there people were watching them. Istvan had always felt watched, had felt there was, just out of his line of vision, someone observing him, but in the past nobody else around him had seemed to feel that way. It was reassuring in a way to know that now he was feeling something that everyone else was feeling, that as far as they were concerned he was right.

Over the course of several weeks the veil became more and more prominent for Istvan, fading away into a burst of light out of which came figures from his past who spoke to him. It was, though he did not know why, either always the dead or people that were dead to him: at first he might see the face of his brother, even the face of one of his fellow prisoners, done over in white lines and in light like an inverted self, but something about that seemed to trouble him and whatever was sending him these visions seemed to sense this, adjusted itself slightly to fit what his mind would bear. Why was it reassuring for him to see the faces of the dead rather than the living? He didn't know. He suspected that it wouldn't be reassuring for most people, might even make some of them lose their minds. But for him perhaps it simply helped him to distinguish between the world of the penal colony and this other, newer world.

As time went on, the light slowly faded, this new world took on color and depth, and had it not been for the pain that filled his head when it came and the fact that he could recognize the faces as the faces of the dead, he might not have known which world he was seeing. *But why*, he wondered, *do I see my mother?* She might be dead, but he didn't know for certain whether she was or not; maybe it was as he had thought before, that she was simply dead to him. Or maybe she really was dead and the vision was telling him this by dressing itself up in her face and speaking in her voice.

But more and more often the face that came to him, the face that slowly gelled and came out of the light and created a world around it, was the councilman he had killed, Tim Fischer. The man came to him with a broken head and a strange clomping stride. He spoke in the same voice Fischer himself had used, though how this might be possible Istvan could not say. For a long time the voice remained strange, simply repeating what Istvan himself said but in a fashion that ran all the words together, as if it were repeating something it didn't understand.

"You're dead," Istvan might say.

"Yourdead," Fischer's voice would echo back, the head slowly oozing blood.

"What do you want to tell me?" he asked, and the voice repeated it back. It was a little like being in a nightmare, but fascinating too. *How can I understand it?* he wondered. *How can I make it understand me?*

The bursts of power were coming more frequently, and the faces when they appeared seemed more and more attentive, as if they were paying close attention just to him. He found they looked closest at him when he turned numbers about in his head, built structures and patterns with them, as he'd been doing since he was a boy. What interested them about that, he didn't know. Were any of the others feeling it? He didn't think so. He couldn't tell for certain, but each of the several dozen other prisoners seemed to take in the bursts in a different way. And as these bursts increased, people changed in a way that Istvan thought of as their true selves bubbling further out. They became rawer, more erratic, in a way that he understood. And for him, despite his visions being all the more intense, he felt like his true self was already closer to the surface. He could cope with it better than they could.

One of the prisoners, a man named Brian Conn, couldn't cope with it at all. It was after lunch. Several prisoners walked the perimeter of the inner circle, a few of them worked out on exercise machines, a few others were still sitting at the tables and reading. Bill and Waldron were talking, mumbling away, their conversation getting more heated as Istvan felt the pressure in his head increasing, the burst of energy starting to come. The veil sprang up again, then the world it contained, and Istvan stayed there as silent as he could, not wanting to speak to the face belonging to Councilman Fischer in front of the others but also not able to see or even really hear the two men sitting next to him. He stayed there with his jaw clenched, staring into the bloody face that stared mercilessly back at him, feeling at a far distance the touch of someone, either Bill or Waldron, he couldn't tell which. Seconds passed, or minutes, and then the face bleached out again and fell into the void of blankness and the veil became tattered again and he could see the real world again, through the veil, and could hear, too, a sound that sounded like screaming, but was quickly cut off. Waldron was gripping his shoulder hard, not—as he might have thought—because he had noticed that Istvan was having one of his visions, but rather because of what he was seeing in front of him. "What the hell?" Waldron said. He was staring straight ahead of him, and Bill, too, had turned around and was staring, so Istvan stared as well. Conn was there, a few tables over, and for a second, perhaps two, Istvan had no idea what he should be looking at. And then he saw the handle of the fork rising from Conn's forearm where he had plunged it in.

Conn opened his mouth and screamed again. He reached down and tugged the fork free and blood began to pump up from the wound, quicker than Istvan would have thought possible. He plunged it in again, a little farther up the arm but just as deep, and screamed yet again.

"What the fuck's wrong with him?" asked Bill.

But Istvan couldn't think of a way to answer this question that would make sense to Bill. There was too much to explain, and Istvan never knew what words to use. It was as if Conn had touched the other world and he had brought some of it back with him and it had lodged inside his brain. And then it had turned that part of his brain inside out and made it into something else. He didn't think it meant any harm, that it was just trying to figure out a way to speak with them. But even if it didn't mean harm, it did not understand how much it could do with a brain without breaking it.

"We have to stop him," said Waldron, and started toward Conn.

But by this time, the fork was out again, and plunged deep into his throat, slicing open his carotid artery and puncturing his windpipe. Waldron reached Conn as he wavered and fell off the bench. He pressed his hand to Conn's neck as the blood spurted through his fingers and as the man sucked for air and quickly died.

Waldron kept holding his hand there, staring at Conn as if he were looking at a ghost. The others had to come and pull him away and make him stand back. But after doing that, they didn't know what else to do. They all just stood there, a few yards away from the body, motionless, not knowing what to do next.

Conn, thought Istvan, staring at the man, memorizing his face. There would be a new face that would come to him now in the other world, he knew. He would now have a visit from the freshly dead.

They must have been there only a few more seconds when the alarm sounded, calling them back to their cells. A few of them went back immediately, but most of them just milled about until an echoing voice issued from the loudspeaker attached to one of the struts of the dome.

"Return to your cells," the voice said. "You have thirty seconds. This is your only warning."

With that, most of the rest began to move, though one or two remained. Bill led both Istvan and the still-stunned and bloody Waldron back to their cells. Istvan sat on his bed until the cell door clanged shut, and then approached the bars, holding on to them and staring out. He caught, down the hall, a fluid flash of black as four or five guards in riot gear rushed from the normally closed security door that led to the next ring through their ring and into the central circle. Then there was the sound of cries; Istvan could not see them, but imagined them setting upon the prisoners who had disobeyed with their truncheons. And indeed, a few moments later two guards rounded the corner dragging an unconscious and bloody prisoner between them. They let him flop down on the hallway, not far from Istvan's cell. Their faces were covered with plastic shields, the light bouncing off them, which almost—Istvan thought, a little astonished—made them look like they had no faces at all. Or like their faces were made of light. Just like the faces of the other world! One of the guards kicked the prisoner once and then both turned and went back around the corridor and into the inner circle. A few moments later, all the guards went through again, carrying Conn's corpse out of the penal colony and into the outer ring. The door closed and then there was nothing but silence.

Or almost nothing but silence. Through it, just below it, below even the beating of his own heart, Istvan could hear the whispering of voices, very difficult to hear, almost impossible. But he heard them. He couldn't make out what they were saying, but he tried to listen to them nonetheless.

22

Henry Wandrei was unfortunate enough to be on monitoring duty when the convict went crazy. He was there before the monitor, watching Istvan, making sure once again that yes, he had been right, it really was Jensi's brother, when suddenly his head began to hurt. *Goddamn migraines,* he thought. Must be something to do with the artificial atmosphere in the dome—he'd never suffered from migraines before. He closed his eyes tight, pinched the bridge of his nose, and waited for the pain to subside. After a few seconds it did, even if only just slightly, and he opened his eyes to see suddenly a strange flicker on one of the monitors. He adjusted that camera slightly and at first couldn't believe what he was seeing. He focused in and then thought *Oh shit* when he realized what he was seeing was a man's arm with a fork sticking out of it.

And then he watched the man's hand close around the fork and tug it out of the arm, which in some ways seemed like a very sensible thing to do, even if the arm did start bleeding profusely. What was less sensible was the fact that he immediately stuck it in again, even deeper this time. Henry had never seen anything like it. There hadn't been a single disturbance since he had arrived: no real fights, almost no suicides, and very little violence except the rare times when the guards were sent in to retrieve one of the inmates and bring him to the interrogation chamber. Since Hell was the last stop, most of the convicts had already been pretty thoroughly wrung out before arriving here, and most were political prisoners rather than hardened cons.

He was reaching for the button to alert the guards, watching one of the other prisoners rushing toward the man who was stabbing himself with the fork, when the man tugged the fork out again and buried it in his neck this time, and then pitched backward off the bench.

After that, he could see very little; a man was leaning over the injured prisoner, perhaps trying to give him first aid, and was blocking the camera's view of him. He did not remember having pushed the button for the guards but he must have for there was a voice in his earpiece now, talking to him, asking him what was up. Stuttering, he tried to explain what he had just seen—prisoner inflicting violence on himself for no discernable reason and having collapsed, probably gravely injured—and then the man who had been administering first aid moved back and the camera could see again and there was no question in his mind but that the man who had stabbed himself was dead.

Henry sat there, a little shocked or perhaps a lot shocked— hard to say. He stared numbly at the body, just as all the prisoners were staring, standing in a circle around it. There was Istvan again, he could see him. He didn't look traumatized or stressed, seemed hardly surprised, just stood there with his face expressionless, staring on. And then, suddenly, he thought he caught the flicker of a smile.

He's crazy, thought Henry. *Maybe they're all crazy.* He was glad that he was not one of the guards, that he wouldn't have to be one of the ones to go in there.

He had to stay watching the prisoners until one of the monitors showed him the guards lined up behind the door, ready to go in. Then he triggered the alarm, telling the prisoners to return to their cells. A few of them did, but most of them were still standing there, still in shock maybe. So he followed protocol and turned on the loudspeaker and turned the volume all the way up and gave them their one warning. There was a little confusion, but in the end all of them returned to the cells except for one. He considered issuing the warning again, but no, he knew the rules, he wasn't to do that. So he closed the cell doors and then called down and warned the guards that there was a corpse and one loose inmate but that that inmate looked stunned, wasn't likely to be a threat. And then, when he'd had acknowledgment, he opened the doors and watched them rush in.

They beat the loose inmate unconscious. There was no need for it, no reason to do it, and it made Henry think again that he'd made a very bad choice by taking this job, by coming to this planet out in the middle of nowhere to live in the outer circle of a penal colony that not only the prisoners but the guards, too, called Hell. He watched two guards—he couldn't tell which two because of the riot gear they wore—drag the unconscious man away and deposit him in the ring with the cells in it. Meanwhile, the three remaining guards milled around the corpse.

Henry's earpiece crackled. "What are we to do with the body?" asked their leader. On the monitor Henry saw him turn and stare up at one of the cameras.

"What do you usually do with the bodies?" asked Henry.

"This is the first one I've had, sir, since they converted the morgue to an interrogation room," the man said.

Don't call me sir, Henry wanted to say, *I'm not one of you.* But he knew if he said it, it would only confuse the man. Plus, he wasn't absolutely sure that it was true. In a sense he was as guilty as the soldiers who had beaten the loose inmate unconscious. "Isn't there a protocol?" he asked.

"Not that I'm aware of, sir. Before, we left them in the morgue and someone collected them."

"Who collected them?" asked Henry.

"I don't know," said the man. "Someone from the other complex, the one we don't talk about."

"Well, we can't leave the body there," said Henry. "Bring it inside and put it somewhere until we can figure out what to do. The interrogation room, maybe. I'll contact the commander and see what he suggests."

Once the body was inside, lying flat on one of the metal tables in the interrogation room, Henry established the link. It took a few minutes for it to go through, the satellite that directed the signal first having to assure itself that the link was authorized and then having to encrypt the signal and send the decryption code securely to the vessel circling the planet. It had always seemed strange to Henry that almost all of the military personnel lived not within the outer ring of the prison but in orbit around the planet. It wasn't as though there wasn't enough room for them here. But maybe they felt freer where they were. Or maybe from their vantage they could keep watch not only over the penal colony but over the other complex that had been built not far away. Henry had no idea what it was or what purpose it served—he had only caught a glimpse of it when the shuttle landed him here, and then if the light was just right or the darkness deep and hazeless he could see its glimmer there at a distance. But he knew it was there, and knew if it was out here in the middle of nowhere whatever was going on inside of it wasn't anything he wanted any part of.

Eventually the line crackled and he saw the face of one of the ensigns. A thin, awkward fellow with a prim mouth. *Orthor*, read the name over his pocket.

"Supply ship isn't here yet," said Ensign Orthor. "It won't arrive for a few weeks. You should have more than enough to last you until then."

Jerk, thought Henry. "That's not why I'm calling," he said.

"Oh?" said the ensign. "Then why are you calling?"

"I need to talk to the commander."

"About what?" Henry didn't answer, just stayed silent and staring until the ensign said, "Let me see if I can raise him."

The screen went blank. When it lit up again, it showed the face of Commander Grottor. He had a crew cut and a craggy face, his cheeks covered with pockmarks that most people would have had surgically corrected. A scar, too, ran from one side of his nose through his lip, the skin splaying out slightly.

"Jenkins, no?" he said.

"No," said Henry. "Wandrei." He couldn't help but feel that the commander had deliberately gotten his name wrong.

"Wandrei, of course," the commander said, and gave a broad but lifeless smile. "Well, what do you need?"

Henry explained.

"A fork, you say?" said the commander. And then said, "Doesn't sound like a man with all his marbles."

"No indication of disturbance or madness until now," said Henry. "Most of these men have their spirits broken. Last thing most of them are up to is any violence toward others or themselves."

"And yet, here we are. I wouldn't worry too much about it, Jenkins. You're not to blame."

"Wandrei, sir," said Henry, and watched a flash of irritation cross over the commander's face. "I didn't think I was to blame. I'm just not sure what to do with the body. Shall we bury it? Incinerate it?"

The commander hesitated for a moment, finally shook his head. "Probably we should have someone take a look at it, just in case. Store it for now."

"Store it?"

"You've got a morgue, don't you?"

"We had one, sir, but it was replaced by the interrogation room."

"Ah," said Grottor, "I see. Well, put him in a refrigerator."

"We only have the ones we use for food."

"Well, clear one of those out and put him in. It'll only be for a few days."

"A few days?" said Henry, imagining one of the guards waking up and stumbling into the kitchen and opening a door on a corpse.

"Maybe sooner," said the commander. "We'll do what we can." He reached out and clicked the screen off.

23

Ensign Haley still wasn't sure if she should be flattered or insulted. She couldn't decide if Grottor was using her or not, and she wasn't altogether sure how much or how little of the truth he was telling her. She also wasn't sure if she could ask him.

You're relieved of your duties, he had said to her in the privacy of his cabin. *I have a more important task for you*. He'd explained to her how she would continue to sit at the same console that she'd sat at before, but he'd arranged for an ensign off the bridge to handle her formal tasks, and then she'd be allowed to do what she was supposed to do.

"And what's that?" she'd asked.

"Why, draw, of course," he said. "Doodle and draw. Don't think about it much. Anything that comes to mind or half to mind, just draw it and then vid it over to me."

"You want me to spend my time doodling, sir?"

He nodded. "You really don't have any idea, do you?" he asked.

"Any idea of what, sir?"

"You didn't recognize what you drew?" he asked.

"No," she said. And then said, "Well, it looked like the Unitologist symbol."

"That's right," he said. "But it's much more than that. Can I share something with you?" he asked.

"Umm," she said, startled. But the hesitancy with which she'd responded had made him clam up again.

"It's tied to our work on the planet," he had said. "What you're doing, Ensign Haley, is important work. It might not seem so, but it is. You'll have to take my word for it. We need to be careful who takes advantage of it."

She had laughed. "You must be joking, sir," she had said.

But apparently he was not, for here she was now, sitting at her console, scribbling with her stylus on her digital pad. She had been doing it for more than a week now, and spinning each doodle over to Grottor as soon as she felt she was ready to move on to a new page.

Grottor's response had been impassive at first; then, slowly, he had begun to express his disappointment. "No," he finally said, "that's not it. That's not helping at all."

"Perhaps if you'd tell me what you'd like me to draw," she said, "then I could be of more help."

He shook his head. "No," he said. "If it's to be of any use to us at all, it just has to come."

But ever since primary school, she'd been trained to please and she was incredibly frustrated that now, somehow, she couldn't. She tried to second-guess what Grottor wanted. He'd been initially pleased when she drew some version of the Unitologist symbol, and so she drew it again, and saw for the briefest moment a flicker of excitement when he saw it. But the excitement quickly faded.

"Stop thinking," he scolded her. "Let it just come."

Let what just come?

It might have gone on much longer like that, might have gone on just like that until the moment when Grottor, frustrated, gave up on Ensign Haley and returned her to her duties, but Grottor, luckily, was not a man to become easily frustrated, and, also luckily, something happened first.

They were, Grottor would realize when he looked at the data later, at the point in their loop where they were directly above the man-made facilities on Aspera's surface. They were also, due to sloppy navigation on Ensign Orthor's part, closer to the surface than they usually were. And finally, instrumentation would reveal, there had been a burst of energy from the planet's surface. From the Marker.

Suddenly Haley had given a little cry and clutched her head.

"Headache?" he heard Orthor ask. Every time the man spoke, it filled Grottor with irritation. It was partly because he knew the man was a plant from Blackwell, but in addition the man was simply irritating. Even toying with that technician down on the surface, Wandrei, pretending not to remember his name, didn't help much.

It must have been a bad one. Ensign Haley had her head in her hands for twenty or thirty seconds, and seemed a little dazed after. What was it? he wondered. Simply a migraine? Why had it seemed to come along so suddenly? He watched her for a while. For a few moments she was still and then she picked back up her stylus and continued her task.

"Ensign Haley," he said.

She raised her head, gave him a tired look. "Yes, sir?" she asked, her tone flat.

"Leave the bridge and take a few moments to gather yourself," he said.

For a moment, he thought she was going to protest, as she had before, but instead she gave a curt nod, spun what was on her pad over to his vid, and stood up to leave.

She was halfway to the door when he realized what she'd sent him.

"Wait a moment, Haley," he said.

She stopped and paused on the far side of the bridge, waited while he took a closer look.

A new series of equations. *Crystallization counter-sequence,* the gray man had called one part of the first set, or something similar if not exactly that. He recognized a few of the equational gestures that he'd seen alongside the first sketch, but he didn't know enough to be able to judge how important or genuine they were. He would have to send them along, see what the gray man felt they amounted to. The image alongside them didn't look at all like the Marker but there was a small rough sketch of the Marker lower on the page and he realized that the rectangle he was seeing was a cutaway, a cross section from the Marker.

"Leave the bridge, Ensign Orthor," he said.

"What?" said Orthor. "I'm not the one with the headache," he said.

"Sir," said Grottor, flatly.

"What?" said Orthor.

"It's: 'I'm not the one with the headache, sir,'" said Grottor. "Leave. That's an order."

Orthor stood, face livid with suppressed anger, but left. "Now the rest of you," Grottor said. "All of you. Except you, Ensign Haley."

There was a moment of stunned silence and then the bridge crew started up and cleared up, a dull rumbling going through them. It took them a few moments, but soon he was left alone with Ensign Haley.

There was a long silence, which she finally broke. "What am I supposed to do, sir?" she asked.

"Do your task," he said.

"My task?"

"Draw," he said. "I want you to sit in that chair and draw until you can no longer see, and then I want you keep drawing."

Confused, she sat and began; almost immediately it was clear that something was happening. She quickly entered an almost trancelike state, and what came pouring out was complex and strange: equations and models, plans and structures. He had always known she was special, but he hadn't realized just how special.

She drew for hours before it began to fade and just became ordinary doodles again. He was not disappointed with the results. And, more importantly, neither was the gray man.

24

There was a static, a whispering, when the bursts came. It stayed with Istvan for more than a little while, even once the visions had begun to fade, and within it, if he listened hard enough, he could hear voices. They were incomplete and partial, but they were voices, he was sure of it. Or nearly sure. And they were not, as the other voices had been, merely a squashed repetition of words he had said himself. No, these were voices. Now all he had to do was train himself to listen hard enough so that he could hear them.

He took to sitting in his cell, on the edge of his bed, his feet flat on the floor, his hands on his knees, just listening. It reminded him of sitting on the edge of his bed late at night when he was a boy and practicing blanking the world out. There were the general noises he could hear around him—the sound of footsteps, the voices of the other inmates, a rustle or creak here or there—but these he tried to learn to unlisten to, to tune out completely, and, in a certain manner and after a few days, he succeeded. Then there was the sound of his heartbeat, the noise of his own breathing, the noises coming from his body and stomach. These, too, he learned to unlisten to, first dulling them and then reducing them to nothing at all. It came slowly, and had to be redone every time he sat down again, but it could be done. And then, once in that space of silence, he had to sharpen his ears still further, had to not only make them listen to the rumble of whispering voices beneath everything but to home in on just one of them, to pick it out, to start to hear its words.

It took six days, days in which he hardly ate, hardly even moved. At first his fellow prisoners were worried about him and clustered around him, but after he ignored them for a few hours, they gave up, left him alone. Occasionally one of them would come back, Waldron mostly, but wouldn't stay long, and though he found it an irritation to have someone shaking him, someone trying to talk to him, he quickly learned to ignore this as well.

And then, late in the sixth day, his ears caught hold of the tail of a voice and reeled it closer until he could hear it. It was incomplete and partial, but it was a real voice, speaking its own words, starting to say something. He massaged it, caressed it, until it grew a little, became a little louder, and he could hear that it was addressing him. *Istvan,* it was saying, *why won't you talk to me?*

But I don't even know who you are, he said. His lips were moving, he knew, whispering the words, but he could feel the words being uttered in his head as well.

Ah, there you are, said the voice. *Now you hear me.*

I've been trying to talk to you all along, Istvan said.

And I've been trying to talk to you. It just took us a while to find the right tongues.

Indeed, as they spoke the voice became stronger, more confident. It stretched and scratched against the sides of his mind like an animal and slowly grew larger, and he knew that now he'd be able to find it again, hear it again, whenever he went searching for it. And late on the seventh day, when the burst came again, he felt less pain this time. It was as if his head had been filled with living, thinking fire. The veil fell over things, tattered at first and then becoming blazing with light, as it always did, and then even more quickly resolving into another colorful world. There was the face of Conn, his lips almost blue, his neck bloody. He hovered there just in front of him, staring.

"Hello, Conn," Istvan said.

And this time instead of letting the face take his words and use them as his own, Istvan imagined the voice that he had been hearing drifting up from where, despite its growing size and power, it huddled and crouched in the background, and threading itself into the dead man's throat until Conn opened his mouth and spoke with it.

"Hello," Conn said. The voice was strange, not quite properly synched with his lips, and he spoke with a wet burble as if his throat was still partly filled with blood. Air, too, hissed softly out from the holes in his windpipe.

There, thought Istvan. *Now we're getting somewhere.*

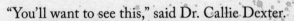

25

"You'll want to see this," said Dr. Callie Dexter.

Briden turned away from his computer and looked at her. "All right," he said. "You have something you want to show me, go ahead and show me."

"Vectors," she said again.

"You've already told me about the vectors. You did that a few days ago."

Dr. Dexter nodded. "I have more data now," she said. She tugged on his chair until it rolled closer to her monitor. "I've charted every surge since the vector of our Marker shifted. And I've also correlated it with the way it continues to broadcast even when not engaged in a surge. Before, when a surge came, it would send a wide-range blast of energy up into space, always a different vector as if it was looking for something. But then something changed."

"It's no longer broadcasting into space," said Briden.

"No," said Dr. Dexter. "Now it's a more focused blast, like a burst of energy being propelled out of a gun. It still spreads and widens a little, but much more slowly. And now it's always oriented in roughly the same direction."

"All right," said Briden. "It's changed. So what?"

Dr. Dexter smiled. "Here's the vector for the Marker from Aegis VII," she said, "which, incidentally, has been firing its pulse simultaneously with the Marker here. It's millions of miles away, so the system is quite wide by the time it reaches this far. But even so, if you calculate the center point of the wave you find that it seems to pass exactly through our planet."

Intrigued now, Briden simply nodded.

"Here's the last one from the project we're not supposed to know about, the one on Kreemar. The reason we know about it is because its signal is also oriented toward the planet we're on, and seems also to be coordinated with the other two."

She pulled up a topographical map.

"The planet's surface," she said. "Satellite photos. You don't know how hard it was for me to get this—had to speak directly to Commander Grottor himself."

"You should have gone through me," said Briden.

"I told him I was going through you," said Dr. Dexter. "Otherwise, he wouldn't have given me anything."

"You have no right—" started Briden.

Callie turned away from her screen and smirked. "Oh, relax," she said. "We're all on the same team. You'll get the credit if things work out well, and if they don't, you can tell them you had nothing to do with it. If you're nervous about it, link with him right now. I'm sure they won't hesitate to yank it away."

When Briden, fuming, didn't say anything, she turned back to her monitor. "Here we are," she said, touching the screen with one finger. Briden could see the specific shape of the compound perhaps two inches across, a gray blot on the yellow-red surface that was the rest of the map. "Marker is approximately right here." She moved her finger slightly. "The vector carries us forward along this path," she said, dragging her finger, "which brings us right through here."

She stopped on another gray blot. The penal colony. He knew it was there, saw it sometimes looming dimly on the horizon if he looked out the right window. But he had never been to it, let alone inside of it. It had nothing to do with their purpose for being on the planet.

"You think it's broadcasting to the prison compound?" he asked.

"I didn't say that," she said. "And it's not a broadcast exactly. It may be pulsing to something beyond that, on the other side of it, maybe even something miles away. But I've had the computer calculate the center point of each vector exactly and when we do that it looks like this." She touched the screen and three sets of lines appeared on the map. They intersected there, right at the prison compound.

"Oh my God," said Briden.

"Nifty, right?" said Callie.

"That's not exactly the word I would have used," said Briden. "What do you think it sees there?"

"There you go, treating it like a person again. It doesn't see anything. It doesn't want anything. The Marker is a mechanical device, you know that as well as I do. It's been programmed to look for something."

No, thought Briden, *she's wrong. It's much more than that.* But to Callie he only said, "What's your best guess?"

"My best guess? That's not very scientific, Briden." But when Briden didn't rise to take the bait, she raised her eyes upward and seemed to examine the ceiling. "I don't know," she said.

"Maybe there's something significant about the location. A certain kind of current or force there, a magnetic flux, perhaps even something we don't quite have the instrumentation to detect."

"It could be anything," said Briden.

"Not quite anything," Dr. Dexter corrected. "But it could be a lot of things."

He sighed. She always had to be right. "So what do we do?"

"Do? What else can we do but go look for it?"

"Somewhere in the middle of a penal colony," he said.

"We go where our data takes us," said Dr. Dexter. "We're scientists."

Briden hesitated, then nodded. "I'll speak with the commander," he said. "We'll see what we can arrange."

26

"Help? You need help?" asked Istvan.

"I don't need help," said Bill, mumbling it.

"Who are you talking to, Istvan?" asked Waldron.

He ignored them. They were in the world that wasn't important. They weren't part of the world that really mattered.

Yes, said dead Conn. *Help me.*

"But how can I?"

"Istvan, are you all right?" asked Waldron, placing his hand on his shoulder.

He shook him off.

We need you, said dead Conn, and as he spoke his face slowly changed, becoming smooth. The wound in his throat slowly closed, and the throat changed, too, losing its Adam's apple. A moment later it was clear that his face was no longer a man's face but a woman's. A moment more and Istvan recognized his mother. *I need you,* she claimed.

Nice trick, thought Istvan.

"What do you need me to do?" he asked.

Come be with me.

"What do you mean come be with you? You're right here."

His mother shook his head. *Find me,* she said. *Come unto me.*

"I'm trapped here," said Istvan. "I'm a prisoner, I can't leave."

"We all are," said Waldron next to him. "You're no different from anyone else." But his mother just looked at Istvan as if she hadn't understood what he had said. Then she smiled. *It is you,* she told him, *who will help change things.*

But now she was speaking in riddles. How was he to help her if he didn't understand what she was saying? And thinking that introduced a little seed of doubt into him. He hadn't liked his mother much when she was alive; why should he listen to her when she was dead? Well, it wasn't his mother exactly, a part of him reminded himself, but someone or something else. *Then what was it?* the rest of him wanted to know. But that was the problem, wasn't it? Because he simply did not know. Maybe it wasn't even real: for many years, ever since he was a kid, he'd had a hard time telling what was real from what was not, even he knew that. And yet it felt real, didn't it? And he wanted to listen to what was said. So why should he be afraid?

And yet he was a little afraid. Maybe it was too much for just one man, especially if he was that man. And he was trapped here: whatever it wanted him to do, how was he going to get out to do it? And how was he to know how to do it even once he was out?

"Why me?" he asked.

Because you can hear us best, said his mother. *You can teach us. You are teaching us to understand the others through you.*

Us? he wondered. But there was only his mother, and another seed of doubt was introduced.

And then the burst came—a strong one this time. He heard

Bill scream somewhere near him, the sound penetrating even into this other world. He felt a finger within his brain, touching it, prodding it, and then it felt like his head had caught fire and melted into slag. The world went strange and he could see, suddenly, both worlds equally, but one through his left eye and one through his right, overlaid on one another, but both still fully present. And then he found himself lying on the floor, staring up at the ceiling, both worlds in full carnival around him, as his fellow prisoners shouted or sweated or yelled or simply stood there, slowly banging their heads against the wall.

27

"You want us to what?" asked Henry.

On the vidscreen the commander's eyes shifted slightly to one side, the only sign Henry could see that he was at least a little uncomfortable with the request as well. "Mr. Jenkins, I know it's an unusual request," he said. "But it's very important. In fact, a great deal more important than the safety of the prisoners, or even, frankly, I regret to say, of you and the other personnel."

"And you can't tell me anything more about it?"

"I'm sorry, it's classified," said the commander.

Henry tried again. "This is probably not the best time," he said. "The prisoners are acting strangely. Everyone is on edge and some of them even seem to be teetering on the brink of something. Whatever is happening is affecting some of our people as well. Tempers are short. I keep on getting the feeling that something's about to erupt."

"Whether it's the best time or not doesn't matter," said the commander. "You will do this, Wandrei." And Henry realized that there was no debating the point; the commander was serious enough that he'd neglected to humiliate him by calling him by the wrong name.

He nodded. "How long will they be here?"

"I don't know," said the commander. "Perhaps a day. Perhaps a month. As long as it takes."

"How many of them will there be?"

"They can bring as many of their people as they feel they need. There'll be at least one—Briden: he's the leader."

"And these are scientists? They're the ones working not far from us?"

"That's right," said the commander. "I don't suppose it will hurt to admit to that, if it makes you feel any better. You're to give them any and every assistance, no matter how you feel about whatever they request. If they ask you to tear down a wall, you tear down a wall. If they ask you to cut off a prisoner's hand, you cut off the hand. You're to follow all their orders as if they were my own."

"Can I ask what they're likely to request?" asked Henry.

"You can ask, Jenkins," said the commander, "but I can't tell you."

"Classified?"

The commander shook his head. "I simply don't know," he said. "Nor do I know how this request ties in to their project exactly. But I do know that they must be given every leeway."

"What if they want to kill a prisoner?"

"Then let them kill the prisoner," said the commander without hesitation. "The men you have there lost their rights a long time ago. They're no longer really people as far as the state's concerned."

"What if they want to release a prisoner?"

The commander hesitated more at this. "You release him into their custody," he finally said. "But you get in touch with me immediately as well. You understand?"

When Henry nodded, the commander broke the link. Henry sighed. The job that was supposed to be temporary, a way of earning a little money so he could start some sort of business of his own back on Vindauga, was becoming more and more complicated. And there was something wrong with the atmosphere here: his head hurt almost all the time, seriously throbbed. In addition to the brief piercing headaches, he was having something like aura migraines now as well. Strobing, throbbing headaches that moved like a psychedelic veil across his vision, obscuring sight in first one eye and then the other. Maybe it was just the stresses of the job that caused it, or he wasn't eating properly, but he couldn't shake the feeling that it was tied to this place, that he'd be okay if only he could just leave.

Nor could he shake, now that he was thinking about it, the feeling that the commander was out to get him. Was this all a trap? Or was he being paranoid, just feeling trapped because he was living in the outer circle of a penal colony? Even though he wasn't a prisoner, he felt like one. And perhaps if he handled this situation wrong, even without meaning to, it would be a simple matter for the commander to order him to be moved from the technician's desk where he now sat and put into a cell on the other side of the wall. There were so many empty cells. Any of them could be waiting for him.

He shook his head. What was wrong with him? Why was he so worried? He tried to laugh, but it sounded wrong, more like someone choking.

He called the six guards and the other technician in, explained to them what was to happen. He watched the anger and suspicion and paranoia manifest itself on their faces, only slowly subsiding. Henry regarded them each attentively with part of his mind, wondering *Which of these men is going to crack first?* If he knew for certain, he could have the man put in a jail cell, just for their own protection. But how could he know for certain? He'd have to put all of them in jail cells just to be safe, and even he knew that if he started putting men in cells, then the remaining men would quickly put *him* in a cell. Before they knew it, everyone would be in a cell, and then they would all slowly starve to death.

He shook his head. What was he thinking? This wasn't how he usually thought about things. No, he had to keep his head clear, especially now, especially in this time of stress, when he might need all his resources. He had to remember to be himself.

28

Jensi waited until they were a few hours in to the flight before asking Swanson where they were going. The big Swede just shrugged. "Probably the same trip as we've done before," he said, "but the captain's always closemouthed about where we're going. Has to be, I guess."

For most of the day they passed through the solar system, the captain letting the *Eibon* move slowly along. Jensi overheard one of the crew saying they were heading to the nearest shockpoint and when he asked Swanson about it an hour later as they did the rounds of the cargo hold, the man nodded and said yes, that was no secret. They would go there and then from there they would go to the Venus shockpoint and then they would go elsewhere, to a place that *was* secret.

"There are only a few shockpoint nodes reachable from the Venus node," said Jensi. "It's got to be one of those."

Swanson smiled. "I thought so, too, first time we went," he said. "But there's at least one more node than people know."

One more node than people know, thought Jensi later, lying in his berth, listening to the drunken snores of the Swede in the bunk below him. Shockpoints were costly to build and took a long time. So the penal colony had not been hastily thrown together but was probably the result of years of planning. Either that, or the result of tremendous resources. Maybe both. The *Eibon*, too, he had noticed, was not your ordinary cargo freighter. The ship was state of the art, one of the newest models with all the trimmings. He had congratulated the captain on being able to afford such a ship, but the man had just shaken his head.

"Not mine, son," he said. "Belongs to the powers that be."

The powers that be, he thought in his berth. That was always the problem: the powers that be, though who they were and where they were to be found was often hard to say. They were behind things, lurking there, almost as if they occupied another world, safe and protected from the jolts and shocks of the world that ordinary people had to occupy.

The node they approached seemed to be under construction, but the captain just plowed through the warning systems as if they didn't exist. And indeed, they didn't seem to exist for them: none of the alarms went off and no barriers went up. They were able to drift slowly into the node and then there was the strangeness of entering a kind of tunnel of energy, the disorientation and near panic that came with it, and then the arrival in a new portion of space, the strange reorientation of the stars as other stars, since they were elsewhere.

But where exactly? The sun was not quite right for the Aspera system. For a moment he thought he'd made a mistake and joined with the wrong crew, accidentally murdered a man for no reason, and that he was just as far away from his brother as ever.

"This is where we're going?" he asked Swanson.

The man shook his head. "No shockpoint where we're end-ing up," he said. "We just got close. Now it's another two weeks of travel through normal space and then we'll finally get there."

For the two weeks of travel, there was very little for either him or Swanson to do. They could only check the supplies and boxes so many times in a day before beginning to feel ridicu-lous. And so they drank. The ship was well-stocked with alco-hol and Swanson had brought a few cases of his own in addition, and Swanson was always eager to start in, so it was up to Jensi to keep him sober long enough for them to do their minimal rounds. Perhaps that had been Talbot's job, too, when he was still alive.

Swanson became more and more voluble over the course of the two weeks, but it also became clear that he knew very little. He didn't even know the name of the planet they were going to and hadn't been curious enough to try to figure it out. The captain himself was slowly warming to Jensi, though he also seemed a little concerned about him.

"Suppose I should have done a security check on you before taking you on," he said to Jensi early one evening, staring at him thoughtfully. "That's what the powers that be would have wanted. But we were in a rush, as you know, because of that damned Talbot going and dying on us. Plus Swanson vouched for you. Had I done a check, what do you suppose I would have found?"

"Nothing," said Jensi.

The captain nodded. "Nothing," he said. "I'll accept that. We'll just have to say that I did the check after all and that's what I found."

A few days later Swanson had the captain down to the supply

room and opened a bottle with him. They joked back and forth between themselves, talking about other runs, earlier runs, back when the captain had been in command of a very different ship, an old, raggedy freighter that was years out of date.

"And look at you now," said Swanson. "Look at us now." The captain sat there with an enigmatic half smile and just kept drinking. Jensi sat on the edge of a box a few feet away, observing the conversation but not really being part of it.

"The thing I don't understand," said Swanson, once he'd had a few, "is why did they choose us? They could have had any captain they wanted for the prices they were offering. Why us?"

The captain shrugged. "Just luck, I guess," he said.

"Just luck?" said Swanson. "No," he said. "You've had luck before, but it's mostly been bad."

"Maybe it was time for my luck to change."

"Or maybe they knew you could be discreet," said Swanson, tapping the captain on his chest.

The captain didn't seem to take the tap badly, but did say, "Not all of us in this room are so discreet," at which Swanson seemed to take the hint and stopped talking.

They kept drinking, Swanson the most, followed by the captain. Jensi was having just enough to keep up appearances, watching carefully for the captain's gaze to go glassy and his hand to begin to wobble.

After a while, Swanson crawled off his box, lay down on the floor, and passed out. The captain put down his glass and stood, straightening his jacket, but Jensi stopped him. "There's still some in the bottle," he said. "It'd be a shame for it to go to waste."

Halfway through the next bottle, he'd gotten the captain to

talk openly. He wouldn't quite say the name Aspera, but he'd hinted enough about confinement and treason and the price of freedom that he didn't have to for Jensi to feel confident about where they were going. He kept prodding the captain, encouraging him, but either he was exceptionally discreet or the man really did know almost nothing about Aspera. He'd done deliveries, but he'd always stayed in orbit; the only ones to go down to the planet's surface were the freight specialists.

"And in this case it'll only be Swanson," said the captain. "They'd have had to clear you back at the spaceport on Vindauga if we wanted you to go down. You can load up-top in orbit, but you can't go down."

So there was another problem he would have to face, he thought after the captain had left, as he was slapping Swanson and trying to coax him awake, trying to get him to return to their quarters. He had to figure out a way down to the planet. Maybe he could prepare a box, slip himself into it. Or maybe Swanson could end up sick and then he'd have to go. But the former option involved a certain amount of risk, particularly if he was caught, and the latter would draw attention to him as well.

He managed to get Swanson awake enough to talk about the delivery process itself, though he had to keep shaking him to keep him talking. He hoped Swanson wouldn't remember any of it in the morning, and suspected he wouldn't after seeing how the man was the next day after previous drunken occasions. The process was this: they were to link first to a military ship in orbit, which would either give them permission to contact the penal colony or not. Then they would start taking loads down in the shuttle. Typically Swanson would land outside the colony, in a small dome that had a breathable atmosphere, and then he and Talbot would unload. There was usually a military ship already landed there, with two soldiers, and once he and Talbot had unloaded everything, the soldiers went over the manifest and carefully divided the items into two piles.

"Why two piles?" asked Jensi.

Swanson shrugged. "I don't ask about these things," he said. "If they want to divide them into two piles, such is fine with me. But if I ask about it, maybe they will ask me to help them move the boxes."

He looked at Jensi, his eyelids heavy, as if awaiting a response. "I see," said Jensi finally, not knowing what else to say.

This seemed to be enough. Swanson nodded. "Talbot, he didn't ask about it, either. But he thought about it," said Swanson.

"And what did he think about it?"

"He didn't have to think much about it," he said. "We always saw the other sets of lights when we were preparing to land. There's another complex on the planet besides the penal colony."

"What is it, another penal colony?" asked Jensi.

Swanson gave a sloppy shrug. "Why would they need two penal colonies?" he asked. "No, Talbot didn't think so. He thought it must be something else."

"Like what?"

"Who knows?" said Swanson, and then his eyes started to close. Jensi shook him. "What?" asked Swanson, coming to with a jerk.

"If it's not a penal colony, what did Talbot think it was?"

"I don't know," said Swanson. "But he figured it this way:

they had us land near the penal colony and unload there, not near the other complex. That meant that the other complex, whatever it was, was something that they wanted to hide more than the penal colony."

Some sort of black ops operation, thought Jensi. *But much more hush-hush than a secret penitentiary in which they illegally imprisoned and perhaps even tortured traitors. What could it be?* Whatever it was, it was something deadly serious, and perhaps something to stay away from.

"Where is Talbot, by the way?" Swanson asked.

"Talbot?" said Jensi. "He couldn't make it."

Swanson smiled. "Too bad," he said, and fell asleep.

He pulled the man's boots off, tucked the blankets up around him. So, he couldn't officially board the shuttle. And even if he did manage to get on the shuttle there would be two soldiers down below waiting to make sure he got back on again and left. And if he hid himself in a box, there were apparently about equal chances he would end up at some sort of secret compound rather than the penal colony. And to top it off, there was only a day, maybe two, left before they arrived.

29

"What are you looking for exactly?" asked Henry.

"We'll know when we find it," said Briden curtly.

"At least he hopes we will," said Callie Dexter, and winked.

There were six of them in all, with Briden and Dexter clearly in charge. They had arrived only a few hours after the commander's call, bringing with them a vehicle full of equipment, which they had promptly started stringing all through the space that Henry normally occupied. Some of them were sitting on the floor, others standing idly by. Briden had immediately commandeered his desk and chair, which made it so that Henry had to watch the monitors standing. He wasn't doing a very good job of that, though, since he was distracted by the newcomers.

"How dangerous are they?" asked Briden. "These are killers or what?"

"A few weeks ago, I would have said not all that dangerous," said Henry. "They're political prisoners rather than rapists or murderers. They feel very strongly about whatever their cause was but usually are fairly ordinary apart from that."

"A few weeks ago, you said," said Briden. "What about now?"

"Now, I don't know," he said. "They're restless, something's wrong with them. I can't predict how they'll behave."

Briden was staring at him strangely. He came a little closer, took him by the arm, spoke softly. "How do *you* feel?" he asked.

"Me?" said Henry, surprised. "Fine, I guess." He tried to keep his eyes from darting around. What if this was a trap? What if all this had been set up as a way to trap him? Maybe that was why the project was classified. He tried to push the thoughts down, swallowed.

"No . . . anxiety?" asked Briden, standing too close to him and narrowing his eyes. "No changes in behavior?"

"Uhh," said Henry, not sure what it was best to answer. "I'm all right," he finally said. "It's a stressful time."

Briden raised one eyebrow. "I can see you feel it," he said, his voice even softer now. "Are you a believer?"

"A believer?" asked Henry.

Briden reached into the neck of his shirt, pulled out his icon, a small twisting shape, the Unitologist symbol. "Altman be praised," he said.

"No, sorry," said Henry almost too quickly. "I'm not a believer. Not that I have anything against it."

"You will be," said Briden, slowly tucking his icon away, a smile still frozen on his face. "You're feeling it already, but you just haven't admitted it yet."

And with that he turned away, went back to directing his team and setting up the equipment, leaving Henry a little shaken and not quite sure what to do with himself.

. . .

It's here, thought Briden. *I'm sure of it.* Whatever the Marker wanted them to find was to be found here, and he, Briden, was going to be the one to find it. He had been chosen to do so. His calling was a sacred one, and he could almost feel a holy crown there shining on his head, invisible for all to see except the truly sacred, the truly chosen. He would find it and he would do whatever he needed to do to protect both it and the Marker from all unbelievers.

It had been a mistake to approach Wandrei the technician as he had, but he had felt something, detected something in the man. He knew that Wandrei felt something, just as he, Briden, felt something. Everybody felt a little bit of something—that was how powerful the Marker was, reaching out to believers and unbelievers alike—but for most it was nothing significant: a headache, a little anxiety, or nausea. More and more people, though, were sensing a call to Convergence, a call to lose their life so that they could find it, so that they could find a larger sense of unity and life in the one. Already six people among their number had let go of their lives, or had had them taken away by a well-meaning soul, and Briden had made very certain that their bodies were prepared and preserved for the day they might rise again. Yes, he understood that the work here was holy.

And there was Callie Dexter beside him suddenly. She was his affliction, the thorn in his side. She did not believe and he knew better than to speak to her about his belief: she would not understand it. She would mock him and would try to use it against him. No, she was there as a test for him, something for him to fight against and overcome, but quietly and subtly and with great care.

"We're all set?" Briden asked.

Callie nodded. "All the monitoring equipment is in place. Now we just wait for a surge."

"Yes," said Briden. "But there are things we can do in the meantime."

"Things? Like what?"

"We need to get a feel for the place," he said. "We need to walk out there and sense its energies."

"Energies?" said Dr. Dexter. "What sort of mystical bullshit are you trying to feed me?"

"I mean, measure for any anomalies," said Briden, backtracking. "Magnetic abnormalities, pressure irregularities, any unusual readings of any sort. Anything that can tell us what's there, what the Marker is looking for."

"There you go again," said Dr. Dexter. "Always thinking of the Marker as human."

Briden bristled. He *wasn't* thinking of the Marker as human. Sentient yes, but hardly human: it was far beyond human. "It's just a metaphor," he said. "I don't mean anything by it."

Dr. Dexter gave him a hard stare. "I wish that were true," she said. "All right, let's see what we can find."

30

The voice and the changing face that went with it were with Istvan almost all the time now, very quiet most of the time, but still something he could hear and understand as long as he was listening in the right way. It was like having a brother again, only better because it wasn't going to abandon him as his brother had done. No, this was a new friend: someone, he felt, that was willing to be with him forever, someone with whom he could spend the rest of his life.

It was beginning to teach him things. He could feel it sometimes touching his brain lightly, smoothing parts of it out, scrunching other parts of it up, and doing so in a way that was beginning to build something within him. It was a strangely intimate sensation, as if someone had their hand in his head and was caressing his brain softly, and he wondered if he shouldn't be afraid. He was, admittedly, a little afraid at first, but then it stroked a particular part of his brain and the fear diminished at least a little. There were shapes and figures beginning to form, strange twisted and watery shapes that he could not only see but that he felt he understood, that he felt somehow, if he just had the right tools and the right training, he could build. It could be glorious, the voice whispering in his head told him. *Glorious. The next step in evolution. Marvelous Convergence, the extension of consciousness from bodies to a place both within and between bodies.*

It was wonderful, so wonderful that he almost didn't feel the pain as the burst came, stronger than it ever had been before, and took him into the other world. He could hear, behind that world, in the world before, the groans and cries of his fellow convicts and knew that somewhere they were feeling it, too, though not in the same way as he was. Where the fingers in his brain moved delicately, stroking and rearranging in a way that he found at once sharp and exhilarating, they must have felt like their heads were being torn off. Indeed, once the burst faded and parts of his vision started to return, he did see that the man roughly across the table from him had beaten his head over and over against the surface of the table until that head had cracked open. Blood was pooling on the surface of the table, slipping over it and toward Istvan. Istvan watched it come, unconcerned, not moving even after it began to drip slowly into his lap. *Was the man dead?* he wondered. *What had been the convict's name again?* And then he decided that it didn't really matter. He wasn't dead yet, but he'd be dead soon.

The alarm went off, sending them back to their cells. The other convicts looked almost in shock, some of them wandering aimlessly about, others just staring at the body, one hitting his head over and over again with his hands. But slowly they began to come back to themselves and move. Istvan braced his hands on the table, to either side of the pooling blood. But before he stood, the voice said something to him.

Wait, it said.

"Wait?" he said. "Why?"

But for once it didn't answer. He looked around him, at the other convicts moving back to their cells, at the dead or dying man across the table from him. What did the voice know? If he listened to it, he'd be beaten by the guards, maybe killed. He again started to stand.

Wait, the voice said again.

He stopped, confused. Why should he wait? What did he gain by doing so? No, it was a mistake. And yet, he waited.

The loudspeaker crackled out its warning, giving him thirty seconds to return to his cell. He counted it down, and then counted a minute or so more before he heard the cell doors clang closed. *Now it is too late,* he told himself. *Now you are in trouble.*

He raised his hands and put them behind his head so that they wouldn't think him a threat. He waited. A minute later the doors to the outer ring opened and the guards came in.

Only they didn't rush this time. They were moving more slowly, dressed in riot gear, and were flanking four people, two men and two women, dressed in ordinary clothing.

New prisoners? he wondered at first. But no, their hands were free, they were at ease and relaxed, and they were carrying various pieces of technical equipment. The door closed behind them. Slowly they moved through the ring of cells and toward the central circle.

One of the guards raised his weapon. "Shall I neutralize him, sir?" he asked.

One of the four people in the middle, a man just approaching middle age with salt-and-pepper hair who was apparently their leader, shook his head. "No need to bother him unless he becomes aggressive. Leave him as he is."

The scientists came forward, sweeping their way into the room, moving back and forth, the guards awkwardly flanking them and sometimes bumping into them as they moved in unexpected directions. Istvan just stayed there, watching them come.

"Check and see if that one is dead," said the apparent leader.

"Will do, sir," said one of the guards. He came forward and examined the man slumped across the table, then stripped off one glove and pressed his fingers into the man's neck. "He's dead," he said.

"Ugh," said one of the others in the group, a woman. "Ghastly." But despite saying that, she came forward and stared at the body with some interest, as if fascinated. She looked up at Istvan. "What made him do it?" she asked.

Istvan hesitated a moment, then shook his head. "I don't know," he said. "I didn't see it."

"Of course you saw it," she said. "You were sitting right across from him."

"I heard it," he said. "But I didn't see it."

Two of the guards were assigned the body. They dragged it away by the arms, leaving an irregular smear of blood in its wake. The other guards and the people with their machines kept circling around, slowly narrowing their focus until they were all standing around Istvan.

"Right here," said their leader. "I'm sorry," he said to Istvan, "but you'll have to move."

You can move now, said the voice to him, and he saw again

Conn's ghastly face flash up before him, his strange smile. *You can go back to your cell.*

Istvan nodded. Very slowly he stood and stepped out from the bench. "I want to go back to my cell," he said.

Distractedly, their leader nodded. "Yes, yes," he said, "go on, then."

Hands still up, he walked away. The guards' eyes followed him, as did their weapons. He could feel their eyes still on his back as he went slowly out of inner circle and into the cell circle and then stood by the closed door of his cell, waiting.

31

"Right here," said Briden, pointing at the instruments. "Right where that fellow was sitting." He turned to Callie Dexter. "I'm right, aren't I? Some kind of anomaly? Something that responds in a particular way to the crystalline structure of our Marker?"

"Seems so," she said.

He smiled. "So directly under the floor, I'm assuming? We get something in here and we start to dig."

Callie shrugged. "Not enough data to know for certain," she said.

"Sure there's enough," said Briden. "It led us here, didn't it? There's nothing here on the surface, so there must be something below."

They put the one loose convict back in his cell, then sent someone back to the Marker compound for a contact beam and an engineer to operate it. It took an hour, maybe more, but finally they were there and cutting through the floor.

The going was slow at first, the engineer working the contact beam and some of the guards recruited to shovel out the rubble.

There was a certain amount of danger, Briden knew: they might break into a cavern or other space without breathable atmosphere and then those standing near the hole might well be killed, which was why he stood at a little distance away. Callie Dexter, though, was up close and leaning in, curious, watching the work. He imagined her eyes bugging out and her gasping for air and it gave him a certain perverse satisfaction. He smiled, though he did eventually call for breathing equipment, just in case. But no reason to stop the digging while waiting for it to arrive.

They went down three feet, maybe four, without finding anything beyond dirt and rock shot through with veins of crystal. Maybe that was it, the crystal? Or maybe there was something there, deeper down? They needed another pulse, something they could correlate and trace and make sure they were on the right track, but it might be hours, or even days, before one came.

Another eight feet. The contact beam ran out of fuel and they replaced the cartridge, and then it overheated and the engineer hauled himself up out of the hole by a rope, shaking his head.

"We'll have to let it cool down," he said. "A few hours at least. Besides, it's time to sleep."

"We should keep going," said Briden. "I'm sure we're nearly there."

The engineer wiped his face with his hands. "There's nothing down there," he said. "Nothing but rock. You're wasting your time."

Briden was eager to keep going, but looking at the face of

the engineer and his fellow scientists he realized it was prudent to wait. "All right," he said. "A little something to eat, a few hours of sleep, and then we can start again."

They would find it, Briden was sure they would find it—it was waiting for them, the Markers had led them to this spot: it had to be there. This was a test of faith, a test of *his* faith. If he was to be their prophet, he had to persist, had to go on.

He pushed at the food in front of him, stirred it around his plate, but ate very little of it. Many of the others had already gone off to catch a few hours of sleep on the spare cots in the guards' quarters or alongside the technicians.

"Penny for your thoughts," said Dr. Dexter. She was still sitting across from him, observing him closely as if he were a specimen. He shook his head.

"Briden . . ." she said, and for once her voice was gentle, a little hesitant. "You have to realize that there may be nothing there."

"But the readings," he said. "You saw them as well as I did. We traced them as close as we possibly could—"

"The readings have been slightly different each time. Maybe they're there for a moment and then not. Or maybe the Markers are off somehow. Maybe they're trying to broadcast to something that no longer exists."

But no, he thought, it couldn't be that way. It *had* to be real. He'd invested too much of his life in this project. He *knew* it was real. The Marker was speaking to him, he could feel it when it pulsed. Unlike Callie, he had faith. He believed in this, believed in what he was doing. There *had* to be something there.

"Look," she said. "I said it earlier. We need more data—"

"Data," he groaned. "What good will that do us? We know where we should be. We need to dig. We need to keep digging until we find something."

"What are we going to find?" she asked.

"How should I know?" he said. "But I'm sure something is there. The Marker wouldn't lead us here if there wasn't."

Callie just looked at him, not speaking.

"What?" he finally said.

"Nothing," she said.

"Why are you staring at me?"

"You don't want to hear it," she said.

"Tell me."

Anger flashed in her eyes. "All right," she said. "You're obsessed. You've lost your objectivity. You've let your feelings run away with you. You've convinced yourself that that Marker is a living thing. You don't know if you're coming or going, Briden. You don't know if you're engaged in an act of scientific discovery or an act of worship."

But I do know, thought Briden. *It* is *an act of worship. How can you be so blind?* Trembling, he managed still to keep his temper, but said nothing.

When Callie spoke, her voice was calmer. "I know you're trying," she said. "We're all trying." And then she reached out and touched his hand.

He pulled his hand back as if he'd been bitten. Gathering his plate and utensils, he stood and left.

Another test, he thought. *She's just another test. Here to confuse me. She's not right, I'm right. The Marker believes in me, not in her.*

He stalked his way up and around the ring until an hour had passed, maybe more, and his legs were sore. Then he sat in the control room, leaning his elbows on the desk, waiting until enough time had gone by that he felt he could wake the others up and start them digging again. He tried to gather himself, tried to bury the irritation and doubt Callie had made him feel. *Not Callie*, he told himself, *Dr. Dexter*. How could she unsettle him so?

But soon, he told himself, everything would change. *Soon everyone will know that I was right and she was wrong, and then we'll see who unsettles whom.*

They dug deeper, another sixteen feet before the contact beam burnt out entirely. The engineer came up shaking his head. "Not made for this kind of work," he said. "It's better for just clearing up small piles of rubble. You need something larger, a borer. Something you can sit in."

"A borer," said Briden. "Well, let's bring one in."

The engineer shook his head. "We don't have one," he said. "We'll have to get one sent in."

"Let's do it," said Briden. "How long will it take?"

"A month," said the engineer. "Maybe two."

A month? Two? "There has to be another way," he said.

The engineer shrugged. "We've got another contact beam or two," he said. "We could burn those out as well, maybe get a little deeper. But I have to tell you: there's no indication that anything's there. The rock that's there, it's been in place probably for millions of years. There's no evidence that it has ever been disturbed."

Another test, thought Briden, tightening his lips. But who was to say that whatever was there, down below, hadn't been there just that long. The Marker technology could be eons old.

"Go get them," he said. "And order a borer just in case."

The engineer sighed and left.

And that was when it happened. Another pulse, a strong one, which left Briden lying on his back right next to the hole that had been dug, almost falling in, his head throbbing, his vision almost obscured. For a moment he saw something or someone, but he couldn't make out their features. And then for a flash it was his dead father's face, and then that, too, vanished and he was panting, lying there, staring into Callie's eyes.

"Are you all right?" she asked.

He opened his mouth to speak, but nothing came out. Near him a guard had fallen to one knee, and was groaning. One of his own researchers was tearing at his hair. From the cells he could hear the cries and howls of the prisoners and realized that one or maybe two or maybe more of them were probably in the process of beating themselves to death. More corpses. More souls opening themselves to Convergence. As he himself would do as well. Only not yet.

"Did you feel it?" he finally managed to say.

Callie nodded. "I felt something," she said. One of her eyes, he noticed, was leaking tears, but only one of them.

"Wasn't it glorious?" he couldn't stop himself from saying.

She scowled. "Don't be a fool," she said and pulled him up.

The guards were scattered and confused. The two other scientists were slowly calming down, one of them standing there with tufts of his own hair in his hand, the other massaging her temples with her fist.

"It's changing," said Briden. "It's growing stronger."

"It's becoming more dangerous," said Dr. Dexter. "We need to be careful." She gestured around her at the little patches of mossy tendrils clinging to the floors and walls. "You see what's happened to the corruption?" she said. "There's more of it now. It's spread with the signal."

"Then it's part of the Marker," said Briden. "We shouldn't be trying to clean it up, we should be encouraging it to grow."

Cassie shook her head. "It's just a by-product," she said. "We should get rid of it. We need to be careful."

She unstrapped her portable reader, getting the feed from the computers in the control room, checking the signal, figuring out where the exact center of this one was. She stood beside the hole, adjusting the apparatus until it was right.

"Interesting," she said.

"What?" said Briden.

"Try yours before I tell you," she said. "Let's see if we end up with the same reading."

He took out his reader and turned it on. The other two scientists were doing the same with theirs. He waited for the new data to load, chose it, then waited for it to compute the nexus point and determine his location. At first, when the distance was still great, it looked just fine, as if he was exactly where he was meant to be, but as the machine dithered and the map scale became more precise he realized that no, he was nowhere near the nexus, was perhaps a hundred feet away from it. He looked at Callie's screen, saw the same.

"We needed more data," said Callie. "Told you."

He nodded, began to move here and there, toward where he thought the new nexus was, Callie alongside him, the two other scientists following behind, still a little shaken. *It moves*, thought Briden. But what was it? What did that mean? Perhaps it was something they couldn't see, something they wouldn't be able to catch hold of. But still he kept walking, kept following his reader.

They came to the wall at the end of the inner circle but they weren't quite there. It was on the other side of that, somewhere in the cell ring. He exchanged a look with Callie and they both headed for the opening into the cell ring and started down it, tracking down the hall. They passed half a dozen cells until, finally, they came to the one that his machine told him was where the nexus had been.

Inside, a young man sat on his bed, his feet flat on the floor, his hands flat on his knees. His eyes were closed and he was breathing slowly in and out in a very measured way.

"It's here now," said Briden. "If we start digging right away, maybe we can catch it this time."

"Briden, no," said Callie Dexter, taking his arm.

"What do you mean, no?" he said, turning to face her, angry. "Who's in charge here? If I say dig, we dig."

But she pulled him back, pulled him away from the bars of the cell. Half whispering, she said, "Don't you recognize him?"

Confused, he turned and looked back at the man sitting serenely in the cell. He was just one of the prisoners, so what? And then the man turned and opened his eyes and looked at him and smiled.

"He was sitting at the table when we got the first reading," said Callie. "He was sitting exactly where we dug."

"No," said Briden.

"And now here he is, sitting just where we got our most recent reading." She sounded at once excited and confused, her objectivity momentarily shot as well. "Briden, we're not looking for something buried. We're not looking for a piece of equipment. We're looking for that man."

PART FOUR

32

He would listen to the voice, he would follow what it said. After all, it had not led him astray so far. No, quite the opposite: it had broken the bonds of his imprisonment. It had plucked him from Hell and brought him here.

"Are you comfortable," the lead scientist asked him. What was his name again? Barden? No, Briden. He nodded.

"Can I get you something?"

He waited for the voice of the dead to tell him what was needed, but it didn't say anything. Briden was staring at him; Istvan was not exactly sure how much time had passed. He shook his head. "Not now," he said.

"Maybe later?" asked Briden, strangely eager.

Istvan nodded. The movement felt odd. When the voice was more distant from him, everything felt false, slightly off. He felt too much like he had felt growing up. Like the world was in charge of him rather than he being in charge of the world. He didn't like that.

Briden was sitting across the table staring at him. Much like the small gray man had done. What did Briden want exactly?

"What is it like?" Briden asked.

"What?" said Istvan, surprised.

"It chose me, too," he said. "It reached out and touched me, and I knew I would become its prophet. Did it do that to you, too?"

Not knowing what Briden was talking about, Istvan hesitated, then nodded. Briden broke into a smile.

"What does it want from us?" he asked.

"Want?" asked Istvan.

"It's here to save us, isn't it?" said Briden. "It wants only our own good. It wants to bring us to Convergence. Has it told you what Convergence will consist of? Has it told you when it will come?"

Confused, Istvan just stared.

Briden watched him, expression open and waiting. When Istvan didn't respond, a flicker of irritation passed over his face. "You can tell me," he said. "I'm one of the chosen."

"Chosen for what?" asked Istvan.

"Is this a test?" asked Briden. "Are you toying with me?"

Who was this man and what did he want? Istvan listened for the voice to tell him what to do. It was speaking, it was always speaking, but it wasn't talking about the man in front of him, wasn't telling him what to do. He tried to stare his way through this world and see the other world, see the face of one of his dead and feel the voice in his mouth, but the veil wasn't ready to fall. He could not make it come.

"It chose me, too," said Briden, defensively. "If it hadn't chosen me, you would still be in there."

That was true, in a matter of speaking, thought Istvan. But even when Briden had been staring right at him he hadn't seen him. It had taken the other scientist, the woman, to recognize him. But to try to calm the fellow, he nodded.

It did calm him. Briden smiled and leaned back in his chair a little. "Now the question is what does it want us to do?"

But Istvan had a hard time paying attention. Inside his head the voice had started to speak again. *See me,* it said. *Understand me. Share me.*

"See me," he muttered.

"See you?" Briden said, surprised. "But I do see you. I'm right here, sitting across the table from you."

"No," said Istvan, "See him. I want to see him."

"Him? Who is him?" asked Briden. And when Istvan just stared, he said, "Do you mean it? Do you mean the Marker?"

Did he? What was a Marker? He didn't know for certain and the moment in which the voice seemed like it was giving him specific direction had faded into a quieter recital, not things he could hear exactly or know why they were important, but he still could feel his brain taking them in.

"All right," Briden said. "Yes, why not. You'll see it. That makes sense. We'll have to ignore a few security protocols, but I am after all the director of this project. This is much more important than a few security protocols."

The vid near the wall chirped. Briden glanced at it briefly. When he turned back there was yet another look of irritation on his face. "You'll have to excuse me a moment," he said. "This won't take long."

He stood and approached the monitor. When he accepted the link, Istvan could see a woman's face, the face of the female scientist who had seen him and recognized him.

"What is it, Dr. Dexter?" asked Briden. "I'm busy."

"The prisoner's not in his quarters," said the woman. "Do you happen to know where he is?"

"First of all," Istvan heard Briden say, "he's not a prisoner. He's our guest. Second, yes, I do know where he is. He's here with me."

"What's he doing there with you?" asked Dexter. "Why didn't you follow protocol?"

"I needed to talk to him," said Briden. "And I didn't think that protocol applied in this case."

"No? Why not?"

"I don't have to explain myself to you, Dr. Dexter," said Briden.

"No, actually you do," said Dexter. "And be careful what you say. You can be sure that it will all appear in my report."

He started to retort, then apparently reconsidered. Istvan watched him take a deep breath. "You still don't understand, do you?" he said.

"Understand what?"

"The work we're doing here. The nature of it. How important it is. There is no turning back now, Dr. Dexter."

"Briden," she said, bridling. "You can't just—"

But that was all she had a chance to say because Briden had cut the feed.

He came back to the table, his smile restored. "Now where were we?" he asked. "Oh yes, you wanted to see it. Follow me."

It was late, the workday mostly done. The few scientists still seated and working within the control room turned and looked at them when they entered. Most of them turned quickly back to what they were doing, but one or two kept staring for a time. Briden ignored them. He simply walked across the room and over to the observation window on the other side, drawing Istvan by the hand after him.

"There it is," he said, and pointed.

Through the window Istvan could see it, a strange twisting obelisk, blackish red and with a reddish glow, inscribed all over with strange figures. Or not so strange, really, for as he looked at them, he began to see in them the warp and weft of the other world, the material which the veil was made of when it fell, even the very lineaments and workings of the faces that came to him in that world. If he was allowed to look at it long enough, he felt, he would even begin to see how these signs and symbols formed the hiss and mutter of the voices that came to him. Yes, here was the thing that brought everything together, that made everything make sense. Here was the key to everything in existence.

"It's beautiful, isn't it?" said Briden.

Istvan nodded. It was hard to take his eyes off of it, but he slowly dragged them around to look at Briden. "I want to go in there," he said.

"There'll be time enough for that," said Briden. "Can't do everything all at once."

"No," said Istvan. "Now."

They stared at one another for a long moment, Briden with a certain curiosity, Istvan steadily, his gaze hard. Finally Briden sighed and turned away.

"All right," he said. "If that's what needs to happen."

He slid his keycard through and entered the code. As the

door slid open, more of the scientists turned to watch them. Then Briden ushered him in.

"Not strictly protocol," he said, almost as if he were talking to himself. The door closed behind them.

The room itself was not the same as in the rest of the complex, Istvan saw. It had a floor made of solid stone, and the bottom part of this chamber had been cut out of the rock, with man-made walls built up on top of it. The Marker rose in the middle of it, at once brutal and majestic. He could almost feel the energy emanating from it. Just looking at it made him dizzy.

"There," said Briden. "Now you've stood in the same room with it. Let's go."

But Istvan ignored him. He began to move slowly toward the Marker.

"Istvan," said Briden. And then louder, "Istvan!"

He felt the man's hand on his shoulder and shook it off. He kept going. Briden said something, but Istvan could hardly hear it over the sound of the voice guiding him forward, leading him toward this thing of great beauty.

It was in his head, too, he now felt, or something like it anyway, all the necessary details and plans were stored up there now: that was what it had been doing as it prodded his brain. It had been making itself a space within him.

But there was Briden, grabbing his arm again and spinning him around. This irritated him, made him bare his teeth at him. But Briden hung on. *Not now,* he was saying, *we have to clear it first for the sake of—*

And then the door behind them opened and Dr. Dexter came in. She looked angry, her face flushed and red.

"Briden!" she shouted. "Even you have to know that this goes far beyond the boundaries of—"

But Istvan had stopped listening by then. Briden was listening though, distracted enough so that Istvan could wrench himself free. He stumbled onward, toward the Marker. He cast a brief glance behind him, saw the two scientists shouting at one another, Briden's gaze darting back and forth between Dr. Dexter and him.

And then he was at the base of the Marker itself. He reached out and pressed the flat of his palm against it and he felt the veil of that other world falling over his gaze again, a tremendous power behind it. In the distance, someone was shouting. Slowly, carefully, he opened his mind up, unfolding it gently. And then he closed his eyes and waited.

For a long moment, nothing happened. And then he felt something flowing through him, sorting through his mind in a million ways at once. The other world rushed up and blotted everything else out as if it never had existed—and who knows, maybe it never had. He looked up and there, where the Marker had been, was now the face and body of murdered Conn, six or seven times as large as he had been in life. Conn was staring at Istvan, looking down at him. He bent farther down, brought his face closer until his head obscured much of Istvan's gaze and Istvan was standing in his shadow. And then, blood still dripping from his neck, he smiled.

Suddenly there was a rush of energy that made Istvan's body vibrate to the very core. All around him, he heard the sound of screams. His mind cleared itself in a burst of white light. He neither knew who he was nor where he was, nor even if he existed. And then he collapsed.

33

It came in a burst big enough that even Grottor felt it. It made him shudder. He steadied himself on the rail, waited for the feeling of vertigo to pass. Orthor clutched his head and gave a little cry and then began beating his head against the desk. Others on the bridge were struggling as well, looking dazed or confused or even crazed, and Grottor told himself once again that if it was this bad up here, thank God they weren't on the planet itself.

When it finally died away, the first order of business was to get Orthor to stop beating his head against the console. The man's forehead was bruised and the skin had begun to split; in just a few minutes he had done himself serious damage. But it also gave Grottor an excuse to have other crew members bundle him off and put him in the brig, thus killing two birds with one stone. Now Blackwell would have no eyes and ears, would not know what he and the gray man were planning.

Only then did Grottor turn to Ensign Haley. She was scribbling madly away, as if possessed, and mumbling under her breath as she did so. She kept spinning him image after image, all of it obviously connected to the Marker, followed by several pages of equations and instructions. He immediately spun them along to the gray man.

By the time she was done, five or six hours later, she was exhausted and shaking, ready to fall apart. He helped her back to her quarters and helped her lie down.

"But," she was saying, "I . . . the—it's still calling me to—"

"Shhh," he interrupted. "There'll be other times."

Thirty minutes later, he had the rest of the crew back on the bridge, including a replacement for Orthor. He made sure that everything was okay, then left. He visited Orthor in the brig and found him suspicious and resentful and paranoid. He had torn most of the bandages off of his head, and he kept asking clumsily veiled questions meant to try to determine what had happened in his absence. Grottor stonewalled him, then left.

He'd only been back in his own quarters a few minutes when the gray man contacted him by vid.

"These are very good," he said. "Very helpful. They teach us a lot."

"What do they teach you exactly?" asked Grottor.

The gray man smiled. "Too early to say," he said. "But we need more. What are the conditions that led to this?"

"I'm not certain yet," said Grottor. "A headache, I believe."

"What caused the headache?"

"I don't know," said Grottor. "What normally causes a headache?"

"Check the Marker readings," said the gray man. "But don't

stop there. Find out what's going on down on the planet and how it correlates with what's happening with her drawings. If other data is an indication, there'll be a connection."

"Other data?"

The gray man smiled. "Need to know basis," he said. "Find out what you can, get her to do more. If it gets too dangerous, get out. Above all, keep both her and whatever's happening down on the planet a secret. Nuke the planet if you have to: if we get enough out of her, we'll be fine without it."

34

"They're not responding to our hail, sir," said the communications officer.

"No?" said the captain. "Well, keep trying. While we're at it, we might as well move into orbit." He turned to the navigator. "See to it."

From near the back of the bridge, Jensi watched. He wasn't supposed to be there exactly, but when he'd arrived nobody seemed to give him a second glance. He was curious to see the planet from the air, curious, too, to get a sense of who or what might be down there, who would answer the hail.

Apparently no one.

"You have the right frequency?" asked the captain.

"It's the same frequency we used before."

"Same coding?"

"Same coding."

"Try other frequencies," the captain said. "Other codings as well. Maybe they had to change it and neglected to tell us. See if anything comes up."

But nothing did. At least not at first. They were just turning

\mathbf{243}

into orbit when the communications officer started picking up something on one of the distress channels.

"Play it aloud so we can all hear," said the captain.

"But captain—"

"Play it," repeated the captain.

He put it on.

This is a warning, it said. *This sector has become quarantined. All landing on Aspera is forbidden. Anyone and everyone must turn back. No exceptions.*

After a moment of silence it repeated, on a loop.

"Does that apply to us?" asked the navigation officer. "Or is that just something they set up to scare the unauthorized away?"

"Considering that we can't get anyone to respond to our hail," said the captain, "I think it does apply to us. Something must have gone wrong."

They kept trying to raise someone, without success. The captain stood placidly, apparently unconcerned. *Shouldn't we turn around and leave?* Jensi wanted to ask, but he wasn't supposed to be there on the bridge and his brother was, after all, down on the planet. He wanted to know what had happened to him.

"What do we do, captain?" asked the navigator.

"Continue to establish orbit," said the captain. "We have to figure out what to do about the supplies we were ordered to deliver. If we don't deliver them, we won't get paid."

"But what about the quarantine?"

"We won't send a vessel down until we can raise someone," he said. "We'll be careful."

And so they established a high orbit, hanging in the sky, still trying to raise someone. Without success.

"Shall I continue, sir?" asked the communications officer.

The captain hesitated, finally nodded. And so the officer went through each channel again, still without success.

Maybe there was a prison break, thought Jensi. *Maybe they've taken over.*

And then, there on the screen in front of them but growing larger, a tiny disruption in the space in front of them. "What's that?" asked one of the crew. Nobody answered. They were slowly gaining on it, the disruption gaining in size to become an object. Slowly it resolved into a ship.

"A Sovereign Colonies gunship," said the navigator finally.

"What is it doing here?" asked the communications officer.

"It's laying down orbital mines," said the navigator. "They're sealing off the planet."

"Hail them," said the captain. "There must be some kind of mistake."

At first they didn't answer, but when the navigator repeated the ship's numbers and used the emergency frequency, someone finally answered.

"Grottor here," the man said. He wore the insignia of a commander, his face hard and craggy.

"Commander Grottor," began the captain. "We have three months of supplies aboard. We cordially request . . ."

He trailed off. On the screen, the commander had lifted one hand to stop him, and was shaking his head. "I'm sorry," Commander Grottor said. "You happen to be in the wrong place at the wrong time."

The captain stood there looking confused. On the screen they could see some smaller objects gravitating toward them. At first it was difficult to tell what they were exactly.

Oh shit, thought Jensi, *the mines* . . .

He turned and began to run.

Behind him the bridge had gone into action. The captain barked orders as the navigator began to swing the ship around, but Jensi knew it was going to be too late. He kept running, as fast as he could, yelling as he went, raising the alarm. He passed over the elevator and slid down the ladder to the lower decks.

Halfway down, the first mine struck and he lost his grip, falling, clanging down the shaft. Above, there was a sucking sound as the atmosphere began to rush out, and he was nearly dragged back up the ladder until the bulkhead shield rose and cut off the leak. He stood up and stumbled down the corridor, found a locker holding an Astrosuit RIG with oxygen storage, and struggled into it. The helmet began assembling itself automatically around his head. From above came the sounds of screaming.

A few more people had had the same idea as he had and were making for the escape pods as well, rushing toward him. Another explosion came, this time on the lower decks, and Jensi and the people running toward him were sucked backward. He watched them spill out through a jagged hole and into space and nearly went out that way himself, but managed to catch hold of one raggedly imploded edge and held on while the pressure equalized.

He pulled himself back into the ship. The artificial gravity was disabled now, so he had to use his zero-grav boots to find his footing. The sound, too, had gone strange, rushing out with the atmosphere. Everything now sounded dampened, almost nonexistent. The noise of his boots clomping toward the escape pods was more a vibration that could be barely felt rather than an actual sound. Almost the only thing he could hear was his own panicked breathing. He hurried forward down the corridor, floating now with chunks of debris, only to see open space where the first set of pods should have been, though the next pods seemed intact. Behind him he heard a muffled noise and then was nearly knocked off his feet by the shock wave that came with it. *I'm going to die,* he thought, and then disengaged his boots and pushed off.

But without gravity it was hard to do it right. He was, he immediately knew, directing himself too high, was likely to spin out the open hole and into space. He tried to stretch and curl to change his trajectory but little seemed to happen, and he was going out and drifting away. But then there it was, a piece of debris floating up above him and he pushed it as hard as he could. It stopped his momentum and sent him sideways at a slower pace and he got close enough to the outer hull that he could turn on the antigravity boots and let them slowly suck him to it.

He quickly clomped his way along the hull and worked his way around to the underside, running along the roof and down the wall to the remaining pods. One had its door open and he saw, lying slumped in its entrance, Swanson. His eyes were bugged out and he was dead from lack of oxygen. *Another man dead,* he thought. He dragged the man up and out of the way and climbed in.

The door levered slowly shut behind him. He webbed in and braced himself and then pressed the release and the ignition. The craft darted out, already spinning, twirling down through the atmosphere. He hoped it was small enough not to draw the mines or that they would disintegrate in the atmosphere before they hit him. Twisting quickly planetward, he held on for dear life.

35

"What the hell was that?" asked Dr. Dexter. Her eyes were wide and she looked terrified.

"So you finally felt it?" Briden asked. His head throbbed and he could barely stand. "It has to yell to you before you'll hear it. I've been hearing it all along."

"It's not a person, Briden," she said. "It's dangerous. Maybe there's something wrong with it. We need to shutter the project before it kills us."

"Shutter it? Are you mad? We're just starting to get somewhere."

"Where we're getting is that," said Callie, gesturing to Istvan who was lying on the ground beside the Marker, shivering, his eyes rolled back into his head. "It's knocked him senseless."

"No, he'll be okay," said Briden. He approached him, checked his pulse. "Just some kind of fit," he said, standing back up. "He'll snap out of it."

"Briden, the Marker is not a good thing. It means us harm," said Callie.

"Don't be ridiculous," he said. "This is the key to our salvation."

Callie shook her head, laughing bitterly. "You're so obsessed, you can't see what's right in front of you," she said. "You want this to be a religious experience. It doesn't matter to you what evidence there is to the contrary or what it actually is. Evidence be damned, you've already decided what it is."

Briden just shook his own head and turned away. He knelt beside Istvan and began to slap his face lightly, watching his eyes. After a moment Istvan's eyelids fluttered and his pupils fell back into place and his jaw unclenched. "There," said Briden. "There." He turned and looked up at Callie. "You see? He's just fine."

"Fine, is he? Briden, we have to shutter the project. You need to let the commander know right away."

Istvan was coming around, looking at Briden. The latter reached out, stroked the side of Istvan's face. "What did you see?" he asked. "What did it tell you? What does it want from us?"

Istvan didn't say anything.

"Briden, if you don't tell Grottor, I will," said Dr. Dexter. When Briden didn't answer, she gave a little stamp of frustration and headed toward the door.

"Dr Dexter," he finally said, just as she was reaching it.

She stopped and turned, only to find him pointing a pistol at her, slowly walking toward her.

"What are you doing?" she asked.

"What I should have done a long time ago," he said.

She raised her hands slowly. "You shouldn't do this, Briden," she said. "You're not thinking straight."

"Oh no, Dr. Dexter," he said. "I know what I'm doing. Now turn around and walk. Straight through the door and across the control room and out that door, too. I'll tell you when to stop walking. I'm in charge now."

"Are you?" asked Callie coolly over her shoulder. "Seems like the Marker might be the one in charge."

He marched her through the control room, the scientists inside stopping their work to stare in astonishment at the procession they made, and out into the hall.

They walked until they came to the security station. "I'd like to remand the prisoner," said Briden to the man inside.

"Prisoner?" said the security officer, wrinkling his brow.

"Yes, man," said Briden, "right here."

"But that's Dr. Dexter," said the officer.

"Of course it's Dr. Dexter," he said. "She's a traitor. She needs to be confined to the brig."

The officer stared back and forth from Callie to Briden. "If you don't do it, he'll probably just shoot me," she finally said.

The officer shrugged. He took her by the arm and led her into the brig and closed the door.

In the Marker room, Istvan lay immobile on the floor, staring up at the two horns rising far above him. Dead Conn was there, poised upon the tips, and then his mother, and then the politician he had shot, Fischer. Their faces shuffled over one another to become one face. The voice, too, seemed a blend of all their voices, a multitonal voice that seemed both high and low at once.

The other world was the real world, he now knew. It was what really mattered. But the Marker existed in both worlds; it was the thing that bridged the gap.

Do you understand now? the three ghosts that were one above him asked.

Yes, he tried to say. *Yes, I understand.* But the words did not come out. And yet the Marker heard him say them nevertheless.

There was movement around him—strange shadows flitting—that it took a moment for him to begin to make things out. These were the scientists, he realized slowly. Maybe four of them, maybe five, come to check on him. One pressed his fingers to Istvan's throat and said something. Another was lifting one eyelid even higher and peering in, as if to look inside his skull. He tried to ignore them, to think of them as something like buzzing flies, but they were still there, an irritation.

We are not right, said the ghosts. *Or rather, we are right, but now we must become something else. We need you to make us whole and make us new.*

"Make you whole," mumbled Istvan. "Make you new."

"What?" said one of the scientists. "Did he say something?"

"Say something, see something," said Istvan.

We will use you as a vessel, said the ghosts. *You will take our image, the image of not only what we are but of what we might become, and you will share it.*

"Share it," mumbled Istvan.

"Did he say sheriff?" asked one of the scientists. "What would that even mean?"

We must be free, said the ghosts. *We must be free.*

Slowly the vision faded. Or didn't fade so much as simply

slip into the background. It was still there, the triple ghost still with its flickering faces, but the faces were changing much more slowly now, every couple of seconds rather than several times a second. And it was subdued and quiet enough that Istvan could see the scientists better, and hear them, too.

"Are you all right?" one of them asked.

Was he? What did the man even mean by that? He hesitantly nodded. One of them was holding a hand out to him, offering to help him up. He waved the hand away.

"Not ready yet?" the man said. "Sure, give yourself a moment. No point rushing things."

"I'm staying here," said Istvan.

"Of course," said the man. "No reason to move until you're ready."

"I'll never be ready," said Istvan. "This is where I live." He needed to be here until the ghosts were free, until he had accomplished his task, his *purpose*. A strange twinge of confusion came to him with that word, *purpose*. But why?

"You can't stay here," the man reasoned. "You can't just stay on the floor."

He shook his head. Of course he could stay here. Why couldn't he?

"You're not thinking properly," said the man. "You're still in shock or something. I think three of us can carry you out of here and put you someplace where you can rest."

"I can rest here," he said. "And there is no time for rest."

"Come on," the scientist said, reaching out again with his hand.

"If he wants to stay here," said a voice it took him a moment to recognize as belonging to Briden, "then he can stay here."

He looked over at Briden and smiled. Yes, Briden understood. Some of it, anyway. And then Briden was there kneeling beside him, eyes shining.

"It wants you to stay here?" he asked.

It? What did he mean by it? Couldn't he see the ghosts? Istvan gestured at them, but Briden only saw the Marker.

"Yes," he said, placing a hand on his shoulder. "I understand."

No, thought Istvan. *He doesn't exactly understand.* But it didn't matter, it was close enough. Briden would let him do what he wanted, what needed to be done. He would live here, at the base of the Marker, and he would learn from it until it had taught him all that he could know, and he would teach it the little he knew and then he would go out in the world and preach for it until everyone understood and more Markers began to arise and there was the dawning of a brighter day.

36

The brighter day began with a murder, followed shortly by a suicide. In the penal colony, a man by the name of James Colbert who had become more and more moody, who was keeping more and more to himself, wrapped his arms around the neck of another inmate, by the name of Ken Dollar, and choked him first unconscious and then dead. The other inmates, once they realized what was happening, tried to drag Colbert away, but it was too late. And while they were seeing if there was anything to be done to save Dollar, Colbert wandered, mumbling, along the edge of the crowd. He was being closely watched by several of the other inmates, but not closely enough that he couldn't, when they were distracted by the attempts to revive Dollar, suddenly take off at a run for the wall and try to run through it so hard that he cracked his own skull and damaged his brain. He was soon dead as well.

Henry watched the murder, horrified. He called the guards in the middle of it. By the time they were assembled near the door, Colbert had killed himself as well. Henry signaled the alarm to send the convicts back to their cells, was surprised when this time all but one or two of the men kept milling about, making no effort to return to their cells. He waited and then started the loudspeaker message, giving them thirty seconds' warning, but they ignored this, too.

What now? he wondered. Ever since Briden and his men had come, the prisoners had been on edge. And it hadn't subsided when they left, taking Jensi's brother with them. No, it had just gotten worse. With the guards and technicians as well, he thought. Fights had broken out; one of the guards, a normally stolid, experienced fellow named Marshall, had almost bitten another man's ear off. He'd been thrown into a room and locked in, where he'd proceeded to shout and scream, throwing himself against the walls. When they finally opened the door to let him out the next day, they found him sitting in his own filth. He had slashed open his palm and had smeared the walls with blood. But it was not just smears, Henry realized on closer examination. He'd been drawing symbols, creepy odd-looking things that didn't look like any language that Henry had ever seen.

He'd called Commander Grottor and told him. The commander grunted, then told him to take a vid of the walls and send them along immediately.

"What am I to do with Marshall?" he asked.

"Marshall? Throw him in a cell. Put him out there with the other prisoners."

He had, but had kept him locked in his cell just in case. One of the other prisoners, a man named Waldron, would bring Marshall food and slide it through the slot at the bottom of the bars; sometimes Marshall'd eat it and sometimes not. He kept worrying the wound on his hand, splitting it open, and when he could get it to bleed again, he'd paint more of the symbols:

on the floor, on the back wall, on the sheets, even on his own body.

What had done that to him? wondered Henry at the time. And then, looking at the screen, at the two dead bodies and the men milling about, *What has done that to them?*

The guards were still standing near the door, awaiting instruction. Their leader opened a link, asked Henry what the problem was.

"The prisoners won't return to their cells," he said.

"What?" said the man. "How many of them? One? Two?"

"More," said Henry. "Almost all of them."

"That's all right," said the man, his nostrils flaring. "We can take them." He seemed to relish the idea, which made Henry realize that if he opened the door someone, maybe a lot of people, were likely to end up dead.

"Go back to your quarters," he said. "I'm not going to open the door."

"C'mon, Wandrei," he said. "Open it."

"No," said Henry. "Go back to your quarters. That's an order."

With some grumbling, the angry men drifted away and Henry turned back to watch the screen. *What am I to do with the bodies?* he wondered. Henry watched the prisoners still milling about, still wandering, sometimes nearly stumbling over one of the corpses. He watched two of them grab one of the bodies and drag them over to the hole that Briden had dug. They released it and it went tumbling down the hole. Then they went back for the second one.

Good enough, Henry thought, and turned his attention elsewhere.

Istvan stayed there beside it, caressing it, staring up at it. It was listening to him, responding to him. It was a beautiful, gorgeous thing, and what it was doing to his mind was gorgeous, too. It was changing him, making him more like it, and he was changing it, too. It was learning how to talk to him and then was sending its voice all around, looking for brains like his.

But his brain was special. What his brain understood, the other brains felt as pain. He watched the others, watched how they reacted, the confusion on their faces, the way their eyes lit up but without a real glow. Their brains started to break when the Marker touched them, for the signal was meant for brains closer to his, not for brains like theirs.

And the signal was growing, getting stronger. The scientists who came often to stare at the Marker and stare at him, too, could feel it mostly as pain, though one or two had a little more flexible cerebral matter and seemed to begin to see hints and traces of the ghosts that Istvan saw now all the time. The scientists whispered back and forth, too, spoke of what was going on outside the Marker chamber, bringing him news. More and more people were going mad, they said, though what they meant by mad exactly he wasn't sure. There were fights for no reason, strange acts of self-harm and suicide. Order was beginning to fall apart; the social structure of the compound was beginning to collapse. But that was okay, thought Istvan. You always had to tear things down before you could build them back up again.

There were scientists who always came to see him, Briden among them: a group of the committed, the faithful. They clustered around him, waiting for him to move or speak. One of them recorded his gestures, his words. Only they weren't his words exactly: he only said what the ghosts were already saying if only the scientists could see them and hear them. *Why can't they?* he wondered. He didn't know the answer.

Other scientists, though, never came in. He saw them in the control room, keeping to their monitors and systems or standing near the glass. There were two camps, he dimly began to realize. Briden was in charge of one, the group that believed the Marker and its possibilities. Of this group, some of them were Unitologists, committed to the project for religion. These, Briden chief among them, were zealous. Istvan sensed in them a willingness to go to almost any extreme for their cause. Others were simply scientists and either atheistic or unconcerned about religion, but these still saw in him a kind of unique catalyst, an essential component for activating the Marker. He was, for all these, something special, something to be treasured.

The second group was the enemy, according to Briden. Even though Callie Dexter was imprisoned, she seemed to lead that group, shuttling messages back and forth to them. These scientists were the ones who largely stayed in the control room. They wanted to shutter the Marker project. For them, something was desperately amiss, and they claimed to object to the idea of bringing in a convict with a clear mental derangement as a key part of the project. But with Dr. Dexter imprisoned, they seemed to have lost a certain amount of their will and were somewhat ineffectual.

Callie had managed to smuggle a fair amount of equipment into the cell. The guard, confused that she was there at all, seemed happy to accept her notes and carry them to one of her contacts in the control room. He would come back with notes from them that explained what had happened and what was currently going on, and she would write responses, sending them off with the shambling guard again.

And more than that: one of the infiltrators in the Marker chamber managed to get close enough to Istvan to scan his brain waves for several hours and then sent her a memory stud with the data. Entering that, she charted Istvan's derangement, trying to understand just how damaged he was. His brain waves were highly abnormal, the sequence irregular and the waveform variable. No question about it: he was an extremely damaged individual. Worse, she realized, comparing these with the Marker pulses, the Marker seemed more responsive to his brain waves and perhaps was even adapting to them. Having Istvan near the Marker was not good for it. It was sharpening the signal, making it more intense. It was perhaps no coincidence that dementia had increased: the signal had risen. Was it because of Istvan? Hard to say. The researcher in her reminded her that the dementia had always been there and it might have developed this way on its own in any case. Though things had definitely gotten worse around the time Istvan arrived.

Through the slot in the door, she asked the guard to go

fetch Briden. He sidled slowly off. She waited, looking over the data again. Yes, she was right, she was sure of it; the Marker effects were getting worse.

A few minutes later the guard was back. "Can't come," he said.

"Can't or won't?" asked Callie.

The guard shrugged.

"Do you think you could let me out?" she asked.

The guard shook his head, but slowly, as if he might be able to be convinced.

"What if I told you it was a matter of life and death?" she asked.

"Whose life?" the guard asked. "Whose death?"

"Everybody's," said Callie.

The guard's eyes narrowed. "What do you mean?" he asked.

"If Istvan isn't removed, the consequences will be dire," said Callie. "Go tell Briden that. And tell him it was from me."

For a moment the guard looked confused, and then he shuffled off again.

This time he came back with Briden. The latter looked irritated. His hair was a mess and his jumpsuit smelled. He looked like he hadn't bathed in days.

"What is it now?" he asked through the slot.

She tried to explain, but halfway through he cut her off. "Istvan's fine," he said. "We need him. The Marker speaks to him."

"But he's changing the signal," said Callie. "The Marker's becoming more enabled, but in the wrong way. The signal was weak before. Now it's tuned and affecting nearly everybody, and symptoms of dementia, which were subdued before, seemed to have become more acute, even torturous. It was always sending out something that encouraged dementia, but it's suddenly become much, much worse."

"That's ridiculous," said Briden. "The Marker is glorious. And Istvan is its prophet."

Callie shook his head. She bent down, brought up an audio log, played it for him. It was Istvan's voice, rambling slowly on.

We must be made whole again. You must take us and carry us and make us again. And when we are in that place and new-made, from there you must carry us and make us again.

She clicked it off.

"So?" said Briden.

"Can't you hear what he's saying, Briden?" Callie asked. "The Marker is teaching him how to reproduce it. And what's more, my data suggests the Marker is rewiring his warped brain. Look at how many dead we already have, how many suicides."

"Collateral damage," Briden said.

"Collateral damage? Really?"

"Besides, I don't think there have been that many more suicides or dead than usual in circumstances such as these."

"Are you serious?" said Callie. "Briden, you're willfully turning a blind eye."

"It's you who are blind," said Briden.

"No," Dexter said. "Briden, you have to believe me: the Marker is dangerous. And with Istvan near it, it's probably even more dangerous."

"Blasphemy," said Briden.

"It's not anything of the kind. Besides, if you won't stop it, I will."

Briden smiled. "Do your worst," he said. "You're imprisoned in a cell." And then he turned on his heel and left.

Through it all, Istvan stayed there, beside the Marker. This, the ghost of the murdered Fischer told him, was where he would be safe. If he were to stay here, beside the Marker, then it would protect him.

"From what?" he asked.

The Marker did not seem to have a ready answer for this question. All around him, through the haze that was the real world, swarmed the other world; swirling and dynamic, full of ghosts and beauty. Now when the veil fell, it fell quickly and all at once. He could see in the Marker the shape and image of himself. He belonged here, with it, with the Marker. Though he looked human and flesh and blood, he felt he was more akin to this twisting tower of stone than to these people gathered round him, staring at him. They were built wrong. He could tell just by looking at them. The Marker wasn't talking to them. It was talking to *him*.

It will keep me safe, he told himself. And saying that somehow made him think of Jensi, whom he hadn't thought of for a long time. Jensi had protected him, had kept him safe. Or had for a while, anyway, until suddenly he couldn't or wouldn't do it anymore. When he thought about that part of it, it made him angry. He had needed Jensi's help, but where had his brother been? Jensi had even been there when the joke with

Councilman Fischer had gone wrong—he had seen him in the crowd, but had Jensi saved him? Had he prevented them from dragging him away and here? No, he hadn't. He had failed him.

But the Marker would not fail him. It had said it would protect him and so it would. The Marker had power and it was giving its power to him. He was, in some senses, becoming it.

We need to reproduce, the dead were saying, the Marker was saying through the dead. *There need to be more of us. We cannot live on this planet all our lives.*

No, thought Istvan. *You can't.*

We must call out louder, and hope for them to hear us and take us into themselves. As you have done, Istvan.

Yes, thought Istvan. *As I have done.* He could feel the form and shape of the Marker imprinted in his head, a delicate and beautiful structure, as entrancing as his numbers had been. It was the Marker, and he felt an almost overwhelming urge to try to bring it out of his head and to reproduce it in life. Soon others, he knew, would be feeling the same urge.

The dead were there now, in numbers, swirling all around him. All of their mouths were opening and they were singing. *It's time,* they were singing, *it's time!* Yes, he thought, it was time. He stood and the scientists around him looked rapt upon him. Briden was beside him, reaching one hand out and touching Istvan's shoulder.

And then Istvan felt it coming. He lifted his hands high above his head. When he brought them down the pulse came with it.

37

In the penal colony, the prisoners reeled and collapsed. Henry, too, found himself clutching his head, waiting for whatever was happening to pass, and when he lifted his head again it was to see most of the prisoners confused and wandering, much in the same state as he.

But then a few of them became more focused. One man grabbed another and tugged him over to the hole Briden had dug and then both stared down into it. Henry turned on the audio feed, trying to hear what they were saying, but by now they weren't saying anything, they were just staring into the hole. The corruption had spread, Henry realized, growing quickly and rapidly with the last burst, and had squirmed its way down the hole. Perhaps that was what they were looking at? He did hear other sounds, though: a few of the other men groaning, a few scraps of speech, and then also something else, something that he didn't know quite how to interpret. A strange sound like the breaking and snapping of sticks. *Wood?* he thought. There was no wood out there, maybe no wood anywhere in the compound. But it definitely sounded like that. What could it be?

He turned up the volume a little, but no longer heard the snapping sounds. Instead there was a sort of damp, squelchy noise.

And then one of the men closest to the hole flinched and stepped back. He opened his mouth and began to scream.

It was a strong one, and different than what Callie had felt before. When she came to, it was to find that she had unconsciously been beating her head against the cell wall. Her forehead was sore and bloody. *I could have really hurt myself,* she thought. She stumbled back to the machine and observed how it had graphed the pulse, saw how it had shot off the range of the chart. Her cell, too, suddenly had a lot of those tendrils winding through it. They hadn't been there before.

Something new is happening, she thought.

She stood and peered out the slot to see if she could see anything, but the hallway seemed empty. There, too, were more patches of corruption and tendrils, one of them big and long enough to almost seem like a cable.

She called for the guard but he didn't come. She called again, louder, this time beating her hand on the metal door, and this time he came, walking slowly and ponderously, with a strange dragging sound. She heard him long before she saw him, and when she saw him, he was clutching his head, a strange frenzied look disrupting his features in such a way that it seemed like his face was made of parts of the faces of four very different men. He stared through the slot, one eye clenched tightly shut, the other eye darting nervously about in its orbit.

"Are you all right?" she asked.

He didn't answer. Instead he brought his face down hard against the door, splitting his forehead on the lip of the slot. Startled, Dr. Dexter stepped back. He raised his head and she saw, through the narrow opening of the slot, blood cascading down his forehead. He took a strange swooping step and struck his head again, even harder this time, and she was spattered with his blood, blood oozing down the inside of the slot as well. And then he fell out of sight.

She heard a scraping sound that she couldn't place, then the sound of him pulling his way back up the door. Suddenly Callie was concerned he might try to unlock it and come in after her. She backed deeper into the cell, her hands feeling for the wall behind her. The guard's face appeared, the flesh over his eye torn away to reveal a stretch of pinkish bone. He swayed, and then tilted his head back.

"No!" shouted Callie.

But it was already too late. He brought his head down hard and fast and this time she could see the lip of the slot break through his head with a crunch and when he fell away he left, along with the blood, shards of brain and bone. He fell as heavy as a sack and then did not move again. Callie still stayed pressed back against the wall, holding her breath, waiting for him to move again, wondering fleetingly what had been wrong with the man, what had driven him to do what he had.

Then her glance fell to the now blood-spattered monitor, the graph with the lines stretching off it and lost beyond the edge of the screen, and then she thought she knew.

. . .

In the interrogation room, they had left the body covered by a sheet and then had forgotten about it. It had started to smell and the body had grown sodden and had begun to change, parts of it clinging to the sheet and soaking it through with a grayish ichor. Here there were no flies or insects and little bacteria beyond that in the body itself, so the decay was strange and unusual; the one guard who had looked into the room, searching for somewhere to take a quick nap while he was on duty, had quickly gone back out again.

Underneath the sheet something was happening. A tendril of corruption had curled up the leg of the table and felt its way to the head. There was a snapping sound and the body seemed to sit up, the sheet still clinging to it. A leg snapped and slid out at a strange angle. And then the body contorted and fell off the table.

It lay there half-wrapped in its sheet, still changing. The head twisted and opened up. The jaw dropped downward and pushed deep into the body. The legs broke and the skin of the chest stretched and fused between them in a kind of sheet. Soon what had once looked human looked more like a flesh-colored bat.

And then the creature, groaning, no longer human, began to crawl. A moment later, it tested its wings.

The screaming brought some of the other prisoners over to the hole. Henry watched them peer in, his hand near the button to call the guards. One of the men had his friends hold his arms and then he leaned out over the hole and looked down from a different vantage.

And then suddenly something strange happened. An odd batlike creature flashed up out of the hole and wrapped itself around the man's head. The men holding him let go in surprise and he fell into the hole, and everyone who had been close began running back and away, scattering all through the circle and moving toward the cells. Some were even, he could see on another of the screens, up against the large door leading out to the ring in which Henry and the guards were, screaming, pounding against the door, begging to get out.

What the hell is going on? wondered Henry. He summoned the guards and kept watching, zooming in close on the hole. What had it been? How had it gotten in? He kept the camera focused on the hole.

When the guards arrived at their station, he sounded the alarm for the prisoners to return to their cells. He let his eyes flick around to the other monitors. Some were already there; the others, though, made no move to do so. The number of prisoners pounding on the door leading out had increased. They weren't moving.

His earpiece crackled. "All assembled, sir," the leader of the guards said. "Open the door."

"Just a moment," said Henry, his attention back on the hole. He stared at it perhaps thirty seconds, perhaps slightly longer.

"This isn't going to be another of those false alarms, is it?" the leader of the guards asked.

"No," said Henry, half distracted. "I just have to figure out a way to get them away from the door."

"How many of them are there?" asked the leader. "We can take control of the situation, I bet."

"Kill them, you mean?" asked Henry.

"We don't have to kill all of them," said the guard. "We can stun some of them."

Henry opened his mouth to reply, and then stopped. Something was happening on the monitor. Something was stirring in the hole.

This time when it came, it took Ensign Haley's breath away. She hesitated, swaying for a moment, and then slipped from her chair and passed out.

She was standing with a woman dressed all in white, who it took her a moment to recognize as her mother. She was younger than she remembered her, and not ill, but there was no doubt about it: she was her mother. She had the same way of tilting her head when she asked a question and the way she moved and rubbed her hands, too, was just like how her mother had done it. No, it was her mother. There was no reason to doubt it.

Except that she was younger.

And not ill.

But surely there was a way to explain that. She was thinking of ways to explain it, thinking of explanations, when her mother asked, "Would you like to see my garden?"

"I'd be delighted," she said.

And she was. She imagined her mother walking her through rows of vegetables, or walking her through flower beds humming with bees. They would walk and talk just as they had before her mother had gotten sick. But no, wait, her mother wasn't sick now: she must have recovered. That was the explanation. That must be it.

But there were no flowers. There were no vegetables. Instead her mother took her around the corner and she saw, there, sprouting up from the earth a two-pronged thing that looked like long horns twisting around one another. It was gigantic, filling the whole plot of the garden and stretching high into the sky. That wasn't a garden, was it? But her mother was guiding her to the thing and touching it, talking to her about how she grew it, how she cared for it. And then she simply stepped inside the thing and brought her daughter along with her. There she was, touching everything, pointing to each cell and bit of it, feeling her way around and through it.

"Because, you see," said her mother, "the reason I'm telling you this is so that you can be an even better gardener than me."

"Better than you?" she said.

Her mother nodded. "When you grow it, when you have your turn, it will be even better."

When she woke up she was not on the floor but at her desk having scrawled into it her pad pages and pages of notes. They had all gone, she knew, to Grottor. But what would he do with them?

She tried to go back and look at old scrawls from earlier, to try to understand what was happening to her, what lesson she was supposed to learn, but they were no longer on the machine. They had been removed. Had she removed them? She didn't remember. Maybe she had, but why would she? Grottor, then? Yes, maybe. But she trusted Grottor. Was she right to? Perhaps Grottor had taken the information from her, removed it and made it his own, and had thought he'd taken it away from her as well.

But she had it all inside, had it all in her head. She could feel it: it was part of her now.

Maybe she would go back to her room and write it down again, write it for herself this time, so that when the time came she could decide what to do with it. She would write it down and send it to friends, people she could trust.

No, Grottor would not be allowed to keep the information to himself. Anybody who wanted to be a gardener was welcome to it.

"I'll be there in a few days," the gray man insisted. "There's no use arguing about it. We need her."

"But she's good at her job," said Grottor. "She's ambitious and smart and now that she's given you what you wanted, she deserves to be left alone."

The gray man shook his head. "There's always more that we want," he said. "And I think she has more to give. I think there's more hidden inside of her than meets the eye. I need to crack her head open in person and get at it. If I'm right, she now carries the key to the next stage of the project."

"But you can't—"

"I can and will," said the gray man.

39

She was going over the figures, looking at the other machines, trying to make sense of all the data and how it related, when she heard something. A kind of flapping. At first she ignored it, then something struck her door and she thought of the guard who had beaten his own head apart. Maybe he was not dead yet after all. Maybe he was trying to get up.

She stood slowly and made her way to the slot, even though it was not cut in such a way as to allow her to see the bottom of the door. But something was happening there; she could hear something, a crackling sound, like the sounds that logs make when they pop and crack in the fire. Not that she had ever seen them—wood was too valuable to waste on a fire—but she had watched the vids when she was a kid.

But that didn't make sense. Who would start a fire here? And if there was one she'd smell it and see the smoke. And if not that, what could it be?

She knelt down and pressed her ear to the door. She could still hear sounds, but not much more clearly. It didn't help any. She stood up again, tried again to look out, still saw nothing.

The noises continued for a while, and then stopped. She

still waited, wondering what to do. And then a different noise started, the sound of movement, something sliding up the door. Yes, it must be the guard, she thought. He must be still alive after all. He must be standing up now.

She backed up a little, just to be careful. Would he be violent like he'd been before? Had the signal faded enough that he might have escaped whatever was troubling him?

His head rose to where she could see it in the slot and she caught her breath. His face was streaked with blood but something else had changed about it, too: the jaw was loose in a way it shouldn't have been. It was hanging wrong. The head was oddly lumpy, perhaps where the skull had been broken, and the eyes had slipped farther in than they had been before.

"Are you all right?" she asked.

He didn't say anything, just stood where he was, staring at her through the slot.

"You should get immediate medical attention," she said. "You're very hurt. Perhaps in shock, too."

She moved a little closer and suddenly he thrust his arm through the slot and tried to grab her with it. Only it wasn't his arm exactly, she realized, but a long scythe. Where had he gotten a scythe?

And then she realized that it was made of bone. It was not a scythe at all, but a part of him.

It scrabbled at the door, trying to get out. It was dragging the sheet behind it, parts of the sheet still adhering to it. It kept scratching, butting against the door.

Down the hall were the guards, still gathered outside the

door to the next ring, the inner ring, milling about, getting more and more irritated and anxious as their leader spoke to Wandrei over vid. One of them, a young blond man named Millar, was more nervous than most. For days now, he'd been itching for a fight, something to sink his teeth into. And now was his chance to have one. But Wandrei was refusing to open the door.

"Calm down," said Ramirez, the guard standing nearest to him.

"I can't calm down," said Millar. "I have to be out there."

"You can't be out there yet," said Ramirez. "We can't go until we've been given approval. It may not even come at all."

"Like last time," said Millar.

"Like last time," Ramirez agreed.

Millar continued quivering: shaking, stretching, nearly bouncing off the walls.

"You're driving me crazy," Ramirez finally said. "You're getting everybody wound up. Look, if you need to get some energy off then take a walk. We won't leave without you."

Millar was off like a shot, rushing down the hall. It felt good to move a little, maybe it'd help. He moved as quickly as he could, following the slow curve of the hall. It didn't help much, but it helped a little.

He went to the end of the hall and the locked door there, and stopped. He was just turning around and starting back again when he heard a strange scrabbling sound inside the door.

"Anyone there?" he asked.

The scrabbling grew louder. A kind of hissing, strangling noise joined it.

He unhooked his truncheon from his belt, hefted it in his

hand. Someone or something was in there, and he was going to find out what it was.

He reached for the door, and then stopped. Whatever it was, was it dangerous? Should he be doing this on his own?

But no, he told himself, he was wearing full riot gear. What could possibly happen to him?

At first glance, it seemed to Henry like he was watching a man's back, the spine clear and pronounced, but there was no head. No, it couldn't be a man, he told himself, he was experiencing some odd sort of perspectival shift, was seeing things wrong. And there were no arms, either, but rather strange flaps of skin, wings almost. And then he saw that yes, they were wings, and the creature took off. He followed it from monitor to monitor as it flew short distances and alighted, searching for something. What was it searching for?

And then another one came out of the hole, too, half fluttering its way to the top and then alighting there on the rim of the hole, waiting for a moment. It was still enough that Henry could see it clearly and see now something that at first he couldn't believe. He understood now why he had first thought it was a human's back: it was because whatever the creature was now, it had once been human. It was formed out of one of the corpses in the hole.

How was that possible? Henry wondered. He shook his head. He must be hallucinating, he thought. But no, when he opened his eyes, the creature was still there.

And then there was further movement in the hole and he saw a strange swordlike object slide out and anchor itself against the floor. More like a scimitar really, though not that exactly, either. And attached to something that was strangely banded but still evidently flesh.

A face and body followed. He could recognize it as the face and body of the man who had leaned over the hole and fallen in, could even see bits and scraps of his prison clothing. He *knew* it was him, but still couldn't believe it, couldn't believe how the man had bent and changed, had been taken apart and then put back together in an incomprehensible way. It was a face and body unlike anything he had ever seen.

40

The creature that had once been a guard roared, clawing at her through the slot in the door. It either did not remember it had the key to the door or, in this state, did not know how to work it. In any case, it did not open the door.

At first she crouched against the back wall, afraid, eyes squinched shut. But slowly her scientific curiosity got the better of her and she began watching it, even coming a little closer. Whatever the thing was now, it had once been human, but she could see little human response left in it, little to suggest it still had a connection to its human side. Even its movement seemed almost programmed, a repetition of certain patterns along a search for living bodies. She could move to one side of the cell or the other and it would turn to follow her, like a flower following the sun.

After a while she was convinced that it wasn't human any longer. Not only that, she wasn't certain that it was a thinking creature at all: it was more like something constrained to draw from a limited set of responses. Was it really alive? It was moving, yes, but it didn't seem to be breathing. If it was alive, it was not alive in the way that it had been before, back when it had been human.

But the important question was first how to get out of the cell and second how to get past it. She had lots of electronic equipment here; maybe she could construct something to broadcast out with, make some kind of distress signal.

She was just starting to sort through her equipment to see what she had when from down the hall she heard a shout and the creature turned. Several shots rang out, and she even saw one of the bullets tear through the creature's chest before it started down the hall. The bullet didn't seem to affect it much at all. It didn't seem to experience any pain. *Interesting,* she thought, as it lumbered down the hall and out of her vision. A moment later, she heard a series of additional shots, and then a series of screams, the latter cut suddenly short.

Millar hit it hard with the truncheon, gave it a blow that should have paralyzed it, but the creature hardly seemed to notice. Abruptly it had leapt and was upon him, its batlike wings wrapping him in an obscene embrace. And then the creature leaned in, but its proboscis knocked against the front of his faceplate. *Ha,* Millar thought, *I'm safe, it can't hurt me,* and he tried to work his arm free so that he could hit the creature again. It knocked up against the faceplate again, and hissed, and then the proboscis darted forward hard and cracked the plastic. *Oh, shit,* he thought. Another blow and the creature was almost through. He tried to shake it off, tried to break free, but it wouldn't let go of him. He screamed. It struck again and this time it went not only through the faceplate, but deep into his brain.

Henry watched as one of the batlike creatures apparently found what it was looking for and swooped rapidly forward, wrapping itself around a convict's head and shoulders. The man, screaming, tried to push it away, but the creature held tight and then pulled him tighter, and then a proboscis shot out of its body and through the center of the man's forehead. The man collapsed, dead, but the creature was still on him, the proboscis obscenely pumping something into the man's head. Then the batlike creature pulled free and waddled off, awkward now on the floor.

But as bad as that was, what followed was much worse. The body itself, already shivering by the time the creature left it, started to transform. Bones and muscles twisted and broke and inverted. Bones pushed out through flesh and changed, thinning, becoming something else. The whole body became something else, something other—became just like the creature with scimitarlike arms that he had just seen crawl its way up out of the hole.

Oh my God, thought Henry and realized that before long all the men in the room would become those things. Panicked, he opened the security door and then watched on the monitor the men trying to push their way in while the guards rushed out, striking all around them with their truncheons.

"No," he said on his headset to the guard leader. "Don't hit them! Get them in here! Save them!"

"What?" asked the leader.

"Drag them in," he said, "and get your men back in as well, but keep those creatures out."

"What creatures?" asked the leader and then he saw one of the shambling beings with bladelike arms. He ran toward it, truncheon lifted over his head, and a few moments later his head had been severed from his shoulders.

Henry turned on the loudspeaker. "Fall back, fall back!" he yelled. Some of the guards did, but a few didn't, and many of the prisoners, too, were still out there. But he saw the batlike creatures and humanoid ones coming closer and felt he had no choice but to close the door.

It slid slowly shut. A body was in the way so he had to use the override to get it closed, and when it did close it slowly tore the body in half. There were men still outside, many of them, and one of them lost his arm in the door. He quickly tried to count the creatures, his eyes flicking from screen to screen, and was pretty sure that they were all there outside. They were safe.

Or so he thought until he heard the sound of screaming from down near the door.

As the alarms went off, Istvan remained calm. He watched people come and go, rushing in and out, and after a while everybody was gone, except for him and Briden.

"Not all of them will come back," said Istvan. "Very few will."

"What?" said Briden.

"It will keep us safe," said Istvan, gesturing to the Marker.

"Safe from what?" asked Briden.

But Istvan did not answer. He closed his eyes and bowed his head and waited.

41

Henry closed the doors to the control room and locked them. It was the only way he could be sure of staying alive. He tried not to listen to the screams and yells, but he could not help but hear them, even through the doors, and he could see, through the glass of the control-room observation portal, the creature slowly tearing one of the guards apart. Then it moved on to another man, a convict this time.

Where had it come from? How had it gotten in? Had he simply missed it?

The guards tried to beat it with their truncheons, but it didn't seem to do much good. The creature just kept on coming. One of them, one of the guards, managed to make it back to the armory and unlock a gun, but when he fired it at the creature it had little effect. It just kept coming at him until it had him in its scythes and was eating away the side of his face. Four or five men were already down. Then another man, a prisoner, plucked up the gun and this time, instead of firing into the creature's chest, he shot repeatedly at the creature's leg until it was little more than tattered mass of tissue that gave out as soon as the creature put weight on it. And yet the creature kept coming, dragging itself forward now with the tips of its scythes until the man put enough bullets into the joint connected to the scythe to break it off. Even then, the creature kept coming, crawling like a worm and trying to chew the man's leg off until one of the others had stamped on it enough times to separate the head from the shoulders. But the torso still moved, as if it were still alive.

So perhaps the only way to stop it is to immobilize it, thought Henry. Cut off the limbs or render them inoperative in some way. Even then, it was still moving, but its ability to attack had been drastically diminished.

The remaining guards and prisoners looked grim and seemed hostile to one another. Eventually, they took the bodies of the dead and put them in a line against one wall.

So the creature was dead, thought Henry. Locking the doors of the control room to keep everybody else out had been premature. They had survived.

He was just preparing to open the door when a wave of pain swept through his head. He grimaced, nearly fainted, and for a moment he could see, standing just beside him, as real as he had ever been when he was alive, his grandfather.

"Papa?" he said.

But it could not be his grandfather. His grandfather had been dead for years. The man, whoever he was, simply smiled and nodded, then reached out to pat his hand. Very slowly he began to fade, vanishing into nothingness.

Henry shook his head to clear it. He was hearing sounds from below, but, still confused, wasn't sure what exactly he was hearing. When he stood up and went to the window he saw that another of the batlike creatures had appeared in the place of a corpse, and that it was huddled over the corpse next to it pumping something into its skull. By the time it moved on to the next corpse in line, the first corpse had already started to shudder and change. Soon the fighting started up again.

It was terrible to watch, but Henry had a hard time looking away. At the end, nearly all of the creatures were dead, but all of the humans were dead, too, and the room was scattered with corpses. Which was not good, thought Henry. Because the next time a burst came, perhaps these corpses would start walking around. And now he was perhaps the only human left alive.

He tried to place a call to the commander, but got no response. What was wrong? Maybe someone or something was jamming the circuit, he thought, or maybe they simply weren't answering.

He placed a distress call on a general circuit and sent it out, hoping someone would hear it and would send help.

But the signal didn't last long. After just a few minutes it went dead. He tried to send it out again, but it was being jammed. He was working on it, trying to figure out how it was being jammed and who was behind it, when a vidlink opened and showed him a picture of the commander's face. He had a stern expression on his face.

"Do you need something?" he asked. "We're a little busy here."

When Henry quickly filled him in on the situation, Commander Grottor simply nodded.

"Things have gone wrong at the other sites as well, all at once," he said, and Henry noticed for the first time that though his expression was stern his eyes were tired and a little puzzled. "God only knows what we've unleashed," he said.

"Sir, what other sites? Are we a site? What does it mean that we're a site?"

"Hmmm?" he said. "Oh, you're at the penal colony. Of course. You don't know anything about that."

"What's going on, sir?" Henry asked.

But the commander said, "I'm sorry, son, but we had to jam your signal. We can't have anyone stumbling onto this. We need to bring it to an end. It needs to end here."

"But you've got to get us out of here," said Henry. "Or me, at least. I may be the only one left alive."

The commander shook his head. "There are bigger things at stake here than your life. I'm afraid you're already as good as dead," he said, and then broke the link.

42

The pod was spinning as it came down, end over end. Jensi tried to stabilize it, tried to straighten it out, but the controls weren't responding. He kept struggling with the stick, trying to bring it under control.

He entered the atmosphere and the ship's apron began to glow cherry-red from the heat. The pod spun backward and he saw the mine following him, and the next time he spun again the mine was closer. He managed finally to get the front end forward and the craft directed and no longer tumbling, but he was still rolling, around and around. And now he couldn't see where the mine was, how close it was, and when it was likely to reach him. Did he dare deploy the thrusters to try to slow the pod down? Or was the mine too close?

Now in the atmosphere, the ship was beginning to handle differently. It was still rolling but more slowly this time. He overcorrected for a moment and rolled in the other direction, but then slowly leveled. He was falling rapidly. Down below, he could see two sets of lights, at a little distance from one another. One would be the secret facility, while the other would be the penal colony housing his brother. Which was which? Left or right?

He stared, looking for a sign to tell him where to go. The lights on the left were clustered a little closer together, which perhaps, he thought, were an indication of a more secure structure, something more compact. Maybe that could be the penal colony? Though perhaps he was thinking about it all wrong. But what else was there to go on?

So he pulled slightly left. Behind him came an explosion and the craft shuddered. The mine had gone off, triggered by the heat of the atmosphere. The pod seemed undamaged, nothing showing up on the monitors. Though the controls were a little sluggish now—so maybe some slight damage, then.

He turned on the forward thrusters to try to slow the craft and they came on with a jolt that knocked his helmeted head against the instrument panel. The lights were getting closer and he was slowing down, though not nearly as much as he wanted. He tried to increase the thrusters but they were already going their maximum. The pod as a craft, he suddenly remembered, was not made for landing on a planet; it was just something to get you far enough away from a damaged or destroyed ship so that another ship could pick you up in a few hours or few days. It had limited controls, limited steering, even limited power of movement. And indeed, he could see that some of the tiles on the apron had blackened and charred. If they were to come free, then the craft would get hotter and hotter until he was cooked.

You can do this, he told himself. He was a picker, he'd taken small craft of all types and quality from the surface of a planet to an orbiting spaceship and back again—he had a lot of experience in this kind of thing.

He fired the forward thrusters again, felt the jolt, and for a moment things began to slow.

What sort of impact could the pod survive? He had no idea. How much fuel did he have for the thrusters? Already half gone, he saw on the monitor, so not much. There were separate indicators for the back thrusters, he realized, so they had a separate source. *Poor design,* he thought. If he had access to all the fuel at once, then he'd probably be able to bring the pod in, maybe even survive.

Which gave him an idea. He aimed carefully for the complex, still knowing that what he might do could very well bring him down miles away. He waited until he was quite close and then turned the thrusters on full and kept them on as long as possible, until the low-fuel indicator lit up. And then he turned on only one thruster and used it to spin the craft around. When he was flying backward, he leveled out with the other thruster, then cut them and turned the rear thrusters on full.

He was flying backward, blind, hoping the rear thrusters would slow him down enough that he'd survive. He couldn't tell how far off course he might be, couldn't tell how far away the ground was, couldn't tell how fast he was going, either, though it did feel like he'd slowed some. He kept the rear thrusters on full, hoping he'd calculated well enough that he wouldn't run out of fuel and speed up again before reaching the ground.

He braced himself for the impact.

. . .

Henry just stared at the blank screen. At first he'd tried to hail the commander again, but there had been no response; they weren't even bothering to answer his calls. Then he'd tried to send out a distress signal on another channel only to find that blocked as well. Maybe if he had some skill in circuits and electronics he could figure out something, some sort of way of working around it, but really, what was the point? Even if he did manage to get a signal out there to reveal his dilemma and his position, the only ships in the area were the military ships attached to the commander, who had just told him he was good as dead. Maybe the other complex had some sort of escape ship, but the prison complex didn't have one; it had been deemed a potential danger. The signal was his best bet, but even if he managed to get a signal past them and to some ship beyond but still somehow close enough to hear it, how long would it take them to come? Two days at least, maybe three. And then they'd have to make it past the commander's ships, get to him, defeat the creatures that had swarmed the prison and made the men in it like them, and get him out. He had water in the control room, but not very much, and no food at all. No, it wasn't going to happen.

What do you do when you know you are going to die? Henry asked himself and found he had no answer. What he was doing now was staring at a blank screen, waiting for something to come to him. But nothing had.

And also there was the question of how to die. He could simply starve to death, growing hungry and then slowly weaker and very gradually fading out of existence. Or he could open the emergency cabinet and remove the pistol in it and fire a shot through his skull. Or he could simply open the doors and let the creatures, still milling about outside, somewhat idly now, make their way in and find him and kill him. There were probably other ways to go about it as well, quite creative ways if he could figure them out. Maybe that was what he would do: spend his last few days figuring out more and more eccentric ways to die.

At last he left the monitor, went and stood by the window. He could take the pistol and shoot out the window, he realized, and then the atmosphere would rush out and his lungs would collapse and he'd collapse, too. It would take probably a few shots since the glass was impact-resistant, but a few bullets fired just right would probably do it.

He could see there, across the rocky plain and at some distance, the lights of the research facility. What were they doing over there? Were they the ones who had caused all this? And if he was being told that there was no getting out, were they being told the same thing? Were they doomed to die as well?

There was, he knew, an ATV just outside the prison, something that the guards used to drive the supplies that landed at the penal colony over to the research facility. Maybe he could drive over there and join forces with them. Maybe together they could figure out what to do and find a way to survive. The menace was, for the moment, contained within the penal colony, at least as far as he could tell, so maybe there was still a safe space. He could drive there, no problem. But the problem was figuring out how to get out and down to the ATV without being killed. He needed a RIG with oxygen, a serious deep-space number, but he wasn't even sure if they had one. At the very least, he needed a good RIG and some O_2 bottles, but those were in a locker down below, with the creatures. He would never be able to get to them without being killed.

And then, looking out the window, he caught a flash of something above him, realized it was something falling from the sky. At first he thought it was on fire, but then he realized that no, it was thrusters he was seeing, it was a ship coming down. He caught his breath and for an instant thought maybe someone was coming to save him after all. But then he thought no, the shape was wrong for it to be a fully operational ship; it was something else. *A rocket maybe,* he thought. But then the thrusters would be on the other side, accelerating it instead of slowing it down. And then he realized that no, maybe it was an escape pod. Not someone coming to rescue him but someone likely soon to be just as marooned as he.

And then he realized it was heading straight at the penal colony, straight at him. It streaked fire as it fell from the sky, and then it struck.

He felt it rattle Hell all the way through. He clung to the wall to keep from falling, then rushed over to the monitors. Most were still operational, but a few were nothing but static now—most of the ones in the central circle were down, so that must have been where the pod had hit. He scanned the other monitors for signs of whatever had struck, but saw nothing.

What's there? he wondered, continuing to peer at the monitors, hoping something would soon appear. *And who?*

43

Jensi groaned. He hurt all over and his faceplate was spidered through with cracks, though luckily still intact. The arm of his suit seemed to be on fire. He slapped at the flame with his hand until it went out. Slowly he unwebbed and pushed his way close to the viewport and looked out.

At first he couldn't make sense of what he was seeing. He had been expecting rock or dust, some sort of barren exterior space, but what he saw instead was different. A dark rounded wall, rising far above him. Cliffs, maybe? No, too regular. He fumbled around the pod until he found the exterior light and then flicked it on to get a closer look. No, he saw, it was a man-made wall. He was inside something.

Carefully, he broke the seal of the portal and crawled out. He was in a domed chamber, fairly large, round. His craft had broken through the dome above, which meant that probably the atmosphere of the planet was not breathable. Hopefully he had enough oxygen left in his suit to get to a contained space. Probably he did, but just in case he crawled back in, came out with two bottles of oxygen that he used to refill his tanks. He took the first-aid kit, too, just in case his injuries went beyond mere soreness, and the flare pistol.

He had struck and destroyed several tables, he realized, and gouged a channel along the stone floor. Not far from where he'd landed there was a large hole, and there were more than a few burnt and charred bodies here, probably people killed, he was sorry to realize, by his landing. It was an accident, he couldn't have known he would land here rather than somewhere nearby—he couldn't even see where he was going—but still he couldn't help but feel guilty. More lives to add to his tally. He just hoped one of them had not been Istvan.

The rest of the room seemed deserted. One of the bodies near the edge, lying facedown in a riot suit, was not charred. Indeed, it seemed a little mysterious that it was dead at all. Or at least it was until he prodded it and rolled it over and saw the hole torn in its chest, as if a cannon had been fired from inside of its ribs. *What did that?* he wondered. It didn't look like a wound from a pistol or a rifle or something that plasma might do. But if not those, what?

The corpse had a lump within its riot suit somewhere down by the waist. Jensi, curious, unzipped it to find a plasma pistol, an older model with a wide beam and with its serial numbers filed off. Obviously something the guard had smuggled in. He picked it up, slipped it into his hand.

The earpiece of his RIG crackled and he got a strange, staticky transmission.

"—ever you are," the voice said, "be careful."

"Hello?" said Jensi. "Who is this?"

The voice began to speak again, but Jensi could hardly hear it: something had struck him hard on the head and shoulders and knocked him down. He could feel it wrapped around his arms and shoulders and digging into his back, trying to cut into his suit, and it was there before his face, pressing against it as well, some kind of antenna or proboscis feeling around his helmet and prodding at it, looking for a way in. It was something alive, clearly, but unlike anything he had ever seen, and he had no doubt that it was trying to kill him.

He felt the proboscis pushing its way against the seal around his neck, trying to insinuate its way through. He rolled over hard, tried to crush the thing between his body and the floor and for a moment the pressure on his back loosened and he forced his arms up and began to tear at the thing, one hand trying to push it back and away, the other managing almost by accident to grab its proboscis, which thrashed in his hand and tried to whip free. He tugged it forward and then snapped it hard and the proboscis went dead at its tip, but the rest of it didn't stop trying to break away and get back at him.

Slowly he managed to pull away from it and move up on it, pinning its body down with his knees. Holding the proboscis with one hand he felt around him for the pistol with the other, hoping it was still within reach. But he didn't find it. Out of desperation he tore the flare gun from his belt and thrust it against the creature's body, but then he wasn't sure where to fire: where was its head? As far as he could tell, it didn't have one—it was just a pair of wings with long limblike extensions and a central body that looked uncannily like a human spine. Where was he to shoot, then?

". . . can make it to the doors," said the crackling voice in his ear, "I'll open them."

Not now, he thought. He pushed the flare gun roughly

against the spot where the proboscis extruded and pulled the trigger. The flare sizzled and burnt through the thing, eating away the proboscis and the flesh around it.

The creature thrashed, then stopped moving.

He stumbled up, dizzy, sweating inside his suit, listening to the sound of his own roughened, restricted breathing. *What the fuck was that?* he wondered. *Some sort of alien? So that's it, an alien invasion? We've finally discovered another life-form and all it wants to do is kill us?* He turned his suit light on and shined it on the creature, the flare still hissing and burning somewhere within its body. The thing was flesh-colored, he saw, and parts of it looked like bits of a human body, but assembled wrong and twisted. It had an uncanny quality to it, like a bad nightmare.

His RIG crackled again. "Are you still there?" the voice asked, still distorted but clearer this time. "Did they kill you already?"

"Not yet," he said. "Who?"

"You can hear me," said the relieved voice. The voice seemed oddly familiar, but he wasn't sure why. It wasn't his brother, he was sure of that. "They've been jamming all the signals out," he said. "It took me a moment to figure out how to send something more specifically directed toward you that they'd be less likely to pick up and stop."

"What the hell is going on?" asked Jensi.

"I don't know," said the voice. "I'm the only one now."

"Only one what?" asked Jensi.

"Only one left alive," he claimed.

Holy shit, thought Jensi. He looked around him until he found the pistol. He picked it up, holding the flare gun in one hand and the pistol in the other.

"Listen to me," the voice in his ear was saying. "You're in

terrible danger. You have to be very careful or they'll kill you. But if you can get to the door, I'll let you in. After that, you'll have to figure out how to get to me, but if you can get that far, maybe you'll get to me, too."

"How do I get there?" Jensi asked.

"Look around you," said the voice. "You'll see an opening in the wall, there's only one. Go straight through and don't turn right or left where the cells are. Straight in front of you there will be the door. When you're getting close, let me know and I'll open it."

"All right," said Jensi. "I'll make a run for it in a moment." He shone his suit light along the wall until the light dropped off and into an opening. There it was. Was it safe to go toward it?

"What are these things?" he asked.

"You wouldn't believe me if I told you," the voice said.

"Try me."

"They're people," said the voice. "Just like you and me, or used to be. Something happened to them. Something changed them."

"You've got to be kidding me," Jensi said.

"I wish I was. I told you that you wouldn't believe me."

Not knowing what to say, Jensi said nothing. Slowly he began to make his way around the chamber, suit light off now, working solely off the glow from the pod's lights. "What happened to change them?" he asked. "What happened to them?"

"I don't know."

"You don't know?"

But either the voice did not choose to answer or the signal had been found again and blocked.

"Hello?" said Jensi. "Hello?" But there was no answer.

His head hurt. He must have hit it in the crash. It was throbbing like crazy. He moved slowly forward, both pistols at the ready, trailing his way along the curving wall, moving as quietly as possible.

There was a stab of pain deep within his skull, as if something had worked a knife carefully between his eye and its socket and then suddenly plunged it deeper in. He swayed and for a moment the dark and gray world was dyed red, and then it slowly faded back to normal.

But something new was there as well, just there ahead of him and facing away from him. Or rather someone. A woman, somehow familiar, her body glowing softly. But no, he knew it couldn't be a woman, couldn't be anyone human—the dome had been cracked open and the atmosphere outside wasn't breathable. Nobody could be alive here.

And yet, she seemed alive and he found himself drawn to her. He approached her carefully, feeling his way along the wall, staring at the back of her head. She was familiar, but no, he told himself again, that was impossible, his mind was playing tricks on him. He was hallucinating. Maybe there was a hole in his suit and something in the air here was adulterating his oxygen supply, making him see things that didn't exist.

Still, he couldn't stop himself from approaching her. She didn't move as he came closer, just stayed exactly where she was until he was standing just a foot or two away, hesitating.

He reached out and touched her shoulder. Suddenly her body seemed to come to life and she turned around to face him, and he saw that the reason the woman had been familiar was because it was his mother.

He pulled his hand away and stepped back.

"You're dead," he said, "you can't be here."

"Jensi," she said. "Help me. Help me become what I can be next."

He pointed both guns at her and wished for her to go away, but she stayed there, staring at him, pleading.

"No," he said. "You don't exist."

"Jensi," she said again. "Help me."

He began to pull back the triggers but found himself hesitating. He closed his eyes tight, shook his head. When he opened them again, his mother was gone and the guns he thought he'd been pointing at her were pointing not at her at all, but at his own head.

What had just happened? What was wrong with him?

After a moment, his headache had passed and he felt gathered and confident enough in his ability to understand the world around him that he could continue on. There was, near the wall, a corpse, the body torn and strange and perhaps somewhat burnt as well—a strange color to it in any case, like the purple gray of meat drying too long in the sun. He would have to leave the wall to skirt around it, but he didn't particularly want to. He felt better having the wall to run his fingers along. *Just a corpse*, he told himself, and began to step over it.

Only, as it turned out, it wasn't just a corpse. As he started to step over it, it moved and hissed and he saw that what he thought was human was not human at all, or at least no longer. He stumbled back and it was after him, waving scythelike blades that seemed to have sprouted from its body, trying to slash him. Running backward, he fired the pistol into its body, but it didn't seem to have much effect. He fired into the head, burning a hole through the skull just above the eye, but the creature didn't fall or even slow down. *Holy shit*, he thought, and began firing into its legs.

It took three or four shots to separate the leg at the knee but still it kept coming, hobbling on one leg and using one of its scythes like a cane. He shot the other leg out and still it kept coming, lying on its belly and pulling itself forward by its scythes. He aimed the flare gun at the fleshy appendage of one of the scythes and fired, and watched the phosphorus flare lodge in the muscle and smoke and burn, until it burnt through the appendage. Even then, it still continued to try to come toward him, dragging itself forward by its remaining scythe, dislocated mouth slavering.

"How the hell do you kill these things?" he asked through his transmitter, but there was no reply. He darted forward and stomped hard on the neck and broke it, and then stomped again, and a third time until the head broke entirely away. And yet, despite that the single remaining scythe kept pulling itself forward, trying to find him. *How can something live without a head?* he wondered. And then he wondered if this, too, was something he was hallucinating.

He stomped on the remaining scythe and broke it off. Even then the thing didn't stop exactly, but simply couldn't do anything to him. He stood there looking at the uneasy torso, realizing he needed some better weapons.

But there was nothing in the pod that seemed useful. Nothing much in the room, either, as far as he could tell—he was, after all, in a prison, not the sort of place where it was likely that heavy weaponry would be lying around. He had just a few flares left. The plasma pistol proper had a number of charges, but it wouldn't last forever. If there were many more of them, he was likely to be in trouble.

How could it be alive? he wondered again. *How could it keep coming at me even after I took off its head?* Whatever these once-human bodies had become it was something very far away from being human. They operated in ways that he could not understand. And you couldn't kill them exactly, it seemed, only reduce them to a certain immobility so that even though they were still moving they could no longer do much harm.

And so what now? What else was there to do but make for the door, hope that the man who had been talking to him would manage to open it before another one of those things found him and tried to kill him?

At first he started off cautiously, trailing his way along the walls, but he quickly thought *fuck it* and began to run. If they were there, they were there, and perhaps moving quickly was as good a way as any of getting past them. He ran along the wall and down into the corridor. He did not turn left or right, but he made the mistake of looking left and saw the line of cells, lights still functioning in this part of the complex, caught a glimpse of a corpse collapsed in one, killed by lack of oxygen, as well as a few of the more humanoid creatures shambling down along the cells, away from him.

He ran forward to the large doors, stopped in front of them, and whispered into his receiver, "I'm here. Open the doors."

He waited, but there was no response. He tried again, a little louder, hoping the noise wouldn't attract the creatures down among the cells. Finally, came a crackling sound:

". . . ny inside, too," it said. "Wave your hand so . . . know you . . ."

What was that supposed to mean? Not knowing what else to do, he followed the part of the message he'd heard and waved his hand.

There was a *thunk* and the doors began to slide open. But on the other side lay, he suddenly realized, not safety, but death.

The room just on the other side of the door was scattered with corpses, some of them torn to bits, others more or less intact. And among them perhaps a half dozen of the humanoid creatures that he'd seen before. The moment they saw him, they hissed and started rushing toward him.

44

He fired the flare gun into the first one and it lodged somewhere near its hip, burning the joint of the leg away but not quick enough for it to fall before reaching him. He turned and ran.

At first he was heading back to the central circle, but no, he realized, there was only one exit there, that was a trap. He swerved and headed down through the cell-lined hallway, only realizing after he'd started that he'd gone the wrong way, toward the creatures that he'd seen walking there earlier. He glanced back over his shoulder but it was too late to correct himself: the others were already nearly upon him.

He sped up, running as fast and as silently as he could. There they were, three of them, up ahead, and he waited to fire on them until he was almost upon them and knew they had heard him. He faded right and they gravitated toward him and he fired the pistol at the one closest to him, trying to take out a limb or a leg, but failing. He fired the flare gun again, and struck one of them in the face, the head suddenly blooming into a ball of fire. And then quickly he veered left, rubbed up against the cells and rushed around them. One of them managed to strike him with his bonelike scimitar, but it was a glancing blow, strong enough to numb his arm and make him drop his flare gun but not enough to cut through his suit. And then he was past them and running farther along the curving hall, hoping he wouldn't run in to more of them.

"I'm still alive and running," he said into the receiver, already mostly out of breath. "Maybe you can hear me, maybe you can't. But if you can, for god's sake, don't shut the damn door."

He kept running, even though his lungs were burning. How much oxygen was left in the suit? The creatures behind him weren't quite gaining on him, but they also weren't losing much ground. If he slowed, eventually they would catch him. And then they would either kill him or make him into one of them.

But he couldn't go far enough ahead of them to make them lose interest in him. They had to keep following him, he had to draw them all away from the door while he circled all the way around and back to it.

And then a terrible thought hit him. What if the corridor didn't go around in a circle after all? What if he was soon going to hit a dead end?

He tried not to think about it, tried just to keep running as long as he could, but the panic made him unable to judge how far he had run. Was he halfway yet? More? How much of his strength should he hold in reserve so he would be able to finish?

He slackened his pace a little and one of them almost caught him. He sped up and then saw it, up ahead: the door. "I'm coming! I'm coming!" he yelled into the receiver. "Get ready to close it!" And then he ran all out and as fast as he could. He yelled "Now!" when he was still a little way away, fifteen or twenty feet or so, and was horrified by how quickly the doors started to close. Would he make it? He gave a last burst of speed and threw himself at them and through them, sliding the last of the way in and watching the door close behind him, crushing one of the creatures as it did so and keeping the rest outside.

45

He lay on the floor listening to his own harsh ragged breathing. After a moment he heard the hiss of air rushing into the chamber and the breather in his RIG shut off. The air here was safe to breathe.

He stood up, retracted his helmet, wiped his face, and looked around.

It was a large room, long, with a door to his right and a door to his left. The walls were smeared with blood and gobbets of gore scattered the floor. There were intact corpses here, and these he was careful with, making sure they were still human before approaching them. One wasn't, but it had been torn apart and rendered harmless. He searched the human corpses for weapons. There were truncheons on a couple of bodies in riot gear, but he found nothing of use.

Which way? he wondered, and for no particular reason chose the door to the right.

It led him down a long, deserted hall to a door marked INTERROGATION ROOM. Near the door was a corpse in riot gear, its head torn from its neck and discarded a little farther down the hall. He gingerly stepped over it and opened the door.

The room smelled of rot, and the table in the middle of it was slimy with ichor or some other foul fluids. He ignored it, focusing instead on the metal cabinets around the walls. He opened these one by one, looking for something to use as a weapon. There were drawers full of gauze, surgical gloves, doctors' coats with faded brown stains on their fronts, a set of scalpels, some equipment related to torture by electrocution. There were empty plastic buckets, surgical tubing. There was one drawer packed full of hypodermic needles, the light glinting off them eagerly when the drawer was opened. There were ampoules of various drugs, some to numb the pain, some to increase it, some to make you unable to talk, others to make you unable to stop talking. *What went on in this place?* he wondered, and thought again of his brother, wondered if he had been brought here and what they had done to him, what they had hoped to get out of him, and, finally, what they had reduced him to.

There were two very large cabinets, and these he saved for last. One was locked, but he beat it open with the butt of his gun. Inside were larger implements of torture: a long curved hook on the end of a ridged metal pole, a branding iron with a self-contained heating apparatus, and a laser saw. He took the latter, switched it on, saw that it offered a foot-long blade. *Yes,* he thought, *finally something useful.*

The other was unlocked, but seemed to be jammed. He tugged on it, then banged it, finally pulled hard enough that it sprang open, making him stumble backward.

Inside was a man. His hand was bloody from holding the door shut, and his face had been smeared with gore. His eyes darted here and there, and even once the door was open he continued to crouch in the cabinet, pressed against the back wall.

"D-d-don't kill me," he said in a small voice.

"I'm not going to kill you," said Jensi. "I don't even know who you are." He reached out, but the man batted his hand away. "Come on now," said Jensi. "There's nothing to be afraid of."

"There's everything to be afraid of," the man said. But, very gingerly, he eased his way out of the cabinet. He looked around the room. "James Waldron," he said, and held out his hand. "I heard you," he said. "I heard you searching through the drawers. I thought it was them."

"Do you know what's going on?" asked Jensi. "How did they get in?"

"They didn't get in. They were already here," said Waldron.

"I saw the hole," said Jensi. "You dug something up, didn't you?"

Waldron shook his head. His eyes were still darting about, unable to focus. "No," he said. "They're us."

"Us?"

"They're not aliens at all," said Waldron. "That's what I thought at first but it simply isn't true. They're dead humans who have been changed, transformed."

"That's what the guy on the radio told me. But I didn't believe him. Are you sure?"

"Who told you? I'm sure," said Waldron. "I saw it happen with Bill Ambler."

"Who is Bill Ambler?" asked Jensi.

"Who *was* Bill, you mean," said Waldron. "First he died, and then I saw him change. I saw his body jerk and stretch and crack, and then he was alive again, though not alive exactly, not in the way we understand that, and not Bill, either. And then I watched him kill Michael Stewart. And then Michael changed, too, and then I ran."

"How many are there?" asked Jensi.

"I don't know," said Waldron. "Too many. But one's too many."

"We have to try to get out of here," said Jensi. "We have to try to find some safety."

"This is safety," said Waldron. "We're safe here."

Jensi shook his head. "There's no food here," he said. "We can't last. We need to find someplace else."

"No," said Waldron, and began to shrink and turn away. He started to babble, words coming out all wrong, offering bits and pieces of the stories of the deaths he had seen. No, he was saying, they must not go out there. One man decapitated, another lifted up on the scythes of one of those monsters, the blades thrust right through his chest. Another struck down by something like a flying bat that wrapped itself around his head and then with some sort of weird proboscis or tentacle broke open his skull. Another—

But Jensi was shaking him, trying to get him to focus. "I know you're frightened," he was saying, "I know you don't want to go. But we have to. It's the only way."

Waldron shook his head. "If I go out there, I'll die."

"I won't let you die," said Jensi. "I promise."

Waldron shook his head reluctantly, but slowly he allowed himself to be led toward the door.

"Do you know my brother? Istvan?" asked Jensi on the way out. "Is he still alive."

"Istvan?" said Waldron, and nodded. He seemed much

calmer now, as if he had accepted whatever fate awaited him on the other side of the door. "He was here for a while. Strange fucker, something really wrong with him. He's really your brother?"

Jensi nodded. "Is he still alive?" he asked.

"They took him away," said Waldron.

"Where?"

"I don't know," said Waldron. "The people interested in him were scientists."

"Maybe the research facility?"

"What research facility?" asked Waldron. "Is there one on this planet? I didn't know. I was a prisoner of conscience—they didn't tell me anything."

"He's probably there," said Jensi. "Unless they took him off the planet. But no, he's got to be there."

"Are you looking for him?" asked Waldron. "Don't bother. He's probably dead and has become one of these things. You find him and he'll try to rip your head off. If I were you, I'd be worried more about saving my own skin than about finding my crazy brother."

"No," said Jensi, as much to himself as to Waldron. "He's still alive. He's got to be. How could I have gotten this far if he was already dead? He needs me. He needs my help."

Waldron shrugged. "You're a fool," he said.

They walked back down the hall, Waldron always behind him, one hand on Jensi's shoulder, always anxious, always nervous.

"How do you get out?" Jensi asked.

"Control room probably has a door to the outside," said Waldron. "I think it was locked. I heard one of the guards say so before one of those creatures killed it. There may be other ways out, I don't know. This is the first time I've ever been in this ring."

"Ring?"

"That's what we call them," said Waldron. "Sometimes we call it a three-ring circus and sometimes it's the three circles of hell. The prison is the two on the inside and this outer ring is for the guards. They watched us from here, controlled us."

"Were you the one who contacted me?" asked Jensi.

"What? No," said Waldron. "How could I have done that?"

"If you were sending a signal, where would you send it from?"

"I don't know," said Waldron. "Must be the control room."

"Waldron, we may be all right after all."

He had a hard time getting Waldron to cross the gore-spattered room. He had begun to mumble under his breath and tried to turn back and screamed when Jensi dragged him across, but in the end they managed it. Through the door on the other side was another hallway, curving slightly. They followed it around, slowly.

And then, suddenly, there was a moment when Jensi felt a wave of pain wash through him. He grunted and stumbled, nearly went down, and his head began to throb. There again was his dead mother, standing before him, looking at him this time. As he watched her a sluglike flicker of blood leaked from her nose and down across her lips. She licked it away.

"Jensi," she said. "Help me. I must arrive at what awaits me."

"You're not real," said Jensi. But he was having a hard time believing she wasn't real. She looked so genuine, so much like she had in life that part of him couldn't quite believe this was a hallucination. It had to be something more.

"Jensi," she said, and reached out for him.

And then something heavy struck him on the side of his head. Woozy and disoriented, he fell to his knees, looked up just in time to see Waldron's boot kick him in the face. He fell back.

"No, father!" Waldron was shouting. "No!" He was waving at the air with one hand, pulling on it as if it were palpable, and flailing about a loose riot helmet with the other. And then his voice changed, becoming nervous and weak, the voice of a little child.

"Where are you?" Waldron said. "Where have you gone?"

"Waldron," Jensi managed to say, as he started to scramble up. "Stop. There's nothing there. You're hallucinating."

But then Waldron turned to him and looked directly at him, a strange glow in his eyes. "Ah, daddy," he hissed. "There you are."

"No," said Jensi. "I'm not—"

But Waldron was already upon him. He brought the helmet down hard, but Jensi brought his arm up and blocked it. Pain shot through his arm, his hand going numb. Waldron kicked him in the side and then Jensi was half up, swaying upon his feet, groping for his pistol. "No, Waldron," he said. "I'm not him!"

"You need to die, father," said Waldron, his voice a strange croon. "And this time you need to stay dead."

He started forward again. Jensi circled, trying to stay out

of reach. "Stop or I'll shoot!" he claimed. He had the pistol out and was aiming it, but Waldron didn't even seem to notice it. He only had eyes for his father.

And there, over Waldron's shoulder, distracting him, he saw the flowing white figure that was his mother. "Jensi," she said. "Why don't you come?"

His concentration had been thrown just enough so that when Waldron rushed forward he found himself unable to get away. He fired twice, trying to hit him in the legs, just trying to bring him down, but the first blast hit him in the stomach and the second in the hip. He fell onto Jensi, but whatever had been driving him forward seemed gone now and he did not strike out.

Jensi rolled out from under him, turned him face up. The wound in the stomach was bad. He moved Waldron's hands to cover it and try to hold the blood in, keep him together. The bullet in the hip must have struck some sort of artery. That wound was pumping out little gouts of blood. He pressed his hand against it to try to stop it, but he knew it was too late.

Waldron looked at him, his eyes hurt and confused. "You promised you'd protect me," he said.

Jensi didn't know what to say. "I'm so sorry," he finally offered.

Waldron stared at him as if he hadn't heard. He lifted his blood-soaked hands away from his stomach and stared at them, the blood meanwhile starting to pump from his stomach. His face was very pale. He let his hands fall.

"What happened?" he managed to ask. And then he died.

. . .

So many dead, Jensi thought again, *so much loss.* He should not have told Waldron he could protect him. He couldn't protect anybody, and if he'd left Waldron back where he had found him the man would still be alive. How many more deaths would he end up being responsible for?

He arranged the body, straightening the legs, smoothing the arms down the sides. He took a moment to contemplate his work, and a moment to dedicate his thoughts to Waldron and wish him well. And then he left.

He was halfway down the hall when the sound brought him back. A strange sound, a sort of crackling noise. He took out the laser saw and headed back.

One of the bat creatures loomed over Waldron's body, its wings enfolding him in a sickly embrace. It had inserted a bonelike tube into his forehead and seemed to be pumping something into him. The body itself was not the same body he had left a moment ago. It had begun to change, transforming into one of the creatures, bone and flesh tearing and re-forming, slowly coming back to life. He turned on the laser saw and rushed forward, arriving just as the flying thing had withdrawn and taken off. He leapt after it, managed to cut through one of the wings. It fell flopping and he cut it down the middle, until it stopped moving completely.

And then he turned to take care of Waldron.

The thing that had been Waldron was already up, hissing, swinging its scimitars. One of them caught him in the side and spun him sideways, knocking him down. It leapt on him, trying to bring its mouth to his neck and he found himself grunting, struggling to keep it away. It gave a cry of what might have been frustration and thrust its blade down at him, just missing his arm. He dragged the laser through the bladelike appendage and severed it, and for a moment its balance was off and it reared up and he could bring his arm across enough to sever its other blade. It still held on to him with the stumps, was still trying to bite his neck, and for a moment it did get its teeth in. He gave a cry of pain and frustration and shoved it off, managed to roll it over so he was on top, and then he very quickly severed its head.

It took just a moment more to separate all the limbs and make sure he was immobilized once and for all. Then he lay there on his back staring up at the ceiling. *Hardly fair,* he thought, *to have to kill the same person twice.* But then again, he told himself, life is never fair. He lay there a while longer, catching his breath, and then he got up and went on.

The control room was only a little farther along. He followed the curve around and there was a reinforced steel door, a plate-glass window next to it. He looked in and saw the back of a man busy taking a piece of machinery apart. The desk in front of him was scattered with circuit systems, some of which he seemed to have joined artificially together with twists of wire. He tried the pad beside the door, but it wouldn't open. He went to the window and knocked on it, but the man didn't seem to hear. So he went back out to the room with the corpses and got a truncheon and brought it back and rapped as hard as he could on the glass.

This time the man heard. He spun around and stared and Jensi was a little shocked to discover it was Henry. But Henry was quite a bit more shocked. He fainted dead away.

. . .

Even when he was conscious again, Henry still couldn't quite believe it. He wouldn't open the door for Jensi at first, just stared at him. Then finally he came over and worked the intercom, spoke with him through the glass.

"This isn't happening," he said. "You're just another hallucination."

"No," said Jensi. "It's happening."

"That's exactly what you'd say if you were a hallucination," said Henry.

"I'm not a hallucination," said Jensi. "I just crash-landed my pod into the prison. You and I were speaking until they jammed your signal."

"That was you?" said Henry. His face was lined and drawn, his eyes still suspicious, but he seemed to be trying to believe him.

"I'm real, Henry," said Jensi.

"But what if you've been sent by them to get me to open the door?" said Henry. "What if I believe you're real and open the door and then they rush in and kill me? It would be smarter just to ignore you."

"Henry," said Jensi. "I've come thousands of miles just to be here. I just had to fight my way through creatures that seemed to feel no pain and had no interest in dying. I met a prisoner named Waldron and then had to kill him and then he came back to life so that I had to kill him again. I've been through a hell of a lot. Damn it, let me in."

Henry stared at him for a long moment, then shrugged and opened the door.

. . .

There were a few more awkward moments after that, moments when he said something that made Henry doubt again that he was real. Once Henry became so suspicious that he picked up a screwdriver and tried to jab out Jensi's eye, and if Henry hadn't been weak from lack of food he might have succeeded. But as it was, Jensi took the screwdriver away and Henry became placid, and remained so for a brief while until he began to be agitated by suspicion again.

Or maybe it wasn't even something he said, but just something else, the side effect of what Henry kept referring to as the pulse.

"What kind of pulse?" asked Jensi. "What do you mean?"

Henry tried to explain it. Scientists had come, he said, and they had recorded it. One of them had explained a little to him, though he didn't think she was supposed to. A pulse, doing something to the brain, created by something called the Marker.

"The what?"

"The Marker. I've never seen it," said Henry. "I don't know exactly where it is or what it looks like. It's in the research facility. Hush-hush stuff."

"What about Istvan?" asked Jensi. "Did the creatures kill him?"

"No," said Henry. "The scientists came and measured the pulse and scanned the area, and then they dug a hole. Once they'd done that, they became very interested in Istvan, and then took him and left." He turned to Jensi and gave him a serious look. "But if the same thing is happening over there that's happened here, he's probably no longer alive."

"He's got to be alive," Jensi insisted.

"He's probably not," said Henry. "I know you've come a long way to be here, but it might be time to admit that."

Jensi turned away. Maybe Henry was right, but he wasn't quite ready to give up. One part of Jensi wanted to become reconciled to the idea of his brother's death, but another part still felt that his brother was still alive, was almost sure of it. Which part was correct? The one that accepted the reality of his brother's death or the part that insisted on continuing to try to find and save him?

"I have to try," he said to Henry. "He may be dead, but I can't give up until I know for certain." He'd had years of frustration over not having been able to prevent Istvan from being taken away, and all those years were gathering together to make him feel that he had to prove himself, that it was now or never.

Henry backed off. "Of course," he said. "Who knows? Istvan may somehow have managed to survive. We'll have to go to the research station to find out, but we were going to have to go there anyway. There's nowhere else to go."

And so they went.

46

They found Henry a RIG and then took the contained all-terrain vehicle through the hostile atmosphere of the planet and toward the research facility. The landscape struck Jensi as strange, more like a moon than a planet: deep reddish-black dust and rock, no plant life at all, no signs of life at all apart from the penal colony and the research facility.

Jensi caught Henry staring at him. "Watch where you're driving," he said.

Henry looked away and shook his head in astonishment. "I still can't believe you're here," he said.

"Neither can I," said Jensi. "And I can't believe the shit that's going on here."

"It's like a nightmare," said Henry.

"It's worse than a nightmare," said Jensi.

For a while they didn't speak much, just drove.

"What do you know about this place we're heading toward?" asked Jensi.

"Almost nothing," said Henry.

"Are we likely to have trouble getting in?"

Henry shrugged. "It's a secure facility, so yes, I'd imagine so. But then again they aren't expecting us."

Or at least they weren't until about a few miles away from the facility itself, when the receiver crackled alive and offered a prerecorded message.

Caution. You have entered a restricted area. Enter your code and authorization. If you do not have a code and authorization, stop your vehicle now and turn around.

"What do we do?" asked Henry.

Jensi shrugged. "Keep going," he said.

The message was repeated twice at intervals of about thirty seconds. Each time they ignored it, kept driving. Thirty seconds after that, a new message came:

You are in danger. Stop immediately or you will be destroyed.

Jensi kept driving.

"I'm going to try to hail someone," said Henry nervously. He was just starting to do so when something struck the ATV. It spun them around, threw the vehicle into the air, brought it down hard to land upside down.

Jensi hung head down in his webbing. The inside of his faceplate was obscured by a fine mist of blood and this, in combination with the cracks that had come from the pod crash, made it very difficult to see. He groaned, shook his head.

He turned and saw Henry hanging beside him, seemingly unconscious. Jensi pressed his webbing release and fell in a heap onto what had been the vehicle's roof, and from there he turned around and worked his way to kneeling. He shook Henry, knocked on his faceplate, but Henry didn't respond.

Carefully he positioned himself to bear Henry's body and then pressed the release for his webbing, letting him down slowly and easily. He dragged him out of the ATV and spread him out on the ground outside.

He connected to him via comlink. "Henry," he said. "Henry, wake up." He checked the suit for tears and holes but there was nothing, and as far as he could tell, manipulating the limbs through the suit, no broken bones. He seemed to be breathing as well.

The ATV, though, was useless. The back half of it had been torn off by a mine or by a rocket, no way to say which, before being flipped upside down. They'd been lucky that the explosion had hit where it had; a little farther up and both of them would be dead.

"Henry," said Jensi. "I can't leave you here, but I can't carry you, either. And I don't know if either of us have enough air to go far."

47

Callie would hear noise through the slot, but it was never anyone human. The creatures would come from time to time and if they heard her they would scrabble at and try to break their way through the door, but she would hold very still and after a while they would go away.

She had been left there on her own for three days, listening to the shouts and screams. Her food had run out at the end of the first day, her water, carefully rationed, in the middle of the second. She was likely, she realized, to die of dehydration. That was better, she told herself, than dying out there, killed by the creatures. All the same, she'd like to go down fighting.

She had examined her equipment, trying to figure out if she could build something out of it, manage some sort of primitive bomb. It didn't seem possible; she didn't have either the right materials or the right tools. And so, not knowing what else to do, she kept doing what she always did, examining her data, continuing her research.

But there was not enough data. Never enough data. What had happened to the guard to make him go mad? And what had happened to him after that, to change his dead body into something else? A parasite maybe? How did it simulate consciousness? Was it tied to the Marker and its broadcasts or was that something entirely different?

No, what she needed was to get to the control room, get back to a place where she had access to all the data. If she had full access, maybe she would be able to figure it out.

But she wasn't even sure if anybody was in the control room anymore. For all she knew, everybody might be dead. She turned back to the data she did have and tried to make the most of it.

She was working over the same figures, the same numbers, yet another time when she heard a noise at the door. At first she thought it was one of the creatures returned again, coming to try to get at her, but then she heard the beep as a keycard was scanned and the lock dropped open. She turned and waited, watched the door open.

It was Anna Tilton, Callie saw, the cryptologist. She was a member of Briden's circle and a Unitologist. Despite the dizziness Callie was feeling, she stood slowly up and tried to look unbroken and proud.

"So Briden's finally decided to free me, has he?" she said. "Finally realized the error of his ways?"

Anna held out a bottle of water to her. Callie took it, her fingers shaking. She had a hard time getting the lid off, but when it finally came, she started to gulp it.

"Not too quickly, or you won't be able to keep it down," said Anna.

Callie had to make a conscious effort to slow down and

stop, but she managed. She held the bottle a moment without drinking, then took a slow careful sip.

"So what changed his mind?" she asked.

Anna shook her head. "No, Briden didn't send me," she said. "I came on my own." She reached into her bag, came out with a chunk of bread, which she handed over. Callie took a small bite. She couldn't believe how good it tasted.

"So what do you want?" Callie asked.

"It can't have been meant to happen like this," Anna said. Callie looked up and saw Anna's troubled, distracted face. "Death and carnage and those . . . things. It's not some religious enlightenment. It's not part of the divine plan, no matter what Briden thinks."

"I think we can agree on that," said Callie. "But why bother to tell me? Why have you released me?"

"Because you have to stop it," said Anna. "You have to stop Briden before it's too late."

48

He waited, trying not to expend too much oxygen or energy, occasionally shaking Henry. How much time had gone by? One minute? Two? Five? When would he reach the point where he would not have enough oxygen to make it to the research facility?

It would be better to leave Henry behind, he knew. If he were just to abandon him and try to make it on his own to the facility, he might have a chance. But he could not bring himself to do so. No, Henry had been there for him after his mother's death and for years afterward, had been a true friend. He was not willing to leave him behind.

And so he sat beside him and spoke to him through his transmitter and shook him until finally Henry gave a little groan and began to come around.

"What happened?" Henry asked. "Where are we?"

"It doesn't matter," said Jensi. "What matters is that we have to go, right now. Can you walk?"

Henry moved his limbs, winced. "Something's wrong with my arm," he said.

"Can you walk?" Jensi asked again.

"I think so," said Henry. Jensi helped him up by his uninjured arm, got him standing on his feet. He stood there, holding one arm in the other.

"All right?" said Jensi.

Henry nodded. He looked dazed, but basically okay.

"We've got to be quick," said Jensi. "We've got to try to get
there before our oxygen runs out and we die."

They took off over the landscape, Jensi leading the way, Henry
stumbling behind. From time to time he would call back to
him, goad him along. They weren't running exactly, Henry was
too dazed to run, but they were moving quickly, Jensi's heart
speeding up.

They were perhaps a quarter mile from the facility when the
warning on his RIG sounded and Jensi knew he had only a
little bit of oxygen remaining. He picked up his pace, hoping
Henry would be able to follow. He shouted to him, encouraging him on. The building had grown large now, and he kept
his eyes open for a door or an airlock, hoping they were coming toward it from the right direction to find one. If they had
to circle the building, there was little if any chance that they'd
have enough oxygen to make it.

He heard Henry's voice in his ear. "You're getting too far
ahead," he said. "I can't keep up."

"Follow my tracks," Jensi said.

"But—"

"I need to find a way in," said Jensi. "Oxygen's almost gone.
It's urgent."

Henry was saying something else, but he paid no attention

to it. He was running now, moving as quickly as he could. The building was only a little way ahead of him, the corner of it, but he couldn't see far or well enough to glimpse a door. Which way should he go?

He flipped a coin in his mind and went left, running beside the wall. He ran perhaps forty yards and then decided he'd made a mistake and almost turned around and went the other way, but had enough presence of mind to realize that if he turned around he'd simply use up whatever little oxygen he had getting back to where he was. He kept going, ran perhaps another thirty yards and suddenly reached a dark opening.

He flicked his RIG light on. It was an airlock, the outer door left open for some reason. He immediately turned around, went back for Henry.

He found him near the corner of the building, weaving and swaying, just starting to turn the wrong direction. He called him and stopped him, then got ahold of his good arm and steered him the right way. His oxygen feed had shut off, having run out, and he realized he had very little time left. He felt lightheaded. There was his mother, standing just next to the building, smiling. *It's a hallucination*, he told himself, *she isn't real*, and he shut his eyes long enough to rush through her, pulling Henry along with him. He stumbled and nearly fell. He was breathing now already exhausted air, the little pocket of it left within his helmet, and was beginning to grow dizzy, but then suddenly there they were, inside the airlock.

He searched for the controls to close the outer door, but couldn't find them. His mother was there beside him, having followed them in.

You always were the smart one, weren't you? she said.

"I don't know," Jensi said.

"What don't you know?" asked Henry.

If you're so smart, his mother said, *let's see if you can figure out a way to get out of this one.*

The darkness was crowding up around him, reducing his vision. He was, he knew, about to pass out. He watched his hand grope around the wall and finally find the panel and press it.

OUTER DOOR MUST FIRST BE CLOSED, said a flashing message.

His mother's face seemed to be eaten away, beginning to collapse in on itself. He tried again, pressing another button.

The message flashed again. OUTER DOOR MUST FIRST BE CLOSED.

"You can't do that," Henry said. "It'd let all the oxygen out."

Henry's voice sounded better than his—maybe he had had more oxygen. "Henry," said Jensi, "will you—"

And then he felt consciousness bleeding away and he collapsed.

A rush of wind, a strange brittle quality to the world around him, as if it could be swept away at any instant. He was standing in the middle of a dark plain, beneath a sky streaked with the reddening rays of the setting sun. There was the sensation of something rummaging around in his head, a kind of blunt and unnamed animal snuffling its way from place to place, sending out little bursts of pain all through his brain. And then there sprang up before him a dead face that at first was unfamiliar but quickly he recognized as the politician his brother had killed and shot. Fischer. The man's head was half destroyed, blood and brain leaking from it to stain his shoulder. One of his eyes was gone, but the other eye stared at him.

"You're like him," the politician said. When he spoke, bubbles of blood formed on his lips.

"Like who?" Jensi said.

"What you have inside is not exactly like him, but it is more like him than the others. What he has inside is right and can be understood. Everybody else is wrong. You are neither right nor wrong."

"I don't know what you're talking about," said Jensi.

"You must come to us. Come to us and we shall make you right." And then the scene behind him began to shiver and dissolved into a torrent of blood.

He awoke from the dream, if it had been a dream, to find himself lying on a metal floor, staring up at the ceiling. Henry was standing over him, still holding one arm, and his helmet had been retracted. His head ached, but he was happy to realize that he no longer felt like he was suffocating.

"You're alive," said Henry.

Jensi nodded, sat slowly up. They were, he saw, in the airlock, both its inner door and outer door sealed.

"You managed to get it shut," said Jensi.

Henry smiled. "Just a question of finding the right button," he said. He nodded toward the inner door. "That door, though, is a more difficult proposition. We need a pass code."

"So, we're stuck."

"Looks like it," said Henry. "We can't go out because we don't have enough oxygen, and we can't go in because we don't have the pass code."

Jensi stumbled up. He went and took a look at the inner door, tried to override it but without success. He examined the door for any emergency releases or other mechanisms but found none.

"So what do we do?" asked Henry.

"Your guess is as good as mine," he said. He took the laser saw out of his pocket but one brief attempt was enough to convince him it wouldn't be able to cut the door open, not before it ran out of power. He put it away.

He removed the gun from his pocket, then grasping it by the barrel began to hammer its butt against the door, a slow regular sequence.

"Maybe they'll hear it," said Jensi over his shoulder for Henry's benefit. "Maybe they'll come get us out."

Henry didn't say anything. *Yes,* Jensi thought, *not likely, I know. But what else is there to do?* He kept pounding, hoping against hope that someone would hear.

49

"They don't die easily," Anna explained. "You can shoot them and they just keep coming."

Callie Dexter hefted the weapon she'd been handed. A kind of plasma rifle, with the barrel modified. When fired, it would, so Anna claimed, send out a stream of energy, but send it in a cutting line rather than focused to a point. "Good for taking off a limb," she said. "Don't bother with the heads; it's the limbs that matter. Once those are gone, they can't move."

"I've never fired a gun before," said Callie.

"Neither had I until a few days ago," said Anna. Her face was drawn and tired. "Don't worry, you get used to it quickly."

They started into the hall, Callie turning in the direction of the control room.

"No, you can't go that way," said Anna, grabbing her arm. "We have to take the long way around. There are several of those things between us and the Marker, and Briden has set up a few guards as well, loyal fanatics who are likely to kill you on sight. We'll have to take the long way around."

So instead they went the other way, away from the control room.

"What does Briden think he's doing?" asked Callie.

"He thinks he's bringing about the next stage of existence," said Anna. "He's convinced himself that he's a prophet, and that Istvan is as well, that together they know the will of the Marker."

"Crazy," said Callie.

Anna nodded. "He thinks those things are servants in the service of Unitology. But they're mindless. That's not what Unitology is about. And there's something strange about them in relation to the Marker. They won't come near it."

"No?"

"It's safe there," said Anna. "That's where he and Istvan stay, dictating to everybody and anybody who will listen the will of the Marker. There's almost nobody left now—most of us have become those . . . things. He's lost his way, but he's got a loyal following of the dead. He's a madman."

Halfway down the corridor, the hallway began to change. The tendril and rotlike substance that had long been found here and there in the halls had started to build up thickly on the floors, a kind of slick organic substance that bunched like a brain. As the hallway continued, it built up on the walls as well. Anna stopped, opened an access panel leading into the ventilation system. "We'll go through here," she said.

"Why don't we just continue down the hall?" Callie Dexter asked.

"Trust me," she said. "You don't want to see what's down there."

The passage was narrow and constricted, and it seemed to Callie very hard to breathe. They had to go on hands and knees, bodies bent low, with Callie pushing the rifle in front of her. The access panel led up a steep incline to the ventilation system itself, and she followed Anna through the ducts, watching their shadows flicker large, listening to the low hum of the ventilators and feeling the turgidly moving air. From time to time, where the ducts intersected, Anna would pause and take out a scrap of paper and unfold it and examine it before deciding where to go. These moments were the worst for Callie, when she felt both cramped by the duct's walls and immobile. It was in those moments that, despite the lights they carried, she felt the duct closing in around her.

At a certain moment, she was certain she heard something behind them. Turning, she saw a brief flash of movement, but then it was gone. "Anna?" she said.

"What is it?" asked Anna.

"Who else uses these ducts?"

"What else, you mean," said Anna. "You see anything, shoot it, and ask questions later."

This did not reassure her, and added to the confined and stifling atmosphere to make her feel highly jumpy.

They continued on. *Where can we possibly be?* wondered Callie. *Are we turning in circles?*

And then she felt something close around her ankle.

She cried out and felt herself dragged back the way she had come, rattling and banging through the passage. She nearly lost her gun but just managed to hold on to it. For a moment the dragging stopped and she dragged herself over onto her back to face it, saw the tip of a thick tentacle curled tight around her ankle, the ropy remainder of it stretching far down the passage. It was, she saw, coiling itself up, gathering itself to pull her farther.

"Shoot it!" she heard Anna yell. "The pustule!"

The pustule? she wondered. And then she saw it, a distended yellow sac farther down the passage, sprouting off the tentacle and partly hidden by the rolls of the curves of tentacle between it and her. *Good,* she thought, *at least now I know what to do.* She worked the gun around, banging it against the sides of the duct passage but finally managing. She aimed, but before she could fire, the tentacle jerked tight and she was flipped onto her stomach and dragged painfully farther along.

It stopped again, the tentacle coiling itself, gathering itself, and she managed to flip over and get the gun aimed. She fired once and seared the wall, then again, and hit the tentacle but not the pustule, and seemed to do no damage. She kept calm. *Third time's the charm,* she told herself. When the tentacle swayed, she could see the hole where it had come from, a deep tear in the wall. If it tried to drag her through it, she knew, it was likely to tear her apart.

She aimed carefully, feeling the tentacle beginning to tense, and fired one last time and this time caught it. The pustule ruptured and exploded, tearing the tentacle in half. There was a roaring sound and the remainder of the tentacle whipped away and back into its hole.

Callie pried the tentacle's tip off of her ankle, saw the red gash it had left. She turned and crawled back the way she had come.

She met Anna after just a dozen or two yards. She was

crawling rapidly her way, but stopped as soon as she saw Callie.

"You're alive," she said. "You made it."

"Don't act so surprised," said Callie. "What the hell was that?"

"One of them," said Anna. "They come in all sorts of shapes and sizes. As soon as we've figured out how to deal with one type, another type appears. Luckily that was one we'd seen before."

"I hope to hell I never see one again," said Callie.

They continued on, crawling through the ducts. At some point Callie had completely lost track of where they were. She began to hear noises that she wasn't sure were there. *Is it a function of the Marker broadcast?* she wondered. Or was it paranoia, plain and simple? Part of herself she felt giving in to the darkness and confinement and beginning to imagine the devil in every shadow. But another part of her, the part that was the scientist, simply observed this struggle from a distance, curious to see what would happen.

Up ahead of her, Anna had suddenly stopped.

"What is it?" Callie asked.

"One of Briden's men," she said. "Or used to be. I had to kill him on the way to find you. Now he's blocking the passage. We'll have to crawl over him."

"What?" said Callie.

"It's the way we have to go," said Anna. "I'm sorry."

"There's got to be another path," said Callie, but Anna had already started forward. Callie watched her crawl to the body and then gingerly bring first her hands and then her knees onto the corpse. But with the body in the passageway she couldn't manage on hands and knees and in the end she had to wriggle through, almost flat. It was uncanny to watch her, the man's body slowly emerging as she passed over it—his staring eyes, the rigor mortis of his mouth.

It was a man Callie had known well, by the name of Dixon. First name, John. She had never liked him but, well, at this point, that hardly mattered.

"Come on," said Anna from the other side of the corpse. "Come through."

She waited a moment, finally sighed and approached. The body had a sour smell to it, but was fresh at least, hadn't yet started to decompose. She pushed her way slowly onto it, trying not to strike his head with her hips or knee. Very slowly she crawled along it, feeling absurdly obscene. There was barely enough room to get by. She wriggled her way forward, then reached out and grabbed his boots and pulled herself farther and finally clambered off.

Anna patted her shoulder. "It's not that bad. You'll see worse," she said, as if that were some sort of consolation. And then she continued crawling forward.

There was, after a while, a sound she couldn't place, some kind of pounding.

"What's that?" asked Callie.

Anna stopped, listened. "I don't know," she said. "Probably one of those things."

"No," said Callie, shaking her head. "It's too regular."

Anna shrugged. "Then one of Briden's crew," she said.

They kept on. After a little while, Callie said, "We need to see what it is."

"Why should we?" said Anna. "It's a waste of our time."

"I'm curious," said Callie. "I want to know."

For a moment Anna looked angry, and then her face softened into indifference.

"Fine," she said. "It's your funeral."

And yours, too, if things go wrong, thought Callie, but she didn't bother to say so.

They found an access ramp and left the ventilation ducts. Down below, in the building proper, the noise was louder. The hall they descended into was deserted, and they carefully tracked the noise down it until they came to an airlock.

"There's someone in there," said Callie. "Somebody who wants to get in."

"It's just those things," said Anna. "Some of them must be trapped. We don't need any more of them than we already have."

Callie crossed her arms. "It's not them," she said. "We already determined that. The pounding is too regular, almost like a code."

She was reaching out toward the emergency release when she heard Anna say, "I don't think I'd do that, Dr. Dexter."

The tone of her voice was odd. Off somehow. Callie turned, saw that Anna was pointing her weapon at her.

"What's wrong, Anna?" she asked, trying to keep her voice level and calm.

"I don't know," said Anna. "You, but, I . . ." She shook her head. "You're with them," she said. "You want to get them out and together you'll kill me."

"Them?" asked Callie.

"Those creatures," said Anna. "You're with them. You're on their side."

Callie shook her head. "I'm not one of them," she said. "Something's confusing you, Anna. You're not being yourself. You came to get me, you need me—there's no reason to kill me." She reached out slowly and put her hand on the emergency release. "I'm going to open it," she said evenly. "Please don't shoot me."

She watched Anna, holding her breath. For a moment there was a struggle within her and then her face contorted and she let the gun barrel dip down. Callie let her breath out, then pulled the emergency release.

50

"Oh my God," said Henry, "it worked."

Jensi was just as surprised as he. He pulled back, groping the laser saw out of his belt, and stood waiting for the door to open the rest of the way.

When it did, it opened on the face of the female scientist who had come to the penal colony a few days before. She looked tired, her face dirty and exhausted, but she seemed very much alive.

"Hello again," said Henry.

"Hello," said the scientist, and smiled. "Dr. Callie Dexter. Who's your friend?"

From behind her Jensi saw another woman, this one holding a gun. "Are you one of Briden's people?" she shouted. "Which side are you on?"

"Calm down," said Henry.

"Anna, it's okay," said the scientist, turning to her. "I know this man," she said, pointing to Henry. "He was a guard over at the penal colony."

"Technician," said Henry.

"It doesn't matter," said the scientist in a low voice. "Just shut up."

"What about the other one?" asked Anna.

"I'm here to find my brother," said Jensi.

"Your brother?" said Anna.

"Yes," he said. "His name's Istvan."

Callie gave a little cry. Anna simply raised and fired her weapon, scorching the wall just above Jensi's head.

"Wait," said Jensi, hiding behind the airlock door. "Wait, wait! What have I done?"

"Your brother is the reason all this is happening," claimed Callie.

"He's the one who did all of this. He unleashed these demons, but there's something more. He wants to make new Markers, spread the evil to other worlds," said Anna.

Istvan? No, Jensi couldn't believe it. How could his brother be responsible? "There must be some sort of misunderstanding," he said. "My brother wouldn't do anything like that." But even as he said it, he saw his brother again standing beside Councilman Fischer, pulling the trigger. Istvan was capable of anything.

"No misunderstanding," said Callie.

"If I can only have a chance to talk to him, I can figure out what's wrong," Jensi said. "I can stop him."

"Why should we trust you?" asked Anna.

"No, Anna," said Callie. "We need everybody we can get." She turned back to Jensi. "If you can stop him, fine," she said. "If not, then I'll kill him myself."

. . .

It took a few more minutes to calm Anna down, but in the end she grudgingly let them come along. Anna led the way, the others following. She took them down a hall, then doubled back and shuttled them into a laboratory while a patrol of Briden's men passed. They came into a corridor and saw a creature stumbling the other way. They simply remained quiet until it was gone and they could move on.

They were getting close to the control room, Callie thought, when, in a corridor covered with some of the strange organic growth Callie had seen earlier, she heard a click and Anna suddenly froze.

"What is it?" asked Callie.

"Everybody get back," said Anna.

Callie inquired again but Anna refused to say anything until the others had retreated to the end of the corridor. "I've stepped on a pressure mine," her voice quavering. "Something Briden's left for us. In a moment I'm going to leap off of it and hope it will just maim me rather than killing me."

"No," said Callie. "Don't. Maybe we can figure out something else to put on it. Maybe it still isn't too—"

But Anna had already leapt. When she came down she was missing both of her legs, which had been blown into bits, and was dead as a stone.

Callie stared at her corpse a moment, then gestured to Jensi. "That work?" she asked, pointing to the laser saw on his belt. When he nodded, she said, "Cut off her arms, too. Last thing we want is her coming back to haunt us."

. . .

Jensi had removed one arm and was starting into the other when his RIG receiver crackled to life. He could tell by the looks on the faces of the others that the same thing was happening with their RIGs.

"Briden here," the voice said. "You should be more careful where you step."

"What do you want, Briden?" asked Callie.

"Ah, Callie," he said. "You should have stayed safe where you were in your cell. You would have had a much gentler death there than you will here. Who are your friends?"

"None of your business," said Jensi.

"It doesn't matter, I suppose," said Briden. "You won't last long. None of you will. If I were you, I wouldn't bother to postpone the inevitable. You'd be better off if you put your guns to your heads now and pulled the triggers."

"Shut up, Briden," said Callie.

"Gladly, Callie," said Briden. "I have much better things to do than to waste time talking to you. Besides, with a little luck your deaths will be captured on tape and I'll be able to watch them over and over again."

They came to another pressure mine but saw it this time and avoided it. Callie led the way, taking a somewhat circuitous path, as if she wasn't completely sure where she was. Jensi had taken Anna's gun, had given his laser saw to Henry.

"I was serious about killing your brother," said Callie.

"I know you were," said Jensi. "Just give me a chance to talk to him first."

They came to a place where the hallway was blocked by

stacks of boxes, a kind of makeshift barricade. Callie stared at it a moment. "We can backtrack and take another hallway," she said. "Or we can break through it. Or we can try to take a shortcut."

"What sort of shortcut?" asked Jensi.

She shrugged, then gestured at the doors behind them. "Some of these rooms connect both to this hall and the one on the other side of it. We cut through one of them, see what's on the other side."

Jensi nodded. "Let's try it," he said.

"It might be a hallway filled with those things," she said. "We might walk out into the middle of them."

"We might," assented Jensi. "But it's worth taking the risk."

He went to the first door in the hall and slid the door open. The room inside was empty, a fairly shallow storage room that did not have another door. He went to the next door and this one was locked. The third door down was open, however, and opened onto a large room, with a door on the other side of it.

"Here it is," he called back, and started in, Henry close behind him, Callie lagging a little ways behind. He crossed through the entrance and took a few steps and only then did he see the man who had been hiding behind the door. He swiveled to face him, raising his gun, but the man reached down to the console in front of him and pressed a button and everything went wrong. He felt his body slow, grow paralyzed. The man suddenly was moving much quicker than he should have been able to move, as if his metabolism had gone mad. He could just glimpse, out of the corner of his eye, Henry, suspended and equally unable to move. *Stasis field*, he realized, and realized, too, that he was trapped.

And then the man at the console was rushing about like mad. He was saying something, but Jensi couldn't hear it, could only see his lips moving too quickly to be read and hear a kind of insectoid whine. There was a rapid burst of energy and the man's head simply fell off his shoulders. Another rapid burst, and the panel he had been standing at erupted in a shower of sparks.

Slowly everything keyed up again and suddenly he was rushing rapidly sideways, returning to the movement he had been in the midst of before the stasis. Henry collided with him, and they came down in a heap.

"Stasis trap," said Callie from above them. "Simple but ingenious. But with a field not quite big enough to catch all three of us." She gestured at the headless technician. "He made a mistake about which one of us to leave out of the field. And a further mistake when he underestimated my willingness to kill him."

They dismembered the body and continued on, following the new hall along. They were halfway when Cassie stopped and ushered them quickly into a side room. They stayed crouched there, listening to the wheezing sound of the creatures passing by, and only once they were ready to go out did Jensi realize that the ducts overhead were broken out and that there was blood spattered across the walls. They slipped quietly back into the corridor and after making sure it was safe, moved forward. Ahead was a strange buzzing noise and Jensi was prepared for some new abomination, but when he turned the corner it was to see a rattling ventilator. The hall curved sharply around another corner and came to an observation theater with a reinforced transparent wall. On the other side of it, in the operation room, stood Briden. He had his arms crossed and was smiling at them. He activated the communication system between them.

"Still fighting it?" he asked, smiling. "Still haven't accepted the inevitable?"

"Shut up, Briden," said Callie.

"I'm here for my brother," said Jensi. "Let my brother go and I'll leave you alone."

"Your brother?" said Briden, momentarily off balance. "And who might that be."

"Istvan," said Jensi.

For a moment Briden looked incredulous, and then he burst out laughing. "He's your brother?" he said. "You've got to be kidding me!"

"What have you done to him?" shouted Jensi. "Give me back my brother!"

"You think he's your brother, do you?" said Briden. "How quaint. Whatever he is now, he's not anyone's brother anymore. He won't even recognize you. He has become a prophet. The Marker has chosen him to spread its gospel. He belongs to the Marker now."

In frustration, Jensi pounded his fists against the glass. Callie was working with the door lock, trying to override it and get the door to open, Henry helping her.

Briden noticed them, gave a deep bow. "Be seeing you," he said, and slipped out a door on the far side.

A moment later the door opened of its own accord and Jensi rushed in and across the operating room. The door on the other side was locked.

"Think you can do anything with it?" Jensi asked Callie.

"I'll try," she said, and started to work on it.

The lights flickered and went off, the room now lit only by the pale glow of emergency lighting. "Callie, did you do that?" Jensi asked. "Knocked some wire maybe?"

"Wasn't me," she said.

"Wasn't me, either," volunteered Henry.

The door they had come in slid suddenly shut. Jensi returned to it, tried to open it, but something was keeping it closed.

"Get out your weapons," Jensi said. "Quick."

"What's wrong?" asked Henry.

There was a scraping, echoing sound somewhere up above them, in the ductwork. Jensi could hear it starting near one corner of the room, moving slowly toward the room's center, near a duct opening, near where Henry was.

"Henry," he called, "move!"

Henry looked up, confused, but didn't move. The grating above him shattered and something large and lanky flashed down through the flickering light and Henry was lifted off his feet. He screamed and screamed, swaying in the air as Jensi rushed forward, already firing but without seeming to do much damage and then Henry was hurled hard against the wall. And then the thing, whatever it was, turned its attention to Jensi.

It looked hardly humanoid, gathered as it was in one distended arm, the rest of its body, head included, remarkably squat. The arm groped toward him and he had to leap back to avoid it. It came toward him in awkward little shuffling hops, and he fired at the arm without much success. He switched his aim and fired at the head, decimating it. And then the creature was shuffling and searching blindly. Jensi took out first one leg and then the other, and then it was little more than an arm, but it continued to crawl and inch about, still searching, still searching.

Jensi gave it a wide berth and made his way to Henry. He was dead, his neck broken, his eyes staring up at the ceiling. One more death, one more loss. Jensi shook his head, still keeping one eye on the inching, throbbing gigantic arm.

"Any luck with the door?" he asked Callie.

"Almost got it," she said. He watched her working, concentrated and focused. She had broken the casing off the control panel with the butt of her gun and had begun to remove and shuffle the circuits. She ran a loose wire between two of them and there was a hissing noise and the door slid open.

"Let's go," she said. "Where's Henry?"

"Dead," he said.

"That thing killed him?" she said. "Too bad. You have to dismember him."

"I can't dismember him," he said. "He's my best friend."

Callie stared at him a moment. "Last thing you want is your friend coming back to kill you. Or me for that matter. But up to you. Come on, let's go."

51

They went straight ahead, moving as quickly as they could until they reached the control room. There, Callie tried to key the door open. They were both surprised when it did open—apparently Briden had been confident enough that they wouldn't make it that he hadn't bothered to rekey the lock.

The control room contained a half dozen researchers, who all froze when they entered. Jensi waved his gun around, fired it once into the ceiling.

"Lift your hands above your heads," he said. "No reason for anyone to get hurt."

They mostly did, except for one man who hesitated. "He's serious, Johnson," Callie said to him. "He won't hesitate to kill you."

Slowly the man lifted his hands.

"There," Jensi said. "Now, the two of us are going to enter the Marker chamber."

"You can't—" Johnson started.

"I've warned you once, Johnson," Jensi said, his voice cold. "I won't warn you again."

Johnson didn't speak again and nobody else moved. They

continued slowly toward the door. "You'll have to keep an eye on them," said Callie in a low voice. "I've got to turn around long enough to press my hand to the keypad."

Jensi nodded. He kept his gun trained at the scientists, sighting down the line of them and then back again. Behind him, he heard the scuff of Callie's boots as she turned. Johnson, he saw, had started to lower his hands and he barked at him to keep them up and in place, and reluctantly he did. There was a beeping behind him, and Callie cursed. Then another, different beeping and the door slid open, and the two of them backed into the Marker room.

Inside it was strangely peaceful, strangely quiet. Istvan stood there alone beside the Marker, very focused, not seeming to notice them. Jensi felt his heart leap.

"Istvan, it's me!" he called.

But his brother didn't respond, didn't even move. Jensi moved closer and repeated his words again, louder this time, and this time he watched Istvan slowly turn toward him, his eyes heavy and lidded.

"Who are you?" he asked. "Why do you look different from the other dead?"

Jensi paused, confused. "It's me, Istvan," he said. "Jensi."

He watched as something changed in Istvan's eyes. "Jensi," he responded. "So you are dead now as well. How did you die? Or perhaps this is not a thing the Marker knows how to tell me in stealing your form."

"Dead? What are you talking about? No, I'm here. I'm real," said Jensi.

But Istvan didn't seem to believe him. He stared at Jensi as if he were staring through him, then slowly shook his head. "No," he said. "How can you be here? You can't be here." He turned and peered up at the Marker. "Of all the things you have made me see, this is the cruelest," he said. "Give me another, not him."

"I've had enough," said Callie. "You've had your chance. You can see how crazy he is."

"No," said Jensi. "I've just found him. He'll come around."

"The time for talking is through," she said. "You've had your chance and failed."

"No!" said Jensi, and stepped between her and Istvan, beginning to move slowly toward her.

"Get out of the way," she said, in a level voice. "It's not pleasant but it needs to be done."

"No reason to kill anyone," he said, still moving slowly forward. "If you'll just give me a few moments . . ." he said.

But Callie was already leveling the rifle at him. He leapt to one side, feeling the burn of it as the beam passed by him to singe the flesh off the outside of one of his shoulders. It hurt like hell. He spun and leapt again, this time into Callie, knocking her off her feet and onto the ground. The breath was knocked out of her, but she continued to hold the gun.

For a moment they struggled, he on top of her, both of them grabbing the gun and trying to pull it away from each other while in the background Istvan stood as motionless as the idol of a savage god. Jensi's shoulder was aching now, and he could smell the stink of his own burnt flesh, and Callie below him had her jaw clenched determinedly and just refused to let go.

He reared up and raised his head and then brought it down hard, slammed it into her forehead. She cried out, her grip loosening. He raised his head again, struck again, and this time her eyes rolled up into her skull and she lost consciousness.

Even unconscious, her hands still gripped the gun. He almost had to break her fingers to get it away from her. He tossed it away from her and it skittered across the floor. Still breathing heavily, he heaved himself up and, clutching his shoulder, stumbled toward his brother.

It had been so long, and he had come so far. Here was his brother at last. Somewhere there, within this strange distracted false prophet, lurked his brother. He was there. He had to be.

He reached out and touched him. At first Istvan seemed not to notice but as Jensi kept his hand there he turned his body a little, trying to draw away from it.

"I've come for you, Istvan," Jensi said. When Istvan didn't respond, he continued. "I'm here to save you, to get you out of all this."

By now Istvan had pulled fully away. Jensi took a step forward, pressed his brother's shoulder again with his hand. "Istvan, it's me, Jensi," he said.

Istvan shrugged him off.

But Jensi was not to be denied. He came closer still and hugged Istvan, wrapped both his injured and uninjured arm around him and held on tighter this time.

"Istvan," he said. "It's really me. Can't you see me? Can't you remember?"

But Istvan was struggling to get away.

"All you have to do is look, brother," said Jensi. "All you have to do is see me."

Istvan gave a little grunt of anger and frustration. He pushed at Jensi's head, but Jensi held on.

"Istvan," he said. "I'm here for you."

Istvan struck him very hard, in the face, but Jensi held on. He hit him again, and then again, and yet again, but still he held on. He hit him harder and harder, Jensi's face growing bruised and bloody, his burnt shoulder cracking and bleeding as well. His head was growing loose on his shoulders, but still he held on.

52

Something was beginning to change for Istvan. The veil that had fallen and had been the scrim upon which he had begun to see the other world was growing more and more tattered, no longer able to hold all the images of that world. There were gaps and tears and the other world was beginning to leak out. The images of his mother, Councilman Fischer, and Conn no longer seeming as real as they had felt over the last few days. No, there was something wrong with them: they weren't real, they were puppets, their motions wrong now, not realistic at all. How could he ever have believed that that was the man he had killed? And how could he have believed they could trade faces with one another?

His hands were still moving, doing something. He was hitting something, he knew, hitting the thing that something or someone was trying to pass off as his brother. No, it couldn't be his brother—Jensi was millions of miles away, safe on Vindauga. He couldn't be here. This was just another deception.

The veil was in tatters now, all but gone. He slowly began to relax. He was less distracted, his motions less mechanical. He began to hit the thing masquerading as his brother less and less hard, and finally stopped hitting it altogether.

When he did, Jensi finally let go. He collapsed, bloody and broken, in a heap. Istvan watched him fall and then stood there looking at him. Yes, it looked like Jensi, remarkably like him, and did not continue to shift and change as the other dead had done.

Istvan hesitated. What if it really was his brother? What if he had killed him?

Slowly he crouched down near him and looked closer, examining the lines of his face. His mother's face had been just as he remembered it, the face she had had the last time he had seen her. It was the face that had been captured in his memory, and this was one of the things that had allowed him to know she wasn't real, that the Marker was talking through her. But here, Jensi's face was different than he remembered.

He reached out and touched the face with his hand. "Jensi," he said. "Is it really you?"

And then the veil came together again, or tried to. He felt a pain in his head and then saw before him, standing on the other side of his brother, his mother. She was there, a ghost, the same ghost he had been seeing for days now, no different.

No, Istvan, she said. *This is a lie. This isn't really who you think it is. It's not Jensi. He's not real.*

"He's not?" he asked.

He could be convinced, he realized. In fact, he would have been convinced if he could not see the difference between this ghost and the man lying on the floor. His mother's face was the same as it had always been, not a bit different. But this man on the floor was his brother but older and bruised and bloody. Which meant that he was not a ghost created by the Marker. Which meant that Jensi must be real.

But how was that possible? How could Jensi have come all this way? And why? In his confused way he couldn't help but realize that if Jensi had come here, had traveled millions of miles to be here, it was for his sake. He had come for him.

So, his brother hadn't abandoned him after all. Quite the opposite. His brother had come for him. His brother loved him and was looking out for him. But if that was the case, then what about the Marker? Did it love him as well? Was it looking out for him? And what about Briden? Was Briden looking out for him, or was he using him?

No, he realized, if his brother was his friend, then Briden wasn't. Briden had urged him on, had held him in the other world, had made him feel important. But Briden was no friend to him. Briden just wanted to use him to get at whatever the Marker wanted to tell him.

It was just a moment's lucidity, the thought quickly rolling under, but it was enough. He had been used and cheated, even if he didn't understand exactly why. Briden had seen what the Marker had done to him and then had fed on that, had encouraged him to fall further out of step with the world and into the other world. The result of which was here, lying on the floor, in the form of his broken and bloody brother.

He put his hands under Jensi and pulled him up, pressing him to his chest. "I'm sorry," he said, whispering into his brother's ear. He wasn't sure if his brother was living or dead. "I didn't mean to hurt you," he said. But Jensi did not answer.

How long he held his brother like that, he wasn't sure. Perhaps just a few seconds, perhaps a few minutes, perhaps longer. He was drawn from his reverie because Briden was suddenly there, beside him, patting his shoulder.

"You are a true prophet," Briden was saying. "I knew you would make the right choice. Our work here is too important to let extraneous details get in the way. The only family you have now," he said as he gestured at the Marker and himself, "is right here."

Istvan stared at him, and Briden's smile flickered just a little. Then as Istvan continued to stare, Briden repeated what he had said. Once he was done, Istvan began to smile.

Very slowly and very carefully Istvan stood up, holding the smile frozen and immobile on his face. Briden was still talking, but he was no longer listening to him. He knew now what he had to do. He had to stand there, waiting for his moment, waiting for his chance.

His mother appeared, stared curiously at him, head cocked to one side. *What are you doing?* she asked. *What are you planning?* But he just shook his head. And then it was the councilman he had killed instead, asking the same things but in a very different way. And then, last of all, it was Conn, who seemed the most interested of any of the three to know the answer.

Briden droned on. Istvan watched his mouth, his throat. When he had finished, he looked at Istvan, waiting for him to say something, but he didn't say anything at all. Briden waited a moment, eyebrows raised, and when there still was no answer forthcoming began to turn away. Which was the moment that Istvan chose to leap on him and break his neck.

Briden went down without a sound, a boneless heap that it was hard to believe had ever been human. His head jutted oddly to one side.

"It seems I was a false prophet after all," he said to Briden's corpse, but the corpse didn't answer.

His thoughts, so briefly lucid, were already beginning to become confused again. He did not know what to do to keep them straight. He kneeled, touched his brother's bruised and broken face. He massaged his neck, trying to bring him back to consciousness or to life.

Perhaps the Marker can help me, he thought. *Maybe it wasn't my enemy. Maybe Briden was the only enemy.*

He shook his head. Did he really believe that? No, he didn't, but he was worried that he might eventually convince himself he did.

He kept talking to Jensi, kept touching him. Slowly, very slowly, his brother's breathing grew less shallow and he began to come around.

"Jensi," he said. "Come back to me. Come, brother."

And slowly Jensi did. One eye was swollen shut and his face was bloody, his cheekbone perhaps collapsed. But he was alive.

"Briden's gone," he said, as Jensi opened his eyes.

Jensi blinked, rolled his head first one way and then the other, then asked "What?"

"Briden's gone," he said again. "Dead, I mean."

"Did you kill him?" asked Jensi.

"I broke his neck," Istvan said in a matter-of-fact way. "Just snapped it."

But Jensi had closed his eyes again. Istvan shook him gently until he opened his eyes again.

"Briden's gone," Istvan said. "It's just you and me. We can use the Marker for good. We can control it. I know how to talk to it and how to make it listen."

"No," Jensi managed to croak. "We can't. It's not something we should touch. We should destroy it."

Istvan gave him a quizzical look. "No, brother," he said, "you just don't understand. It knows me. It grew with me. It changed me. It'll be okay." He gestured all around him. "You see how it protects us from the creatures it has created from our imperfect flesh, just like you used to protect me? The creatures cannot approach us. It will teach me how to control them, and then we can make this world our own." He gave a strange smile, one eye darting about independently. "After that, who knows?" he asked.

Jensi shook his head, but Istvan was staring at the Marker now, his gaze unfocused.

"It will give us a purpose, brother," he said. "It will fulfill us." He lifted his arm and suddenly Jensi felt his head burning, aching as if it were slowly being torn open from inside. Was it coincidence? wondered Jensi. Or had his brother somehow triggered the pulse by raising his arm? Did Istvan really have control over the Marker?

And then the sensation deepened, intensified. It felt like something was scraping fire along the channel of his thoughts, reworking them, modifying them. He saw, before his eyes, a brief flash of his mother, her startled face staring at him, and then she was gone, and he was seeing instead the Marker. But not seeing exactly—it was going on not outside of his head but inside, and it was as if he was seeing how the Marker came together, how the Marker was what it was. It felt like someone was applying pressure more and more strongly to his mind, forcing information into it, and no matter how he fought to think something else, he could feel it there, pushing its way into him. He clutched his head: it felt like something was living inside of him. *The Marker,* he thought, *the Marker.* It's trying to infect me. And when he opened his eyes there was the actual Marker above him, implacable and brutal, the images still in his head, indelibly there.

Jensi turned his head to look away from it only to see Callie writhing on the floor, her face contorted and suffering. He watched her slowly rise to her hands and knees, uttering little cries, and start to crawl until she ran into the wall. She pawed it, seemingly trying to move through it, and when she found she couldn't she began to beat her head against it.

Jensi winced, and then suddenly the pressure in his head faded and he found he could breathe again, the pulse subsiding. He was confused, his head buzzing, but he was still himself.

But Callie didn't stop. She kept striking her head against the wall, harder and harder, her movement more lost and erratic than it had been at first. A stain of blood had begun to spread on the wall and was beginning to drip down.

"Callie, no!" he yelled, or tried to yell. His voice was little more than a whisper, perhaps nothing she could hear. He rolled over and began to crawl toward her, his whole body aching with pain, but it was too late: before he was even halfway there, she had collapsed.

B. K. EVENSON

He continued toward her, but by the time he reached her he knew she was dead. She wasn't breathing, her eyes were open and glassy. Her neck was oddly loose beneath his fingers, her head resting at the same wrong angle as Briden's. *What a waste*, he thought, and brushed her eyelids closed.

When he turned away from her, it was to find his brother standing over him.

"It spoke to you," Istvan said.

"I don't know what you're talking about," said Jensi.

"It spoke to you," Istvan insisted. "Now you have its shape inside you." For a moment he was still, motionless, as if he wasn't inside his body, then he seemed to come to himself. He gestured past Jensi, at Callie Dexter's broken corpse. "What happened to her?" he asked, seemingly astonished.

"You're crazy," said Jensi. But Istvan ignored him.

"Not everybody can be like us," said Istvan. "We have to have followers, too." He walked past Jensi and prodded Callie's body with his toe, sniffed. "I remember her. I liked her. Yes, she can be with us. She'll be a follower. We'll just have to help her along. We'll carry her away from the Marker and put her where it can reach her and then she'll come back to life as one of our servants."

Jensi rolled onto his back, closed his eyes. He tried to push Istvan's words out of his head, but he couldn't. They had wormed their way too deeply in. Callie had been right, he realized: his brother was beyond help, beyond saving. He was mad. He couldn't acknowledge what the Marker was doing, still lived under the delusion that it was helping him even as it attempted to rewire everybody's brains, manipulated the dead into other forms, and attempted to destroy or transform everything around it. It wasn't a friend to humans, nor even a friend to just Istvan. No, Jensi suspected it didn't think of humans as anything but fodder for accomplishing whatever goals of its own it had.

But Istvan couldn't see it. He had been with the Marker too long, and his brain was strange, wrong, off, which probably made it worse, and made him all the more dangerous. No doubt the same thing had happened to Istvan that had happened to Jensi: the Marker presenting itself to him, imprinting itself onto his brain, trying somehow to spread knowledge of itself through the minds of others. That probably meant that others in this complex, and others in the prison colony, had experienced the same thing, that they now carried around with them the plans and the seed for the Marker.

He shuddered. What would happen if one of these people got off the planet? Was there some way the Marker could control them? Would they suddenly have an uncontrollable urge to what . . . share what they knew? If that was the case, then before long maybe there'd be not one Marker, but many, and that would mean the end of humanity.

Or maybe it didn't mean anything. Maybe the images and plans would simply be forgotten in time and it wasn't dangerous. But was that a risk he was willing to take?

It had to be stopped here.

Still, Jensi tried to tell himself, Istvan would never do anything to put humanity at risk. But it rang hollow. Maybe if Istvan was sure that he was putting humanity at risk that was true—Jensi wasn't even completely sure about that. But Istvan was so convinced that he knew what he was doing that he wasn't going to listen to reason, not until it was too late.

And yet Jensi had traveled millions of miles just to find his brother, to protect him, to save him. What was he to do? He could protect his brother, but he couldn't do so without potentially sacrificing everything and everyone else. Not just himself, not just lives already lost on the way to this moment, but perhaps every human life. He wasn't willing to sacrifice all that to save his brother, he just couldn't do it. But the question was, what was he willing to sacrifice to save all the rest of it?

53

"Are you with me, brother?" asked Istvan. Perhaps, Jensi realized, he had asked it before. When Jensi didn't answer he said, "Brother?"

"Of course," said Jensi. "When have I not been with you? We're brothers, aren't we?"

Istvan smiled broadly. "Brothers always," he said.

"Where's my gun?" asked Jensi. "Have you seen my gun?"

"What do you need a gun for?" asked Istvan. He gestured to the Marker. "We have something much more powerful than a gun."

"I'm just used to having a gun," claimed Jensi. "It makes me feel safe. Can you find it for me?"

"But you don't need it," said Istvan. "I already told you."

Jensi stared at him a long moment, pondering. "Istvan, will you do this for me?" he finally said. "As a brother?"

Istvan hesitated a moment and then nodded and went to look for Jensi's gun.

Jensi let out his breath and closed his eyes. *Please forgive me,* he thought, directing the thought into the void. *Let it be quick,* he asked, *and as painless as possible.*

A moment later, Istvan came back with a gun. "Is this yours?" he asked his brother. "It may have been hers, hard to tell."

"It'll do," said Jensi. "Now put it in my hand." And when Istvan started to do so, "No, the other hand."

"But you're not left-handed," said Istvan.

"My other arm is hurt," said Jensi. He turned his head, spat out blood.

"Did I do that?" asked Istvan. "I'm sorry, brother. We'll get the Marker to fix you, to make you whole. It'll make you better, I promise."

Jensi nodded. "Now help me up," he said. "Gently now."

Istvan wrapped his arms around his back and pulled him up in a bear hug. Soon they were both standing, Jensi sagging against his brother's side.

"Istvan," said Jensi. "Do you trust me?"

"Of course I trust you."

"Do you trust me to do what's best?"

"Sure," said Istvan. "You always used to. You always looked out for me."

"Then close your eyes."

"Why?"

"It's for the best," Jensi said.

For a moment Istvan looked confused, but then he closed his eyes.

"You're my brother," whispered Jensi. He slowly raised the gun and held it near his brother's chest, the barrel wavering. "No matter what you've done, no matter what it's done to you, you'll always been my brother. I'm sorry."

He pulled the trigger and the shot burnt its way through Istvan's chest, through the heart. Istvan drew in a huge shocked breath, opened his eyes wide in astonishment, and collapsed, taking Jensi down with him, landing on top of him. Jensi lay there underneath him, feeling the dead weight of the flesh that had once been his brother as the blood and last bit of life slowly leaked out of him.

At one point he passed out. At another point he came conscious gasping for breath, with the impression that his brother's weight was suffocating him slowly. It was a horrible feeling. Maybe minutes, maybe hours later, Jensi struggled his way free. He was in bad shape—his ribs were broken and it hurt to breathe. His arm was broken as well, his face puffy and swollen. Probably there was serious internal damage as well, organs and cavities slowly filling with blood and preparing to fail.

He stumbled his way to the door. When it slid open, he saw not the scientist who had been there before, but more of the creatures. They hissed when they saw him, but hesitated, seemed unable to cross the threshold.

He could feel the Marker still there, prodding his mind, trying to contact him. It was not painful this time, but unexpectedly gentle as if it was looking for someone new to communicate with now that Istvan was dead and that it was finding the composition of his particular mind sympathetic. He did his best to ignore it.

So much to do, he thought. First he had to destroy the complex and everything inside it, the Marker especially. Then he had to sort out some way to wipe out whatever knowledge or information he had felt the Marker put in his brain. He'd be damned if he'd be its host and help it spread itself elsewhere.

And then it was as if he had blinked and fallen asleep on his feet, perhaps only for a second or two. When he was conscious again it was to find the barrel of his gun in his mouth. He had no memory of putting it there, but there was Istvan beside him, smiling, egging him on.

Yes, that's right, Istvan was saying. *Go ahead and pull the trigger.*

Horrified, he took the gun barrel out of his mouth. He pointed it out the door and at the creatures, or thought he did, but no, it was in his mouth again. He took it out, saliva gleaming on the barrel and pointed it again, again at the creatures, but no, it wasn't being pointed at them at all, it was back in his mouth; it kept slipping back into his mouth. What was wrong with him, why was this happening to him, how could it really be happening, was he going mad? And how could he know for sure now what he was pointing the gun at? Wasn't there always a chance, more than a chance, that when he pulled the trigger his own head would explode?

Go ahead, said Istvan next to him, *go ahead. Pull the trigger.*

Was that the taste of gunmetal in his mouth? He tried to step out of the door frame and back farther into the room, but that was a dead end as well. No, the only way to go was forward, but how was that possible? He had to move forward, had to point the gun at the creatures and know, or at least

hope, that he was pointing it at them and not at himself. And then fire. How would that ever be possible?

He stayed there, leaning against the door frame, on the verge of passing out.

And then finally he closed his eyes and pointed the gun straight ahead of him, or at least he hoped so. He tightened his finger on the trigger. He took a deep breath and fired.